CAN'T BUY ME LOVE

SINCLAIR SISTERS 3

JANET ELIZABETH HENDERSON

First published in 2019 by Janet Elizabeth Henderson

© Janet Kortlever 2019

ISBN: 978-0-473-50429-8

Author's Website: www.janetelizabethhenderson.com

Cover design by Janet Elizabeth Henderson

Editing by Liz Dempsey

CHAPTER 1

It turned out the Catholics were right—purgatory was real. And it was a small town in the Scottish Highlands. Oh, sure, the locals called it Invertary, but Agnes Sinclair knew better. She wasn't fooled by the picturesque loch or the rows of crooked white houses. Invertary was where souls came to have the hope sucked out of them—or whatever it was that happened in purgatory. Not being Catholic, Agnes wasn't sure what went on there, but with a name like purgatory, it couldn't be good. All she knew for sure was that she'd only been in town for three weeks, and already she'd lost the will to live.

"You called a security firm to investigate *me*?" She glared at her new boss, Dougal Jamieson, the owner of Invertary's only hotel, and he didn't even squirm.

He tugged down his red tartan waistcoat, which he'd teamed with a pink button-down shirt, and glared back. "I called them in to investigate the *thefts*. The ones you informed me were happening. Was I supposed to ignore them?"

"You were supposed to let me do my job and investigate

them myself. That's why you employed a hotel manager. To free you up to take care of the pub and build your new conference center." The conference center that was still in the planning stage because the land Dougal wanted to build it on was being held hostage by an old woman the town called Satan. Which seemed appropriate, because if this was truly purgatory, Satan should live in it. Right? She really needed to find a Catholic and have them explain this stuff to her.

"You might be the day-to-day manager, but this is still my business," Dougal snapped.

It was clear to Agnes, after only three weeks in the job, that Dougal didn't actually want to let go of the responsibility of managing his hotel. So he'd taken to managing her instead.

In detail.

Every.

Single.

Day.

His micromanagement was beginning to make her skin crawl, and the urge to gag him and lock him in a closet grew stronger by the minute.

Dougal's white brows furrowed as he huffed a breath that made his matching mustache and beard flutter. Her boss was Santa dressed as Elton John, with a booming voice and a deep Highland burr. Talking to him was like having a bad acid trip.

It was on the tip of her tongue to demand to know why he'd hired her when he seemed so set on doing the job himself. But Agnes already knew the answer—her sister's husband had talked him into it. Yep, that's how pathetic she'd become. Even though she'd spent ten years studying part time to get a degree in hotel management and had countless hours of practical experience under her belt, she needed her sister to find her a job.

There were days, like this one, when she second-guessed the decision that'd landed her in her current predicament. She'd been offered a job managing a large hotel that was part of a famous chain, and all she'd had to do to secure the position was have sex with the owner. Agnes had politely declined, kicking his nuts into next week as she did so. Less than twenty-four hours later, she'd been blacklisted throughout the entire UK hotel network, leading her to this moment—a face-off with disco Santa.

She should have had sex with the creepy hotel owner.

Taking a fortifying breath, she reached deep for what little patience ran in her genes. "I know this is your hotel, and I understand that I work for you. But I just want the opportunity to do my job before you decide you need someone else to do it for me."

"This isn't a judgment of your abilities." Dougal's voice reverberated off the walls. "It's an attempt to give you some help. Benson Security can investigate the thefts while you manage the hotel."

What was left hanging in the air between them was the fact the bulk of the thefts had only started after she'd arrived in Invertary. She looked her boss straight in the eye. "I'm not the one stealing from you."

He smacked a beefy hand on her desk. "Did I say that?" He turned to the man leaning in the doorway. The man Agnes had been steadily ignoring since he'd arrived with her boss ten minutes earlier. "Did I, at any point, suggest my manager was stealing from me?"

Agnes tossed her long, straight blonde hair over her shoulder, folded her arms over her gray suit jacket, and tapped her toe. Yes, what exactly *did* the almighty 'security specialist' think of this situation?

The corner of the man's mouth quirked as he uncrossed his arms and ankles and stepped into the room. At about five foot eight or nine, he wasn't massively tall, but he would still tower over her. He wore a black long-sleeved tee with the sleeves pushed up, a pair of dark blue jeans, and brown suede boots. His thick, mahogany hair, shorter at the sides, was pulled back in a rough right parting. He reminded her of a younger Tom Cruise. Only with a nose that'd been broken at some point and set crooked. They shared the same lean, muscled physique, and the same amused sparkle in their eyes.

"What I think," he said, "is that we all need to take a step back and calm down."

And that was all she needed to hear to know he was an ex-cop—it was in his tone. The same tone she'd heard many times over the years. Perfect. This was *just* what she needed. She could have coped with one of the ex-soldiers Benson Security employed—someone taciturn and bad-tempered like her brother-in-law Callum—but not an ex-cop. She'd discovered at an early age that cops had been put on earth purely to rub her up the wrong way.

"I don't need to calm down," she told him. "I'm perfectly calm."

He cocked his head and shot a pointed look at her tapping toe.

"This is impatience." She exaggerated the tapping. "Not irritation." Although, she was getting there fast.

"Look." He spread his hands wide. "I'm sure if we work together, we'll get to the bottom of this situation in no time at all. That's what we all want, right?"

Agnes bit her tongue. What she wanted was for everyone to get out of her office and let her get on with her crappy job. The only job she could get. The job that was right in the middle of bloody Scotland when all she'd wanted was to work her way out of the damn country, not become more entrenched in it.

"Exactly." Dougal nodded decisively as he tugged down his waistcoat—again. "I'll leave you two to sort this out. I have a council meeting to organize. We're going to confront Betty and make her negotiate the sale of the land I need for my conference center. She's holding up progress. This town will die if we don't attract new business." When he reached the door, he turned back to Agnes. "I expect you to cooperate fully with this investigation."

Deep breaths. Think zen thoughts. Don't imagine strangling your boss with his tartan waistcoat...

"Of course." She bit out the words through clenched teeth.

Dougal nodded once and strode off, leaving her with the security specialist who was there to investigate her. Because she would bet everything she owned—which wasn't very much—that she was suspect number one.

It was the story of her life.

* * *

Logan smiled at the woman who clearly wanted him to leave with her boss. "We weren't introduced. Logan McBride." He stuck out his hand. "And you're Agnes Sinclair. I met your sister Isobel when I visited the London office."

"That's nice for you, but you should know that I'm *nothing* like her."

For a minute, he thought she was going to leave him hanging there with his hand out, but grudgingly, she shook it. A strange tingling sensation ran up his arm, and he had the urge to hold on tight and never let go. Reluctantly, he released her. His hand warm from her touch.

Agnes took a step back, a faint pink blush dusting her

cheeks, making him wonder if she'd experienced the same irrational urge to hold on tight. Her chin lifted, and she stared him straight in the eye. "Aren't you going to ask if I'm the thief?"

"Are you?" he said, because she seemed to expect it.

"No." Her green eyes blazed as if daring him to say otherwise.

Logan felt the hairs on the back of his neck stand on end. He'd been with the Strathclyde police force for almost ten years before going to work for Benson Security. In that time, he'd asked people about their guilt so many times he'd lost count, and they'd always clarified their answers. Always. He'd expected her to say something like, 'No, I've never stolen anything in my life.' Or, 'No, I'm not a thief.' To have her reply with just a 'No' had his instincts tingling.

"Okay," he said slowly. "Do you want to fill me in on what's been happening here?"

"Hasn't Dougal done that already?" Her eyes flicked between him and the door, giving the impression that she was fighting the urge to ask him to leave.

"Aye, but I'd rather hear it from you." He motioned to the guest chair facing her desk. "Do you mind?"

Her jaw clenched for a second, telling him she definitely did mind. "Please," she said instead.

Fighting a smile, Logan took a seat. Agnes was a conundrum. She was right when she said she was nothing like her older sister. While Isobel was sweet and soft, and slightly dippy, Agnes was sharp as a tack, prickly, and growing more impatient by the second.

She pulled back her chair and sat on the edge. The lapels of her gray suit jacket fell open to reveal a stiff white shirt underneath. No jewelry. Only a Timex watch with a classic white face and a black leather strap. This woman was all about business. And he was getting in the way of it.

"So," he said, leaning back in his chair, "things have been going missing from around the hotel?"

She slid a piece of paper over the desk toward him. "It ranges from worthless stuff, like soaps and shampoos, to food from the kitchen and jewelry belonging to guests."

He glanced down the list. "What kind of jewelry?"

"The expensive kind," she said evenly, making him think it was an effort for her to remain calm. "We've had things go missing from guest rooms, storage, and back of house. There's no pattern to it. I mean, who steals soap and a diamond ring? It makes no sense, but it has to be someone with access to all areas of the hotel."

He let out a low whistle. "Why haven't you called in the police?" If people's valuables were missing, this was definitely a case for the local cop.

"We want to see if we can sort it ourselves."

"In other words, you're afraid of the bad publicity." It wasn't a question. "So, you think a staff member's behind the thefts?"

Fire flashed in her eyes. "Yes, Logan, I think it's the staff." The 'you idiot' at the end of that sentence was definitely implied.

"Which one do you think it is?" he asked, just to see how she'd react.

Her jaw clenched and unclenched before she spoke. "I don't know. That's what I was looking into before Dougal called you in to take over. Maybe *you* could tell *me* who's been doing this."

He nodded with fake solemnity. "I'll definitely do my best to get that information to you, Ms. Sinclair."

Her fingers twitched on the desk, and her eyes flicked to a heavy glass paperweight with a tiny Eiffel Tower inside it. It didn't take a genius to connect the dots between the paperweight and his head.

"Have you discovered anything that might help me in my investigation?"

"Yes," she said before slowly enunciating the words, "Someone's stealing stuff."

It took all his self-control not to burst out laughing. "Do you want to show me where this *stuff* was stolen from?"

"All over the place." She narrowed her eyes at him. "You were in the police, right? What were you? A traffic cop? Community liaison? Worked with dogs?"

It was too much. Laughter exploded out of him. When he caught Agnes' eye, it was clear she wasn't joking and was waiting for an answer. And she wasn't doing it patiently—her hand had inched closer to the paperweight.

"I was with the Strathclyde Police," he told her, before she started lobbing things at his head. "I made detective, specializing in organized crime, until circumstances brought me back home to Invertary."

"Really?" The incredulity on her face almost made him laugh again.

"Really."

"Have you been out of the job long?"

"You mean, so long I'm rusty and have forgotten what I'm doing?"

She gave him a look that said she thought that was another stupid question. "Well…yeah."

She was just too much. "Look." He held out his hands in supplication. "We both know you're perfectly capable of finding out who's stealing from the hotel. Unfortunately, we both answer to our bosses. And your boss asked my boss to look into things. So how about we work together, get to the bottom of this, and get it done?"

For a minute, he didn't think she'd take him up on the offer, but then her shoulders slumped. "I hate that you sound reasonable. Fine. But I'm in charge."

This was the most fun he'd had with a woman in years. "I'm the one with the investigative experience," he pointed out.

"And I'm the one with the hotel experience."

"How about we share the lead role?"

"How about you just follow my lead? I'm in charge of this hotel." She lowered her voice and muttered, "When Dougal lets me."

"Okay, how about this? Think of me as your consultant. An expert you've called in to assist. Can you live with that?"

"That depends. Are you an expert who follows orders?"

"Is there any other kind?" He stood and motioned to the door. "Why don't we start with you showing me the scene of the crime?"

"Well, seeing as the last thing that went missing was the toilet paper from the downstairs loo…" Her eyes sparkled, letting him know she was messing with him.

"If that's where you want to start," he said, "then who am I to argue?"

"Right answer, Clouseau." She stood, rounded the desk, and strode toward the door. "You coming?" she called back over her shoulder.

With a grin, Logan followed Agnes out of her office—watching her voluptuous backside sway in her staid gray suit trousers.

CHAPTER 2

Agnes would be the first to admit that, when it came to men, she was somewhat shallow. She wasn't proud of it, but she put it down to not having a whole lot of time to invest in dating. Which meant there was no need to get to know guys on any deep level. And when you didn't have time to get to know someone, you chose brawn over brains. Yeah, it didn't sound any better when she tried to justify it to herself. Nevertheless, Logan McBride, as unwanted as his help might be, was definitely eye candy. It made dealing with him a little less painful.

"I gather we aren't starting with the toilet paper theft," he said as she led him upstairs to the first floor.

"I'll save that treat for later." Agnes pointed to an inconspicuous door at the end of the corridor. "That's the main storage closet for the hotel. We've lost some bedding and sundries from in there."

"Who's got keys?" Logan crouched down to take a look at the lock, the action pulling his jeans tight over solid thighs, making the material cup his rear like gentle hands. She began to drool at the sight, losing track of the question.

He glanced over his shoulder. "Are you checking out my backside?"

If he was hoping to embarrass her, he'd be sorely disappointed. Donna was the only Sinclair sister who did embarrassment—much to her sisters' disgust. "Seems only fair. You were checking out mine while we climbed the stairs."

"True." He flashed a cocky smile at her over his shoulder, proving he didn't embarrass easily either. "Ogle away but talk while you're doing it. Who's got access to the closet?"

It wasn't as much fun ogling him when she had permission, so she stepped up to his side and watched him examine the door instead. "Dougal, of course, me, head of housekeeping, and whichever cleaner is on duty."

"So, what you're telling me is that there are several copies of the key floating around. Are they all accounted for?"

"Honestly, I don't know. And neither does Dougal. The locks haven't been changed since he bought the place. And whenever a key goes missing, he has another cut. He keeps no record of how many are out there or who has them or what's happened to them."

He studied her for a moment. "If this was your hotel, you'd know where the keys were."

"Well, duh." Hadn't she already made her point about liking control?

His lips twitching, Logan returned his attention to the door. "I don't think the keys are the issue." He pointed at the scratches around the handle. "The lock's been jimmied."

Agnes leaned over, aware it put her firmly in Logan's space. His scent engulfed her. Spicy and fresh, it reminded her of a walk through a pine forest or…car air fresheners. Hmm, not so sexy when you looked at it like that.

"Why are you frowning?" His deep voice was close to her ear, making her tingle.

"You smell like those little green tree air fresheners you

hang from your rearview mirror. Which kind of cancels out the effect of seeing you in those jeans."

He threw back his head, laughing. It was a delicious sound.

"Time to change deodorant, I think," he said. "I wouldn't want to dull the power my jeans have over women."

"Probably wise." Her attention drifted back to the lock.

There were scratches all around it, and paint had flaked off the door at the point where the lock met the jamb.

"See? Someone's picked the lock. And by the looks of it, tried to force the snib up with a credit card or something."

"That is a seriously amateur job." Agnes was disgusted. She could have done better blindfolded and armed with a ball point pen.

That made him arch an eyebrow at her. "You know how to pick a lock?"

Like she'd admit that to a cop. Even an ex-cop. "So, it could have been a guest, or just someone wandering into the hotel. Which means the suspect pool has opened right up." She frowned. "Well, that's annoying."

"Looks like you might need me after all." His cocky, and very sexy, grin was back. "This isn't the open and shut case you thought it would be."

Agnes rolled her eyes as she straightened. "Come on, Clouseau, maybe you can use your awesome detective skills on the woman who lost her diamond ring."

Without waiting for him, she strode down the hallway, expecting him to follow. The thick, red tartan carpet softened her footfalls, and the cream walls made the corridor feel airy. Gorgeous pencil drawings of the town, framed subtly in matching cream, adorned the walls. The whole effect was one of wealth and comfort. It never failed to astonish her that a man like Dougal, whose taste in clothing could only be termed Scottish Disco, had managed to put together a hotel that was both cozy and classy.

Rapping on the door to room twelve, one of two suites in the building, she kept her eyes on Logan as he crouched down to examine the lock.

"This one hasn't been jimmied," he informed her as the door swung open.

"Oh." Mrs. Edwards smiled widely at them. Today, the older American woman was dressed in a gray velvet jogging suit, sparkly sandals and diamante horn-rimmed spectacles, and there was a white Scottish terrier puppy under her arm. "Did you find my ring?"

"Not yet, but rest assured we're taking its loss very seriously, and we're looking into it." She waved a hand at her sidekick. "This is Logan McBride. He's from the local security company, and he's going to help us get to the bottom of this."

"Pleased to meet you." Logan flashed his panty-melting smile, making Mrs. Edwards simper, and proving that his sex appeal worked across all ages. "What a cute wee pup." As he petted the dog's head, Mrs. Edwards looked like she might faint.

Honestly.

"He isn't mine." Mrs. Edwards sounded breathless. "He's Dougal's. I just borrow him now and then because he's such good company. Aren't you, Arnold?"

Oh yeah, Arnold was great company—until he chewed your shoes or peed on the carpet.

Logan caught Agnes' eye and mouthed, *Arnold?*

"It's Dougal," she muttered, as though that explained it. Which, if you knew the pub owner, it probably did.

"Mrs. Edwards," Logan said, all business and polite charm. "Would you mind answering a few questions about your missing ring?"

"Of course not." She swung the door wide. "Come on in."

Agnes motioned for him to go ahead of her—that way she could enjoy his reaction to seeing the suite for the first time. Two steps into the living room, he tripped over his own feet, righted himself with a suspicious cough that might have covered a laugh, and motioned for Agnes to join them.

"Isn't it wonderful?" Mrs. Edwards looked around the room with pride. "Not many hotels would let you decorate for your stay, but Dougal had no problem with me swapping out the drapes and bedding."

Logan opened and closed his mouth a couple of times before settling on, "Um, that's a lot of…Josh McInnes."

He wasn't wrong.

She'd replaced the curtains with ones printed with massive photos of Josh in his trademark black suit. Cushions with his smiling face were scattered over the sofa, the bedding showed a shirtless Josh lazing at the beach, and on the table were piles of signed photos of the star waiting to be mailed.

"So, um, you're a fan?" Logan said.

Mrs. Edwards giggled like a schoolgirl. "No, dear, I'm *the* fan. I just got voted in as head of Josh's American fan club. That's why I'm here. Part of the job is to collect signed memorabilia and do special interviews with him, just for the fan club. I only intended to stay a week to get it all done, but I fell in love with Invertary, so I've been here a month so far. I can totally understand why Josh moved here. This town is so quaint."

"I don't think it was Invertary you fell in love with," Agnes said. "I think it's the fact that Josh wanders around town and eats in the pub downstairs."

"There is that," the older woman said, her eyes sparkling with mischief. "But I would never bother the man. Unlike some fans, I understand a celebrity needs their space. I only enjoy admiring him from a distance."

Logan cleared his throat. "Can you tell us where you lost the ring?"

Agnes bit her lip to stop herself from reminding him that there was no 'us.' She already knew about the ring. He was the one playing catch-up.

"It was right over here." Mrs. Edwards wandered over to the dining table, which was covered in bags, merchandise and envelopes. "I was making up packages to send to fan club members. Not all of them, of course. That would take a factory working around the clock. These are only for the fans who won a pack. Even then, it would still have taken forever to bag everything, but Caroline McInnes, Josh's wife, rounded up a group of teenagers to help me. Caroline's amazing and very efficient, isn't she?"

The question was aimed at Agnes, who'd never met the famous Caroline McInnes. But the customer was always right, so she answered, "Oh yes, so efficient."

"I gather you took off the ring while you were making up the bags," Logan prodded.

"It kept snagging on the gossamer bags, so I put it in my purse at my feet."

"Who was in the room at the time?"

"Like I said, several teenagers. They kept coming and going, in shifts." She waved a hand toward the door. "I propped the door open. The hotel sent up snacks too, which the teens loved. You don't think it was one of the kids, do you? They were such a great bunch."

"I wish I knew, but we'll do everything we can to find out."

"I'm sure you will," she said as the dog wriggled in her arms.

She bent down and released it, and it ran from the room.

No doubt to find another corner to pee in. How long did it take to train one dog?

"I suspect he's off to find his daddy," Mrs. Edwards said. "Are we finished here? Because I wouldn't mind a nap. I'm not as young as I used to be."

"Of course." Agnes imagined her pulling her Josh curtains, climbing in between her Josh sheets, and putting on her Josh sleep mask before placing her head on her Josh pillow and falling asleep to one of Josh's CDs. She supposed there were weirder things to be obsessed with, but none came to mind.

As the door closed behind them, Logan shot her a look. "I feel like I should rush back to the office and open a file on that woman, just in case she snaps and goes full *Misery* on Josh."

"She's harmless." Agnes headed back down the corridor, expecting him to follow. "Josh knows all about her, and he isn't worried."

"Josh doesn't play with a full deck."

Logan wasn't wrong. "Back to the thefts. If half of the kids in town were traipsing through the hotel to help stuff bags for Josh's fan club, it looks like everyone in Invertary is on the suspect list."

"Not so clear-cut, eh? Maybe I'll be of some use after all."

It took a second to realize he was teasing her, because it wasn't something many people did. "Maybe. The jury's out on that for now."

"Well, while the jury's debating my worth, I'd better make sure the evidence is on my side. I'll get a proper description of the ring and see if she has any photos, that way I can circulate it around the Glasgow pawnshops. Or see if it's turned up online. If you have details on the other jewelry that's been stolen, send it through to me, and I'll add it to the search."

"There's no point in hunting down the other pieces. They

weren't worth anything. The ring is the most expensive thing that's gone missing."

They stopped outside her office on the building's ground floor. "I'll also run some background checks on the staff, make sure no one has a record for theft."

"That's a good idea." Agnes fought the urge to place her hand on her roiling stomach. "Will you run a search on me too?" Had that sounded casual enough? She hoped so.

"No, because I'm pretty sure Lake will have already done it. He has a habit of checking out the love interests of the people close to him, which means Isobel would have got the treatment when she met Callum. I expect he covered you and your sisters as well. And, seeing as he was the person to talk to Dougal about giving you this job, I'd say I can strike you off my list."

Relief made her knees go weak, but she locked them in place. "Good to know." Although, Lake couldn't have delved *that* far into her history. Otherwise, he would never have helped her get the job.

"I think the best course of action in the short term," Logan said, "is to put up cameras and try to catch the culprit in action. Or at least prevent them from taking anything more."

Like she wouldn't have already done just that if she'd been able. "Dougal doesn't want cameras. He says it interferes with the guests' experience while they're here, makes them feel like they're under surveillance."

"Which they would be." Logan leaned against the door-jamb, the image of a man at ease. But the look he gave her was anything but casual—he was assessing everything she did and said. "How do you feel about cameras?"

"If this was my hotel, I'd put them up, but I'd make sure they were unobtrusive, then I'd post notices saying they were there—in places that weren't easy to spot."

Amusement flashed in his eyes. "In other words, you'd skirt the law."

She shrugged. It was what she did best. "I wouldn't break it though." She wanted to make that clear. Her reputation and her future depended on it. As he considered her, she calmly stared him straight in the eye. She refused to shift uncomfortably, and she sure as hell wasn't going to look away. "Why are you asking about this anyway?"

His eyes turned from hazel to dark brown. And just like that, she was back to being aware of him as a man instead of as an obstacle in her way. "I thought we could meet up at the Benson Security office and pick out some cameras."

Oh, that was such a tempting offer. But she was trying to be good. Which meant doing as her boss told her, no matter how wrong that boss might be. "Not without Dougal's permission."

"Strange, I didn't have you pegged as a woman who liked to follow the rules." When she didn't rise to the bait, he carried on. "How about I take responsibility for the cameras? We can tell Dougal it was a strong recommendation from your security consultant."

That wicked panty-melting smile of his was back, and she definitely wasn't immune to it. Not even a little.

"Well, he did say we should work together to get this done."

"He wouldn't call in a security specialist and not expect them to do their job."

Honestly, the man was the embodiment of temptation. A sensual devil coaxing her into sin.

"There's no need for him to know about the cameras," Logan said. "As soon as we find the thief, we'll remove them. What do you say, Agnes, do you want to live a little dangerously?"

Oh, he had no idea how much. "Okay, I'll meet you when

I'm finished for the day. It won't be until late. I have guests coming in mid-evening and no receptionist to greet them, so I'm covering."

"I'll be in the office behind the shop, come when you're ready." Logan pushed away from the doorjamb and headed down the corridor toward the main entrance. But before he disappeared, he glanced over his shoulder and called to her, "Wear something pretty."

Arrogant sod. "This is not a date," she shouted after him.

All she heard was a deep chuckle that vibrated right through her. With a huff and a strange dancing sensation in her stomach, she turned to her office, only to find Dougal's dog peeing on the leg of her desk.

CHAPTER 3

Against her better judgment, Agnes found herself walking up the high street to the security shop as soon as she'd settled her last two guests for the night. She was tired. Her feet hurt. And she'd had to deal with another complaint of missing jewelry, this time from a very whiny woman who wanted instant compensation for the item. Agnes had forced a smile, replying in a polite and professional manner—exactly as she'd been trained. Each word had stuck in her throat, reminding her that there were days when she just hated people in general.

The sky loomed black overhead, heavy with dark clouds that threatened snow. A chill wind rushed up the high street from the loch, and even though she wore several layers under her padded coat, Agnes still imagined she felt the wind go right through her. Tugging her woolen hat down over her ears, she wondered again why she was making this trip. It wasn't like Dougal was going to thank her for the initiative anyway. And she was self-aware enough to know she should probably have kept her current mood away from the public. She wasn't exactly a bundle of seasonal cheer. But still, she carried on, dragging her feet toward the Benson Security shop.

Despite her morose mood, she had to admit the town had done a half-decent job of decorating for Christmas. Large red tartan bows adorned lampposts, while twinkling lights zigzagged between them, back and forth over the cobblestoned street. Their colored lights bounced off the facing rows of whitewashed buildings, old houses renovated to turn them into shops.

Windows were decorated with trees and gifts. In the lingerie shop, mannequins in red tartan underwear wore Santa hats. And the newsagent's window had been sprayed with fake snow. Even the big Presbyterian church at the top of the street had bright wreaths hanging from its doors.

A banner strung across the street proudly proclaimed that the Christmas market was the following weekend and included the town's annual lingerie runway show. She cocked an eyebrow. It was an interesting choice for a Christmas celebration, that was for sure. Of course, Agnes already knew about the market. It was an Invertary tradition and attracted much-needed business to the town. The hotel was booked out for that weekend, and Dougal had been over the details of what the pub was doing during the event. Apparently, they were having Christmas karaoke. She needed to remember to buy earplugs.

Someone with a sense of humor had decorated the Benson Security shop window. It was filled with elves waging war on each other, armed with various stun guns, radios and assorted weapons. There were even casualties. One elf lay sprawled in the fake snow, a pocketknife sticking out of his chest and what looked like tomato sauce blood spilling out from under him. In her current mood, it was definitely a scene Agnes could relate to.

After banging on the door, she turned to watch the street

as she waited for Logan. There were only a couple of other people out, and they were heading into the pub. This place was a ghost town, and yet, sadly, it was positively buzzing compared to the town she'd grown up in. The best thing you could say about Arness was…

She drew a blank. There really was nothing good to say about it. Located at the bottom of the Kintyre Peninsular, the dot of a town suffered from flat landscape, constant wind, and long car trips to anywhere interesting.

Man, she hated Scotland.

What was she doing still living here? What cruel fate was this to work ten years and end up in a worse position than when she started? She was the butt of some cosmic joke that just wasn't funny. When the door swung open behind her, she turned to find Logan looking annoyingly hot in a royal blue crewneck sweater, faded jeans and tan suede boots.

"I hate Christmas," she said.

A slow smile curled his lips. "Well bah humbug to you too." He motioned for her to come inside.

"My sister Mairi's in Canada." She followed him into the warm interior of the shop. "She's freezing her backside off under mountains of snow. Here, we get icy rain and endless darkness. In New Zealand, Christmas is in the middle of summer. Why can't we have Christmas in summer? Nothing happens then anyway."

"This is Scotland," Logan said. "We'd still have rain for a summer Christmas, it just wouldn't be icy." He grinned. "Probably."

She found his grin irrationally annoying. "I hate Scotland. And I hate rain. Cold rain. Warm rain. All rain. I hate *all* rain. And I particularly hate Scotland because all it does is rain."

"Oookaaay." Logan studied her long enough for it to become uncomfortable.

"What?" Hadn't he cottoned on to the fact she wasn't in the mood to be annoyed? Did he have a death wish?

"Have you eaten?" he asked, after what felt like an eternity of him staring at her.

"What's that got to do with anything?" She was there to pick up some cameras. That was it. Then she'd head back to her hotel room and spend another night alone, staring at the tartan carpet.

"I'm going to go out on a limb here and guess you haven't. When was the last time you ate?"

Now that he mentioned it, she wasn't sure. "Breakfast?"

"Figures. Come on, Suzy Sunshine. Let's get some food into you." He snagged his jacket off the back of a chair as they headed through the shop and into the back of the building. Like a numpty, Agnes followed.

Before she knew it, they were in the alley behind the shop, and Logan was unlocking the car. "I don't want food," Agnes whined. "I don't want to go out. There are people out there, and I hate people. I just want the cameras, and then I want to return to Fawlty Towers and continue my sad existence."

"I know you do." He patted her shoulder. "But everything will look much better once you've eaten."

She glared at the hand on her shoulder. "If you pat me again, I'll rip off your hand and smack you with it."

"Right." He opened the passenger door for her. "Get in and stop talking while I still like you."

"I especially hate men," she snarled as she climbed into the car.

Five minutes later, they parked outside a huge stone building that must once have been a church. Now it sported a sign proclaiming it Invertary's spa and restaurant.

"I'm not dressed for this place." She was wearing jeans

and a sweater. This didn't look like the kind of place that had Casual Tuesday.

"Nobody will care. Stop making excuses and get out of the car."

"Fine. The sooner we get this over with, the sooner I can get back to the hotel."

"That's the spirit."

Like a recalcitrant teen, she stomped up the steps to the front doors, frowning as she went.

Logan held the door for her. "Try not to terrorize anyone before they feed us."

Agnes attempted to incinerate his brain with the power of her mind, but it didn't work. Meanwhile, he asked the woman who greeted them for a table for two. As she followed him through the old church, she realized he was right—the place wasn't exactly hopping, and no one turned to look at them. There were only three other people in the dining room.

After they settled at their table, their waitress approached. The middle-aged woman looked like she'd seen life and then some, but she smiled cheerily enough. "Have you had enough time to look at the menu? Can I get you drinks while you wait? Our soup of the day is roasted butternut squash with toasted pine nuts and crispy bacon. And today's special is confit belly and braised cheek of pork, truffle and cauliflower purée, and roast carrots with toasted nuts and brown butter jus. Tonight's dessert is warm pistachio souffle with chocolate sauce."

And just like that, Agnes' hunger made itself known—with a huge stomach rumble that the waitress pretended she didn't hear, but that made Logan chuckle.

She cast him a frown before answering their waitress. "Yes. I'll have all of that. And bread. It comes with bread, right? I really need bread."

To her credit, the waitress politely replied, "Yes, it comes with bread."

"I need wine too," Agnes added. "Red. Lots of it." She knew nothing about wine, so there was no point in asking for it by name. "Something rich and smooth, with no tangy aftertaste."

"I'll get you some Malbec." the waitress asked. The name meant nothing to Agnes. "Would you like a bottle or a glass?"

Agnes glanced at Logan. "You drinking it too?" He nodded, so she said, "A bottle, please."

When the waitress looked at Logan, he said, "Make it two of everything, thanks, Joyce."

"Sure thing, Logan." And with that, she gathered their menus and hurried away.

Leaving Agnes with a grinning man.

"What?" she demanded.

"Never heard anyone order wine like that before."

She couldn't help the burn in her cheeks. Sometimes her poverty-ridden roots showed through, no matter how far she managed to distance herself from them. "I know what I want to taste. I just don't know names and types." She should have done the wine course when she was at college, but it didn't count toward her degree, so she'd deemed it non-essential. And there'd been no room in her budget for anything that wasn't essential.

"There wasn't anything wrong with it." His face softened. "I just haven't heard it before."

They lapsed into silence. Agnes wasn't in the mood for idle chitchat and, thankfully, Logan was smart enough not to attempt it with her. After what seemed like an eternity, their soup arrived, and Agnes fell on it like a lion who'd chased down an antelope, moaning in delight when she tasted it.

Catching Logan's eye as she reached for the bread, which was warm and baked to perfection, she stilled. He was looking at her the same way she imagined she was looking at the bread—like she'd died and gone to heaven.

"It's good?" he said in a low, gravelly voice.

All she could do was nod. Suddenly, the atmosphere in the restaurant seemed far more intimate than she'd noticed. There were candles on every table, soft music playing in the background, and a large open fire roaring on the back wall. In the bay window, a white Christmas tree decorated in rose gold sparkled at them. From the rich hues of the wooden floor to the exposed brickwork and the crisp white linen, it was clear the place was designed for romance. None of her dates had ever taken her somewhere quite so lovely.

But this wasn't a date.

As if reading her mind, Logan said, "It was either eat here or at the pub, and I figured you'd seen enough of the hotel."

Agnes didn't quite know what to do with his thoughtfulness, so she concentrated on finishing her soup, and when the waitress arrived with their main course, she switched her focus to that. It was definitely worth her attention. The confit melted in her mouth, the carrots were deliciously sweet, and the creamy cauliflower made her taste buds sing the 'Hallelujah Chorus.'

Although she actively kept her gaze from Logan, she was painfully aware of his every move. And it distracted her from her food. Honestly, his sexiness should have been a crime. From the way his bicep flexed as he reached for his wine to the way he patted his lips with his napkin. It was all overtly sensual. As though he'd been designed to make every movement an enticement. And it was annoying.

"Stop it," she said. "You're distracting me."

His eyebrow shot up. "Stop what? I'm just eating."

"I know. But it's the way you're doing it. Maybe you should eat over there." She pointed to the other side of the room.

"Am I chewing too loud? Did I slurp the soup?" His eyes twinkled at her, which was also sexy and therefore rubbed her up the wrong way.

"You're being too…sexy. It's seriously irritating."

That slow, panty-melting smile of his lit up his face. "Too sexy?"

"You need to tone it down. This isn't a date, but you're still oozing sex appeal. I'm embarrassed for you."

"We can't have that."

They stared at each other for a moment, and Agnes could have sworn the temperature in the room shot up.

"You're still sitting here," she said, her voice sounding strangely husky. "Shoo. Go sit over there."

"Agnes, I'm not sitting on the other side of the room because you find me irresistible when I'm not even trying."

"I didn't say I found you irresistible, just distracting."

"And embarrassing," he added helpfully. "Maybe you should eat with your eyes closed and solve the problem that way."

She shook her head. "I'd still hear you and smell you."

"And I sound and smell sexy too?"

"I don't think you're taking this seriously. I'm not attracted to you. I'm just embarrassed for you. You need to rein it in."

"I appreciate the advice." But he still didn't move.

With a grunt of frustration, Agnes attempted to focus on her meal.

* * *

Logan honestly couldn't remember the last time he'd had this much fun having dinner with a woman. She was priceless, and she wasn't even trying. She genuinely wanted him to move away because she found his 'sex appeal' annoying. Agnes gave the word hangry a whole new level of meaning.

"So." Logan leaned back in his chair as he toyed with the stem of his wine glass. "Tell me about yourself." Now that she'd gotten some food into her, she didn't look quite as feral as she had when she'd first turned up on his doorstep. The woman wasn't taking care of herself. And for the sake of everyone around her, she really should.

"What is this? A job interview? I'm already employed," she said with a frown as she dug into her meal.

"This is what most people call polite conversation, Agnes. It generally occurs between two people who're sharing a meal, and it doesn't mean anything other than we're civilized. You can do this. I have faith in you. We'll start with something simple. What's your favorite color?"

He fought to stop from laughing when she rolled her eyes. "Can't we talk about politics or religion instead? Something where we can have a decent debate."

She meant an argument. It seemed the food hadn't quite kicked in enough to mellow her out, and she was still looking for a fight. The whole thing was so damn funny. "No, we can't debate. We're keeping this light. It's called small talk."

"I don't like small talk."

"I'm going to take that as a sign you're feeling better just because you didn't say you hated it."

Her lips twitched as though she wanted to smile but wasn't quite ready to give up her mood just yet.

"Okay, I'll start. My favorite color is green. And yours is?"

"Did you know that's the favorite color of most serial killers?"

He couldn't help but laugh. "Is that true?"

"No." Forgetting she was irritated with him, and the world in general, she flashed a mischievous smile. "It's orange. And my favorite color is cornflower blue."

His heart thudded loudly in his chest at the sight of her. She was gorgeous when she was in a bad mood, but a playful Agnes was breathtaking. As the waitress swapped out their plates for dessert, he kept his eyes on the woman opposite him, watching her mellow as her belly filled. Feeling an irrational pride at being responsible for her mood.

"Okay then, what's your favorite food? Mine's haggis."

The horrified expression on her face was priceless. "Nobody's favorite food is haggis. We just eat it because we're Scottish."

"Cross my heart." He made the gesture. "I love haggis. Your turn. What's your favorite?"

"I can't answer. I'm too traumatized over finding a Scots person who loves haggis. Please tell me you hate bagpipes. At least give me that."

"No can do. I've been to the Edinburgh Tattoo three times."

"That is my worst nightmare." She shuddered. "Being stuck in an enclosed space filled with bagpipe players. Or fighting cats. They'd both make the same noise."

"How can you not like haggis and bagpipes? It's in our DNA."

"Not mine. I don't like black pudding, Scotch pies, or oatcakes, either."

"I don't understand it—you sound Scottish, you look Scottish, and you definitely have that special Scottish charm… Wait! I've got it. It's because you grew up so close to the English border. Their proximity's infected you."

"And you're the poster boy for every Scottish cliché in the book. You've got a kilt, haven't you? And I bet you don't just wear it to weddings."

"I've been known to wear it while fishing…or to the odd football game…" He leaned forward and folded his arms on the table.

The candlelight brought out the golden streaks in Agnes' white-blonde hair and made her green eyes shine like emeralds. Her skin, damn her skin, looked like the surface of the palest pink rose petal. It made him want to touch.

"I knew it," she said triumphantly, flashing a wide grin.

Damn, she was stunning.

He cleared his throat. "Here's the thing about kilts. They're made of heavy wool, which is perfect for winter, but then you have the whole draft issue to contend with. So, that makes you think the built-in ventilation system would make the kilt a good summer option, but then the heavy wool makes you sweat. Really, we need a summer kilt and a winter kilt. And the winter kilt should probably come with thermal shorts."

"You've spent way too much time thinking about this."

"A man's balls are no laughing matter, Agnes. They must be kept at the optimum temperature. Otherwise, his ability to think is seriously affected."

She burst out laughing, and damn if the sight didn't make his blood rush south and his heart soften just a little. He wasn't sure why, but he got the feeling that Agnes didn't laugh much, and that life had been far too heavy and serious for her.

"Come on," he said. "We'd better get those cameras and install them."

Just like that, the light in her eyes faded. "I should probably run it past Dougal first."

"No, this time, I'm putting my foot down and saying that, as a security specialist, I highly recommend you help Dougal to get out of his own way by *not* telling him what we're up to."

The look she gave him was so weary and earnest, the weight of it drilled right to his soul. "I'm trying to be good." A pretty pink blush colored her cheeks. "I mean, I want to do well in this job. My future depends on it."

Logan got the impression she'd meant exactly what she'd said the first time. "You'll have done a good job if you get to the bottom of the hotel's thefts and put a stop to them. Trust me, I know what I'm talking about when I say we need cameras. I'll deal with any fallout. Now, what time does he go home?"

"I deal with my own problems, Logan. If anyone's dealing with Dougal over fallout, it's me."

She was wrong, but he let it go. For now. "When does he go home?" he asked again.

"After the pub shuts, about eleven."

Logan glanced at his phone. It was almost ten, meaning they had some time before they could install the cameras. He signaled for their waitress, who looked up from clearing another table.

"You want it on the Benson account?" Joyce asked.

"Aye, thanks."

"You're putting this on a business account?" Agnes sounded incredulous. "Normally, I'd be impressed, but like I said, it's important Dougal doesn't think I'm taking advantage of him or the people he hires, so I'll pay."

"Believe me, no one will think badly of you because Benson Security paid for dinner." Waving goodnight to Joyce, he led Agnes out of the restaurant. "And don't worry, I'll tell Lake about our dinner in the morning. We don't keep secrets." Lake would have his head on a spike outside the Benson Security office as a warning to anyone else who dared try. "Now, we have an hour to kill before Dougal leaves the hotel, and it will only take five minutes to pick up the cameras, so how about I show you the sights?"

"In the dark?"

"They have lights. It'll be fine."

"And…Invertary has sights?"

"Well, there's the castle, but anyone can see that from the road. And the loch, but you live facing it. You can't visit the old mine at night, so that leaves the folly and Betty's gravestone."

"But Betty isn't dead. She was in the pub just yesterday, hassling Dougal about something."

"No, she isn't dead, although there are many who wish it was otherwise. She just commissioned her gravestone years ago. Trust me, you're going to love it."

"This town just gets weirder and weirder."

"Wait until you've been here for years, that's when the really crazy stuff comes out."

"I don't plan on being here that long. One year. That's all I'm giving Invertary."

Pushing down the strange urge to try to talk her into staying longer, he opened the car. "Do you want to see the sights or not?"

"Fine." She climbed in. "Let's go out in the cold and dark to see gravestones for people who aren't even dead."

"Now you're getting into the swing of things," he said as he closed her door.

CHAPTER 4

MacGregor's folly turned out to be yet another homage to the erect penis.

"Men really don't have any imagination when it comes to architecture, do they?" she asked Logan as they stared at the phallic structure.

"I think the guy who built it might have had some issues. If they'd had Viagra back in the day, this would probably have been a bandstand." He shoved his hands in his pockets and grinned at her. "We can go inside if you like. It isn't locked."

"Tempting, but no." Agnes was beginning to think Logan McBride might be her catnip. Being around him was slightly addicting and definitely put her in a better mood. And it wasn't only because he'd thought to feed her—a rare occurrence in her life, as she was usually the one who looked out for the people around her. Well, her sisters, at least. But Logan also made her have fun. He kind of cajoled her into it. And Agnes couldn't remember the last time she'd had fun.

"Well, if you don't want to check out the interior of the

enormous stone penis, we'd better head over to Betty's gravestone. Come on."

He led her through the park to the graveyard, where Betty's monument stood in all its glory. He'd been right—it was hard to miss. Not only because it had yellow uplighting, but also because it was ten feet tall. It depicted a suspiciously familiar man with long hair and a kilt, carrying a woman in his arms. No, carrying *Betty* in his arms.

"Mel Gibson could sue over this," Agnes said. "Or the producers of *Braveheart*."

"Would you sue Betty?"

He had a point. There was a reason the townsfolk called her Satan. Agnes had only met the ancient woman a couple of times, but she'd heard stories that would curl straight hair in a second.

"You want a photo with it?" Logan asked.

"Uh, no. Thanks."

"You sure? I don't mind taking it."

"You're enjoying this just a little too much, aren't you?"

His smile made her stomach do flips. "Just a little."

"Explain something to me," she said, mesmerized by that smile of his. "Why does Betty wear a hairnet when she's practically bald?"

"I think a more important question is why, when Betty took to dying her hair blue, didn't she dye the hairnet to match?"

Agnes covered her mouth with her hand. "She dyed her hair blue?"

"Well, technically, she dyed her head blue. As you pointed out, she doesn't have much hair."

The girly giggle that escaped from behind her hand didn't sound like her at all. Yet it was strangely freeing. "Why did she dye her head?"

"To show Jodie at the spa she had skills. She wanted a job doing hair."

That was just too much. Agnes doubled over laughing, clutching on to Logan's arm to keep herself upright. As she wiped her eyes, she looked up at Logan, who was staring at her as though fascinated.

"We need to keep you well fed," he said. "Not that I don't like bah-humbug Agnes, but this one…she's something else."

Her cheeks burning, Agnes dropped her hand from Logan's arm, still feeling him against her fingers even when she'd let go.

"Okay." He rocked back on his heels. "Guess that concludes this evening's tour of Invertary's highlights. Next time you have a day off, I'll take you to the mine. That way, you won't have missed anything."

"You don't need to take me anywhere else, Logan. Dougal hired you to investigate the thefts, not to keep me entertained."

"This is what people do when they're being friendly. I figure the whole concept of someone being nice just because they enjoy spending time with you is foreign to you, but this is what normal people do when they like each other. They hang out."

They turned toward the area where he'd parked the car, their breaths like puffs of smoke in the air in front of them. Agnes shoved her hands into the pockets of her coat to stop from reaching for his arm. To stop herself from holding him. Touching him. The temptation was almost too much to bear.

"I'm worried you think this is a date," she said, but really, she was more worried about her own thoughts.

"Don't be. I know this isn't a date." His eyes darkened. "Because if it was, I'd be kissing you by now."

She tripped over her own feet, and his hand shot out to

steady her, grasping her arm, making her skin burn through all of the layers between them.

"Logan," she whispered.

For a second, time was suspended as the two of them stood looking at each other.

At last, Logan cleared his throat and took a step back, releasing her. "Let's get those cameras up."

"Yeah," she agreed, feeling strangely disappointed. "Yes. Good idea."

"And, Agnes, for the record, when we do go out on a date, there won't be any confusion."

As they climbed into the car, she realized he'd said when. Not if. But she honestly couldn't bring herself to correct him, even though she knew dating anyone in Invertary was pointless. She didn't plan on sticking around long enough to see if a relationship could work out.

* * *

AGNES SINCLAIR WAS DRIVING him nuts. It took all of his self-control to keep his hands off her. Everything about the woman appealed to him. From her prickly nature and quick wit to her golden hair and curvy figure. Plump. He'd always loved that word, and that's what she was, voluptuously plump. His fingers itched to trace her curves, to fill his hands with her breasts and backside. He broke out in a sweat just thinking about it. Sitting facing her through dinner had been the sweetest agony, but he was going to go crazy if he didn't get hold of her soon.

The desperation to touch, taste and seduce was a warning bell he couldn't afford to ignore. The last time he'd felt this out of control, he'd married the woman who'd caused it and, in doing so, had ruined his life. No, not completely ruined it. Danielle had given him his kids, and he wouldn't change a second of his life if it meant that he didn't have them. So, no, she hadn't ruined his life. She'd just made it bloody unbearable for years.

Although, if he were honest, the fault had been his as much as hers. Going in, he'd known she didn't want the same things as he did, but he'd thought she'd change her mind. The bloody arrogance of youth—it bit you on the backside every time.

It didn't take them long to pick up the cameras from the office then head on over to the hotel. Once they'd both rid themselves of their jackets, Logan picked up the box and gestured for Agnes to lead the way. "I'm sure you've already thought of the best places to put these," he said.

Astonishment flitted across her face. "You aren't going to question me?"

"Why would I do that? You know the hotel better than I do, and I'll tell you if I think there's a better spot for them. Plus, I'm just the muscle." Holding the box under one arm, he flexed the other.

"Are you trying to impress me with your muscles?"

"Is it working?" He would bet from the way her cheeks flushed that it was.

"Let's get this done," she grumped. "Follow me."

"With pleasure. I meant to tell you over dinner, but I was worried you'd bite my head off, that's a pretty jumper you're wearing, Agnes." Pretty was an understatement. The coral color made her skin glow, and the shape flowed over her curves like cream off the back of a spoon. But the jumper was the least of it. His eyes dropped to her rear. "I like the jeans too. They make it hard for a man to think."

"Will you behave?" If that was supposed to be a reprimand, she'd failed miserably, because it sounded more like a sexy purr.

"This *is* me behaving," Logan said.

With a shake of her head, she turned to climb the stairs. "I thought we'd aim one of the cameras at the storeroom."

"Uh-huh." Damn, she knew how to swing those hips.

Glancing back over her shoulder, she frowned. "Are you listening to me?"

"Aye. But I'm enjoying the show too. I'm that rare mythical beast women search for—a man who can multitask."

Agnes burst out laughing, and Logan felt a strange pride that he'd been the cause of it.

They walked along the corridor to the storeroom in silence, aware that guests were sleeping or watching late-night TV behind closed doors. She pointed up at the corner facing the closet and the bulk of the corridor. "How about there?"

Yep, that would do fine. "You got a ladder?"

"No. I was going to levitate to install the camera." And there it was again—that snarky little bite that made him want to kiss her.

She opened the storeroom door and pulled out a ladder. Logan set it up quietly while Agnes unboxed the cameras. They were just wee things, able to be fixed to the walls with heavy-duty double-sided sticky tape, which is why they'd chosen them—it meant no drilling into the walls of Dougal's precious hotel. Unfortunately, it also meant the range they could transmit was shorter, and their lenses weren't great. There wouldn't be a whole lot of detail in the images they got, but hopefully, they'd be enough to identify the culprit.

Logan pointed down the corridor. "One at the head of the stairs, covering the guest rooms. Another facing your office. And a third in the kitchen."

"What happened to *you know the hotel better than I do?*"

"Just proving I have a brain under all this." He waved a hand down his body. "Wouldn't want you to think I'm all looks and nothing else."

"How about you use that brawn of yours to hold the ladder for me?"

That wasn't happening. His mother had brought him up better than that. "As much as I'd like that view, manners dictate I do the grunt work."

"Fine. If it makes you feel all *manly* to climb the ladder, who am I to get in the way?"

"Exactly." Once he was at the top, she handed him the bottle of rubbing alcohol and a cloth. "I'll wipe the area where the sticky tape will be before you hand it up to me." A couple of minutes later, he'd stuck the first camera high on the wall. "Open the app we set up and check if the angle's right, will you?"

She dug out her phone and compared the image from the camera with the corridor. "A little to the left and down a bit." Logan did as instructed. "That's it. Perfect. You really are a mythical beast—you can multitask *and* you follow instructions."

"Oh, I'm very good at following instructions," he purred as he climbed down the ladder to stand beside her. "Especially if I can see the value in doing it." He reached out to tuck a lock of her white-blonde hair behind her ear, but he took his time, lingering, feeling the silk between his finger and thumb. "Isobel has dark hair," he murmured, and most would say it was pretty in itself, but he preferred the color Agnes sported.

"And my sister Mairi has curly red hair, and my other sister, Donna, has honey-colored hair. My family covers all the options."

Her voice sounded raspy, and he wondered if it was an effect of him standing so close to her. He hoped so.

"You've changed your deodorant," she said, making him realize she was breathing him in just as deeply as he was her.

"Is it better?" His fingers toyed with her hair.

"Yeah. It smells like the ocean." She cleared her throat and stepped back out of his reach. "Next camera. Get the ladder. Chop chop."

"Yes, ma'am."

After attaching two more cameras to cover the main guest floor, Logan turned to Agnes. "What about upstairs?"

"There isn't any storage up there, and that's where my room is, so I should be a deterrent to a thief. I think one camera at the top of the stairs is probably enough."

"Sound reasoning," he agreed.

"And *that* doesn't come across as patronizing at all."

That delighted him. "You honestly don't believe in letting shit slide, do you?"

"No." She stared him straight in the eye. "Still think my backside is sexy?"

"Oh, yeah." Even more so than before. Call him a masochist, but Agnes' take-no-prisoners attitude did it for him.

"Let's do upstairs first, and then there's just the kitchen to cover." She picked up the box of cameras.

And that's when they heard it. A little doggy yip followed by a deep rumble.

Dougal was back.

"I thought you said he'd gone home," Logan hissed as he grabbed the ladder and ran for the storage cupboard.

"He had," Agnes snapped behind him.

Heavy footfalls on the stairs signaled that Dougal was very much there and heading their way.

Logan thrust the ladder into the closet as silently as he could, then stepped inside. Agnes came barreling in after him and pulled the door tight behind them. Her phone light came on, and she slowly inserted her key in the lock and turned it, securing them inside, just as Dougal's footsteps arrived on the first floor.

CHAPTER 5

It was a good thing Logan didn't suffer from claustrophobia, or he'd have been going out of his mind. Much like a pantry, the closet was narrow but deep, with shelving on three sides filled with bedding, soaps, coffee sachets, and assorted other things the housekeepers needed to stock their carts. It would have been plenty big enough for one person to move around, but with two people and a large metal ladder, it was a tight fit.

Agnes lifted her phone, typed a message and held it up to him. *I think we should just come clean. Hiding in here is ridiculous.*

But fun. Logan grinned before whispering against her ear, "I thought you didn't want to have this conversation with him? There's a good chance we can get this whole case solved without him having to know anything."

They stood pressed against each other, her back to his front. He could feel the tension in her body as she weighed up the different options before typing again. *If he catches us in here, I'll get fired.*

Logan didn't think so—Dougal might be loud, but he was

all bluster. He wouldn't fire her for this. "We'll just tell him we're on a stakeout," he whispered.

They heard a scraping at the door, and Agnes pressed back against him. He wrapped an arm around her, turning her to face him as he slowly angled her away from the door, wanting to put his body between her and Dougal. His behavior was more instinct than any worry her boss would strike out if he found them.

There was whining, followed by a yip and more scratching. The dog knew they were in there. Logan tried to swallow a chuckle, but it forced its way out. Quick as lightning, Agnes slapped a hand over his mouth and held on tight. Her disapproval was so loud he could almost hear her frown.

"What is it, boy?" Dougal whispered. Well, it was a whisper for him. For normal people, it was their usual voice. The man had volume-control issues and a deep need to hear himself talk. "Is something in there?"

The door handle rattled, and Logan tightened his arm around Agnes' waist, pressing their chests together, making him painfully aware of all her soft curves against his firm muscle. His mouth watered, and his fingers itched to explore. If this temptation was some sort of test, he was worried he'd fail.

"It's locked, boy," Dougal said. "There's nothing in there but soap and sheets. Now, come away. Let's get this over with, so I can get some sleep."

The dog kept scratching and whining.

"Arnold," Dougal snapped. "Come here."

There was another yip and then silence, making Logan hope the dog had done as it was told. They heard a knock and a door opening.

"I'm sorry to bother you at this ungodly hour, Mrs. Edwards, but Arnold left his favorite toy here, and he won't go to sleep without it."

"I totally understand," the woman said. "I can't get to sleep without my favorite Josh pillow."

That set Logan off again. Covering his mouth tight with her hand, Agnes kicked him in the shin to stop him. Unfortunately, the kick must have attracted the dog's attention, and it started scratching at the door all over again.

"Arnold," Dougal called. "Get over here. I have your toy. Look, here it is."

"That's an interesting toy," Mrs. Edwards said. "It's an eggplant, isn't it?"

"Aye, although we call it an aubergine here in Scotland. It's one of them emoji things the kids like. One of the teens gave it to me, and Arnold fair enjoys chewing on it. They also gave him one of those poop emojis, but I don't let him have that one in public. Kids today, there's no accounting for what goes on in their heads."

It was too much. Logan tore his mouth from Agnes' hand and buried his face in the crook of her neck, his shoulders shaking with silent laughter. He would bet she wanted to hit him again but didn't want to lure the dog back to the door.

"There you go, Arnold," Dougal said. "Who's a good boy? Thank you, Mrs. Edwards. I'd better get this tired pup home now. We'll see you at breakfast."

"You know," Mrs. Edwards said, sounding far from sleepy, "you and Arnold are welcome to spend the night here. Save yourselves the trip back home."

She was hitting on Dougal?

This was priceless. Logan almost choked from trying to stay quiet when all he wanted to do was roar with laughter. Agnes pinched him in the ribs. Hard. But it made no difference. He was having the most fun he'd had in years.

"Uh, eh, thank you. But no. Delightful offer, but I have to decline," Dougal blustered. "Arnold can't sleep without his dog bed either. Can you, Arnold? We'd best be getting back." Dougal's voice became fainter as he retreated.

"Oh, well, maybe another time," Mrs. Edwards called after him before her door shut quietly.

Ears straining, they waited until they heard the dull thud of the pub door close behind Dougal.

"You numpty," Agnes hissed as she thumped his arm. "You almost gave us away."

His hands on her hips, Logan grinned against the curve of her throat. He felt like a kid again, sneaking around after hours, hoping his parents didn't catch him. Before he could open his mouth to tell Agnes to chill, he heard a thud in the corridor. They stilled. It probably came from Mrs. Edwards' room, but better safe than sorry.

"We should give it another five minutes, just to be sure," he whispered against the shell of her ear.

A shiver passed through her, and her breathing hitched, before she nodded. His hands flexed on her hips at the realization she was just as aware of him as he was of her. Suddenly, it wasn't the humor of the situation that was foremost in his mind, but the feeling of Agnes' hands spread wide on his chest. Relying on instinct, he nuzzled her throat and elation surged when she angled her head to give him better access. The darkness covered them like an intimate blanket, and the need to be silent heightened their senses, making each touch, each breath, so much more electric.

Breathing deep, he took her scent into him. Wildflowers. Of course, wild, just like her. Slowly, softly, he ran his lips down her neck to her shoulder, pausing where he felt her pulse thunder. Time seemed to stop as they balanced on the edge of a precipice. Should they step into the unknown or retreat to safety? Fingers moved on his chest, stroking. Once. Twice. The decision had been made—they were taking the leap together.

Cotton sheets brushed his knuckles as he pressed her back against the shelves, the cool material a stark contrast to the warmth under his palms. She emitted a sexy little sigh, her hands sliding up and around his neck as Logan gently kissed the curve of her throat. Their breathing became heavier, the sound of blood rushing through his veins so much louder. Slowly, deliberately, he kissed his way along her jaw to her mouth. Her skin was as smooth as he'd imagined it to be, exactly like satin-soft rose petals.

There was a second, a pause, where he hovered over her lips, barely a hair's breadth between them as they inhaled each other's air.

"Agnes?" he whispered the request against her lips.

Her answer was immediate, but it wasn't expressed in words. Instead, her tongue nipped out to taste him. And with a groan, he was gone. Clasping the back of her head, he angled his mouth over hers, threading his fingers through all that glorious, silken hair. They seduced each other with lips, and teeth, and tongue. Slow, languorous, drugged kisses that made his heart beat faster and the world fade to nothing.

Her fingers clasped the hair at his nape, tugging him to her as her leg slid up the outside of his thigh. Logan hooked a hand under it, pressing his hard length against her, swallowing her moan. He was a teen again, lost in a long, stolen kiss. Hoping it'd never end. Praying that she'd let him go further, but not yet, not while the kissing was so damn good.

A brutally sharp rap at the door jerked them back to reality.

"Sorry to interrupt." Mrs. Edwards' voice invaded the closet. "But the soundproofing in the store cupboard isn't the best, and I figured you'd want to move somewhere more comfortable soon anyway. Oh, and the camera wasn't stuck up properly. It fell off the wall. I'll just leave it on the floor beside the door. Night, night, you two. Have fun!"

Logan leaned his forehead against Agnes', smiling at their ludicrous situation. "How did she know it was us?" Damn, but he wanted to keep on kissing her. It didn't matter that they were in a closet and one of the hotel guests was eavesdropping just outside. He just wanted more of the woman in his arms.

"Ears like a bat." Agnes sounded breathless, and he couldn't help but preen. "She misses nothing," she said. "Unless she's talking about Josh at the time. She also makes good use of the spy hole in her door."

It sounded like it wasn't the first time Agnes had been caught out by Mrs. Edwards. "You don't make a habit of seducing men in storage cupboards, do you?"

Agnes growled at him. A sexy sound in the darkness of the tiny space.

"I'm joking. Come on, we'd better fix the camera. Then I need to get home to my kids."

Every muscle in her body went taut. And then she squeezed past him to fumble with the door, throwing it wide as soon as she'd unlocked it. Light spilled into the closet, almost blinding him. When his eyes had adjusted, he discovered Agnes standing on the other side of the corridor, her arms folded.

"Kids?" She sounded far too polite, considering they'd been making out not two seconds earlier.

"A fourteen-year-old son and a twelve-year-old daughter." Her eyes drifted to his left hand, and he felt like kicking his own backside. So that's what was bothering her. He waggled his ring finger. "Divorced. Going on seven years."

"I'm sorry," she said, as though offering her condolences.

"I'm not. What's going on, Agnes?" He took a step toward her, but she hurriedly retreated.

"Nothing. Absolutely nothing. You need to get back to your kids, and I need to get to bed." She blinked up at him with a perfectly bland, professional expression. "If you need to hurry home, I can finish up on my own. In fact, why don't I just do that? It's getting really late. Let me get your jacket for you." And she jogged down the stairs to her office.

There was nothing Logan could do but follow and, before he could blink, he found himself with his jacket in his hand, standing outside the hotel, while she locked the door behind him. For a few minutes, he just stood there, staring at the doors and wondering what the hell just happened.

And then, he went home to his kids.

* * *

AGNES LEANED her head against the closed front door and listened to Logan walk away. "It's for the best," she whispered.

Getting together with Logan when she knew she'd be leaving was one thing, but she couldn't start something with no future when there were kids involved. It was best she stopped things now before someone got hurt.

Taking a deep, shaky breath, she went back upstairs to finish putting up the cameras and found Mrs. Edwards waiting for her.

"I thought you two would be heading to the bedroom, but I saw you go downstairs instead," the woman said, proving she'd been making good use of her spyhole again. She peered behind Agnes. "Where's your young man?"

"He's gone home, and he isn't *my* young man."

"That's not what it sounded like when you were in the closet."

They were silent for a moment before Agnes said, "Probably best if we don't tell Dougal about this."

"My lips are sealed." Mrs. Edwards made a zipping gesture over her mouth. "You know, I thought Logan would stay. You seemed to be having fun." She waggled her eyebrows suggestively.

"Yeah, well, the fun ended. Let's just say things didn't work out."

"Oh, that's a shame. Was it an ego problem? Did you challenge his masculinity?" Mrs. Edwards patted her hand. "Men are such delicate creatures."

Agnes cocked an eyebrow. "I don't think we know the same men."

"It's true." Mrs. Edwards nodded. "They have fragile egos that are easily bruised. That's why they strut so much. It's an attempt to warn people away, so they can't get close enough to damage them. You have to be very careful of their egos— it's the key to a lasting relationship." She stared into the distance. "My dear, departed husband, Harold, used to say, 'Emily, you're a queen amongst women because you know how to stroke a man.'"

Agnes almost choked on nothing and started coughing loudly.

"Oh dear, I'll get you a glass of water." Mrs. Edwards scurried away, passing another guest. Mr. Thompson, who was in his nineties, was in town visiting family. Although his kids had wanted him to stay with them, he'd told them he needed his own space. Agnes suspected his kids wouldn't have looked favorably on the amount of whisky he put away before bed.

"What's going on?" he demanded. "I could hear the racket you're making even without my hearing aids. You do realize it's the middle of the night? The hallway isn't the place to party." Agnes kept coughing while he frowned down at her. "Are you sick? Do you need a hot toddy?"

Mrs. Edwards appeared again, a glass of water in her hand. Agnes took it gratefully.

"It's the flu season," Mr. Thompson told Mrs. Edwards.

"She needs a hot toddy. That will sort her out. Do you want one an' all?"

"Oh, yes, please," Mrs. Edwards simpered.

"Back in a minute." Tugging his dressing gown belt tight, Mr. Thompson stomped toward the stairs and the kitchen below them.

As she gulped down the water, Agnes held up a hand to stop him. "The kitchen's locked for the night."

"Don't worry," he said over his shoulder. "I know the code."

"He has the code?" Agnes looked at Mrs. Edwards, who nodded.

"You know, to the metal number box that controls the lock."

"Yes," Agnes forced through gritted teeth. "I know what the box does. What I don't know is how he has the code." Was there any security at all in this damn hotel?

"Oh, everybody has it," Mrs. Edwards said dismissively. "It's four zeroes. If you stay in the hotel for more than a week, you pick these things up. When I can't sleep, I often go downstairs during the night and make myself a sandwich."

Well, that explained the food missing from the kitchen. No need to put a camera there. But she was damn well changing the lock code.

"By any chance, do you also help yourself to soap and stuff from the store cupboard?" It was worth asking.

"No, I wouldn't do that. Now, do you need more water?"

"I'm good," Agnes groaned as Mrs. Edwards fussed around her, chatting about Josh for endless minutes.

"Here we go," Mr. Thompson called as he came back up the stairs, thankfully interrupting yet another Josh story. "Hot toddies for everyone." He carried a tray with steaming mugs and a huge cake. "And I found a chocolate cake in the fridge. Hadn't been touched yet. It looks like we're in for a treat."

"That's for tomorrow's lunch crowd," Agnes said.

Mr. Thompson and Mrs. Edwards looked so deflated that Agnes just sighed. "What the hell, have at it. I'll get a replacement from the bakery."

"Now that's the spirit," Mr. Thompson said. "Are we having a picnic out here in the hallway? Because I don't think my arthritis could cope with sitting on the floor."

"Come into my room." Mrs. Edwards took his hand. "Have you seen my Josh McInnes cushions?"

"No, can't say that I have."

"Then you're in for a treat." She smiled over her shoulder at Agnes. "Are you coming, honey?"

"No. I need to get to bed."

Another door opened, and one of the young guests from Australia popped her head out. "What's going on?" she said.

"We're having chocolate cake in my room," Mrs. Edwards said. "A midnight feast. It's just like one of those books I read when I was in school. You're welcome to join us."

"Awesome." The woman grinned and called back into her room, "Breanna, we've got cake. Get your backside out of bed."

The door beside the Australians opened and the male half of the middle-aged couple from Holland appeared. "There is very much noise," he said.

"We're having chocolate cake." Mrs. Edwards pointed at the tray. "Would you like to join us?"

He looked at everyone. Looked at the cake. Then shrugged. "For sure." He called into the room. "Marijke, wij hebben lekkere chocolada taart met de buren." He looked back at them with a wide smile. "Everything people say about Scotland is true. You are a very welcoming nation."

"Isn't it awesome?" Mrs. Edwards beamed at him as she

led Mr. Thompson into her room. "Do you like Josh McInnes?" she asked the Dutchman.

"I think he is a singer, ya?" The man looked confused.

"Oh, he's so much more than that," Mrs. Edwards said as they all piled into her room, dressed in various sleepwear.

"Is this normal over here?" Breanna asked Agnes as she passed.

"Nowhere near it," Agnes said.

With a bewildered smile, the Australian closed the door behind her, leaving Agnes with her hot toddy. She sank onto the top step and grimaced as she took a sip. It was good whisky ruined.

"I should never have kissed him," she muttered to nobody.

Kissing a man was fun, but kissing a single father was terrifying. Kids needed stability and sacrifice. You couldn't be selfish *and* have kids, and Agnes very much wanted to be selfish. She'd looked after her sisters for as long as she could remember.

Before she'd left home illegally at fourteen, not the sixteen they'd told everyone, she'd been the one to protect her sisters from bullies. And the one brave enough to sneak into their parents' room while they slept, to take money out of their dad's wallet so they'd have food the next day, instead of him drinking it away. And when Isobel had fallen pregnant at fifteen and their dad kicked her out, Agnes had been the one to leave with her.

It had been Agnes who'd lied about her age to pick up part-time jobs to support them. And Agnes who'd stolen when things got tough—and they'd been really tough when their two younger sisters left home to join them. By eighteen, she'd been responsible for her three sisters and her nephew. The weight of keeping everyone fed, clothed and warm was so heavy at times, she'd wondered if she'd ever get out from under it.

Yeah, she'd had enough of the responsibility and selflessness that went with bringing up kids. Now, she wanted to do all the things she couldn't do when she was younger. She wanted to travel, and she wanted to live a carefree life. But most of all, she wanted the security she'd never had as a child. And the only way to get that was to work her way to the top of her profession.

Which couldn't happen in Invertary.

So, no, starting something with a single father was the worst thing she could do.

Even if he did kiss like a god.

CHAPTER 6

A few short, restless hours after leaving the hotel, Logan found himself walking back through the front door while wondering what the hell he was going to say to Agnes. He was a father, and his kids lived with him. There wasn't a whole helluva lot he could, or would want to, do about that. It didn't mean things had to end between them. People with kids dated every day, and he just had to get to the bottom of why Agnes had reacted so badly when she discovered he was a father.

"Morning, Bernadette," he called to the young woman behind the hotel reception desk.

Barely nineteen, the girl was more interested in the makeup tutorials she did for her YouTube channel than anything else.

"Good morning, sir. How may I help you?" she asked woodenly.

"Are you okay?" Normally she shouted, 'Wassup?' at him.

She glanced behind her toward the open door to Agnes' office and shook her head. "She's in a bad mood," she hissed.

"Well, she can take it out on me." He headed toward the open door.

Bernadette grabbed his arm with a look in her eye that said she was on the verge of hysteria. "Maybe you should come back later, like once the full moon has passed. I hear it affects her."

It was hard not to grin. "I think I can cope with your boss." He patted her hand before striding through the door.

Agnes sat behind one of the two desks, poring over a pile of receipts. She looked up at him, her face such a picture of professional disinterest you would never have guessed they'd kissed only hours earlier.

"You'll be glad to hear I solved the food thefts," she said. "So we can strike that off our list. It seems everyone staying in the hotel knew the code to the kitchen. I've changed it, so there shouldn't be any more missing food. Unfortunately, there's still the missing everything else to deal with. I'll call if anything else is stolen or if the cameras show something new."

With a polite smile, she returned to her work. He'd been dismissed.

Ignoring the dismissal, Logan closed the door behind him and sat in one of the guest chairs. "Are we going to talk about last night?"

Something flickered in her eyes before they turned cold again. "There's nothing to talk about. We got carried away, and it won't happen again."

"I'm not so sure about that." Chemistry like that was pretty hard to resist.

"Look, Logan." She put her clasped hands on the desk in front of her. "I had a lovely time last night, but I don't want to start something that can't go anywhere. I'm only in Invertary for a short amount of time and trust me when I say that

I have no intention of staying here. A relationship with me is a dead end."

He scratched his head. "You're saying it isn't even worth seeing if there's something between us because you're leaving anyway?"

"Exactly." She beamed at him like he was a not-too-bright child.

He motioned between them. "What if this thing has the potential to be something great?"

"There is no 'this thing.' There was a kiss. That was it."

"A pretty spectacular kiss."

"I'm flattered you think so."

"You're flattered?" Was she saying it had been crap for her?

"I have it on good authority that the male ego is a fragile thing, so let's not get into this." She stood, walked over to the door, and opened it for him. "I'd be happy to have the camera feeds go to your phone too. It would be a relief to have someone else monitor them. Just give your number to Bernadette, and I'll get that set up."

"The camera feeds work over localized Wi-Fi. Even with the app, I'd only be able to see the feed if I was in the hotel."

Her smile was frighteningly cold. "In that case, I'll call if I need you."

Logan had no other option but to leave. As he passed her, he paused. "That kiss was damn amazing, and you know it."

"Have a nice day," she said, before the door closed with him on the wrong side of it.

Logan stared at the door for a minute before turning to a fascinated Bernadette. "I don't even know what happened in there."

"She has that effect on everyone. It's spooky. I've been having these weird random pains since she started working here. I searched her office, just in case there was a doll that looked like me that she was using as a pincushion. Nothing turned up. But that doesn't mean it doesn't exist. I just need to look harder."

Logan swallowed a sigh. "Bernadette, have you thought about going to college? You know, getting out of Invertary might do you good."

"Oh, no." Her heavily made-up eyes went wide. "It's just a matter of time before my YouTube channel takes off, and I'm fine right here until it does. This job might not look like much, but they feed me, and when it's slow, Dougal doesn't mind if I work on my videos. How many jobs let you do that?"

"Okaaay," Logan said. "Then can you do me a favor and keep an eye on Agnes? If she does anything out of the ordinary, send me a text."

"You want me to spy on my boss?"

"Well, aye."

"Yes!" She punched the air. "This day is looking up. I can totally do that for you. Do you need photos? I'm awesome at taking photos."

"No," Logan said, deflating her bubble a little. "Just updates." She looked so crestfallen that he added, "But if something merits a photo, I wouldn't say no."

And just like that, Bernadette was back to perky. "I'm on it. Don't worry. I'll keep my eyes glued to her." She handed him her phone. It was pink.

"Great." He keyed in his number before returning it. "Thanks for your help." He strode toward the door.

"Wait," Bernadette called. "Does this mean I'm officially part of Benson Security?"

"In an unofficial capacity," he said with a straight face.

"Awesome." Bernadette looked starry-eyed.

With a shake of his head, Logan headed into the pub, where he was meeting Lake. Maybe his boss could shed some light on how Agnes' mind worked, because he was coming up blank.

* * *

AGNES PRESSED her hand to the closed door after Logan had gone. Surely, he'd gotten the message that she didn't want to start anything romantic. She'd been clear, right? And it was *definitely* what she wanted…mostly…

She'd spent the night thinking about it and had come to the conclusion that this was the only way forward. There was no future in starting something with Logan, so why put them both through an inevitable breakup? Why put his kids through it? Yes, it was definitely the right decision. So why did she have a pain in her chest from sending him away?

Her phone rang, and she glanced at the screen to see it was housekeeping. "The delivery's here," the housekeeper said. "They've parked out front like you asked them to. Although why you didn't get them to park at the back door as usual, I don't know. Are you just trying to make more work for us?"

Agnes smiled, and she knew if anyone could see it, they'd run screaming. "It's just for today. You can carry on with preparing the rooms, and I'll deal with it personally." She hung up before Eileen could complain that the housekeeping deliveries were her job.

"I'm dealing with a delivery," she told Bernadette as she passed. "If you need me, call me on my mobile."

Bernadette nodded and then, for some inexplicable reason, took her photo. Agnes didn't even bother to ask. Some conversations seriously weren't worth starting.

She pushed through the heavy wooden doors and stepped out into the icy December air, instantly wishing she'd thought to grab her coat. The driver climbed down to meet her. A big man with wild hair, he reminded her of Boris Johnson.

"You must be the new manager. Dougal doesn't like us parking out front. And he's very specific about not using the main door for deliveries."

"I know," she said sweetly and held out her hand for the paperwork. "Unfortunately, we're having some work done and it isn't possible to use the back door at the moment. I'm afraid you'll have to take the boxes through the pub and up the stairs to the hotel."

"Why can't we use that door?" He pointed at the hotel doors she'd just come through.

"Blocked."

It was clear he didn't believe her, as he was staring at her as though trying to figure out what the punchline was. "Fine, we do it your way," he said at last. Then he pointed at the guy in the passenger's seat and signaled for him to get out.

Meanwhile, Agnes reached for her phone. She already had Mrs. Edwards primed to do her part, now she just needed to get Dougal out of the pub, so he wouldn't start shouting when the deliverymen traipsed through.

"Dougal," she said once he'd answered, "Mrs. Edwards has a problem, and she refuses to speak to anyone but you."

"I'm happy to talk to her." He hesitated. "But you'd better come with me, seeing as you're the…ah…manager."

Yep, she bet that stuck in his throat. "I can't, I'm sorry. I'm in the middle of something."

"The customer comes first," Dougal barked.

"I understand, but I'm really tied up."

There was silence for a second before his voice lowered. "I don't think it's a good idea for me to be alone with her."

Agnes fought a grin. "Don't worry about that. She's got a room full of teenagers helping stuff goody bags."

He cleared his throat. "Okay. Well, in that case, carry on."

"Thanks, Dougal." She hung up.

When she turned to the deliverymen, they were waiting with a trolley loaded with boxes.

"If Dougal shouts at us," the driver said, "we're pointing at you."

"And they say chivalry is dead." She walked down the street to the pub doors. They were on the corner of the high street and in full view of everyone out shopping. Once there, she propped the doors open for the men to go through. "Be careful with those boxes," she called after them, far louder than necessary. "That's our new toiletry range for the hotel. It's top of the line—people pay a fortune for this stuff. We're lucky to have gotten it."

"If you're changing out the toiletries to something better," Breanna asked, as soon as Agnes stepped into the dining area of the pub, "is that only for new guests, or will we get it too? I wouldn't mind trying that range."

Agnes beamed at her. "I'll make sure they stock your room."

As she watched the deliverymen make their way through the bar, she was pleased to see heads turning to follow their progress and people reading the brand name on the boxes. She could tick part one of her plan off her list. She was grinning when her eyes caught on the last person she wanted to see there—Logan. Just her luck.

* * *

"SHE'S UP TO SOMETHING," Logan told Lake, who sat opposite him in a booth at the side of the pub, not far from where Agnes was grinning a little maniacally after the deliverymen.

Lake glanced over at Agnes and nodded. "Absolutely."

"Just take all the new toiletries up to the store cupboard,"

Agnes called, loud enough for the whole room to hear. "We won't start putting them out until tomorrow."

The deliverymen grumbled something but headed for the stairs up into the hotel.

"Why is she making them go through the pub?" Logan said, more to himself than anyone else. "Deliveries would usually go through the back door."

Louise, who worked in the town's tiny supermarket, stopped beside Agnes. "I can't believe you have the Orion range of toiletries," she squealed. "That stuff is so hard to come by. I couldn't even order the shampoo off their site the other day because it was out of stock." She stared wistfully after the deliverymen. "I don't suppose you'd sell me a couple of bottles?"

"Sorry." Agnes shook her head. "But if you book a room after tomorrow, you'll be able to use the range as part of your guest experience."

"I wish," Louise said with a laugh. "I'd love a night away from the kids. If you change your mind about selling them, let me know."

"Absolutely." Agnes beamed. It was over the top.

"She's still talking too loud," Logan said. "And why is she making such a big deal out of shampoo?" He groaned as it hit him. "I'm an idiot." His brain had been so occupied with wondering about what'd happened between them in the office and why things had suddenly turned cold that he'd missed the obvious. "She's baiting a trap, and she's not being subtle about it."

"Nope," Lake said. "That'll be why she had the lorry park in the street." He cocked a thumb to the window, where the rear of a huge truck blocked their view.

He'd been so focused on Agnes that he'd missed the truck. If Dougal saw that there, he'd have a conniption. Logan glanced around, realizing Agnes had managed to get rid of the hotel owner. She'd staged the whole thing, and he'd missed most of it because he'd been too busy worrying about their weird conversation. Some detective he was turning into.

"She's driving me crazy," Logan confessed. "I'm so busy wondering what's going on in her head that I'm missing stuff." It wasn't an apology, but his boss should definitely know he was falling down on the job.

"Happens to the best of us." Lake reached for his coffee, his too-observant eyes missing nothing. "You know, Agnes has a habit of taking care of her own problems, even when it can get her in trouble. She isn't used to relying on anyone else."

Logan focused in on the man. "What does that mean?"

"Did you read the background report I did on her?" Lake lazed back in the booth, his leather pilot's jacket at his side, and the sleeves of his blue Henley pushed up past his elbows. He sipped his coffee, looking every inch a man relaxed, but his gaze continually scanned the room on the lookout for trouble.

"It seemed pretty standard," Logan said. "Except for the part about why she's been blacklisted in the hotel community."

Lake's eyes turned to steel. "That's being dealt with. Callum wasn't too pleased about his sister-in-law being blackmailed for sex either."

It was on the tip of his tongue to ask to be included in whatever Callum had planned for the sleazy hotel owner, but he didn't have the right. Agnes had made it clear they were nothing but work colleagues. And that knowledge sat in his gut like cement.

"What wasn't in the report?" Logan asked his boss. "What do you know that I don't?"

"More than you're capable of processing."

"About Agnes, dickhead."

Lake did that smile-twitch thing he did, rather than just smiling like the rest of them, before leaning in to rest his forearms on the table. "When Agnes' sister Isobel first walked into Callum's life, I did a deep dig into all four sisters. I didn't want my business partner taking on something he wasn't ready for."

This wasn't news—Lake looked out for his own. "But you must have been happy with what you found. Callum and Isobel are married."

"Isobel's a sweetheart who attracts trouble. Callum can handle that. Mairi, the youngest Sinclair, is a bit of a wild child, but now that she has her business and a man to occupy her, she's calmed down some. And Donna's the sensitive one. She needed someone to protect her, which her husband, Duncan, is doing just fine."

Logan was used to Lake knowing everything about everyone, so he wasn't surprised by his assessment of the Sinclair family. "And Agnes?"

Lake's ice blue eyes met his. "She's the protector."

Something in the way Lake said it made Logan sit up straighter. "What exactly did she do to protect them?"

"See." Lake pointed a finger at him. "That kind of question is why I hired you and why I put up with you calling me dickhead on occasion. Agnes has a sealed juvenile record a mile long."

Logan didn't bother asking how Lake managed to get access to sealed records. His boss had connections that even government intelligence agencies would envy. He would have found court documents child's play to attain.

"Most of her arrests ended without a conviction," Lake said. "But she did community service for one offense."

Community service wasn't uncommon as a punishment for wayward teens. Logan thought back to the way Agnes had denied she'd stolen from the hotel. Just that one word: No.

"What did she steal?"

Lake's eyes flashed approval. "Just about everything that wasn't pinned down. She was the main breadwinner for Isobel and her baby, and then their two younger sisters. She was fourteen when she moved out with her pregnant sister. Seventeen when the other two sisters joined them. Donna and Mairi were still in school."

Logan's mind was going a mile a minute. "Food, clothes, nappies—am I right?"

Lake nodded. "Everything her family needed that she couldn't afford to buy on the money she made from her cleaning jobs."

"A judge would have understood that. I don't see her getting community service for it. Counseling, aye, but a sentence?" He shook his head. "What else is there?"

"Her father was, *is*, an alcoholic. The bastard kind. Beats their mother, who's so out of it on pills I doubt she even notices anymore."

Logan let out a low curse, his mind instantly going to his own kids. "Did he hit the girls too?"

"Only the once. He turned up at their flat in Campbeltown. Agnes was a few days shy of her eighteenth birthday. He wanted money. Social Services had cottoned on to the fact the girls weren't living with him and had stopped him claiming money to support them. Furious, he figured they owed him for the loss of income, and he threatened to have the two youngest girls sent back to him or put in care. Agnes told him to go to hell and that he wasn't getting any money from them—not that they had any to give. He didn't like being told no. And being drunk, he struck out, hitting Donna."

"The weakest link. The bastard."

"Yeah." Lake took a sip of his coffee, his eyes on Logan. "He hit her hard enough to give her concussion. She doesn't remember any of it, but there are hospital records."

From what little he knew of Agnes and her sisters, he guessed she'd gone ballistic when Donna had been hurt. "What did she do to their father to get her arrested?"

"Hit him with a wooden chair. When it broke, she used the leg to beat him senseless. Broke his nose, took out three teeth, damaged the sight in one eye, and pulverized the fingers in his left hand by jumping on it. It took two cops to get her off him."

Logan nodded. "I would have done worse."

Lake inclined his head in agreement while Logan reached for his own coffee, wishing it was something stronger.

"That doesn't explain the community service though. Grievous bodily harm is a serious assault, so she should have been tried as an adult."

"There were witnesses, apart from her sisters, which helped her case. But the flat they rented was owned by a local businesswoman who had a lot of property in the area, meaning she had power and connections. Far as I can gather, their landlady was seriously pissed that the girls had been hurt. She had a word with the local judge on Agnes' behalf, and her word held sway."

"Was the community service connected to a hotel by any chance?"

Lake flashed a rare smile. "Just so happened that their landlady owned a small hotel. Agnes worked out her time there, then went on to paid employment with time off to study. The owner organized other work placements for Agnes too, helping her get all the experience she could, not to mention the money she needed. If it wasn't for deferring her study to help support her sisters, she'd have had her management degree years earlier. I think she planned to work in the woman's hotel when she qualified, but the owner died years ago, and her properties were sold."

It seemed Agnes Sinclair just couldn't catch a break. "What happened to the father?"

"Well, he can't play the piano anymore," Lake said drolly.

In spite of everything, Logan laughed.

"He's been in and out of prison. Agnes and her sisters have nothing to do with either of their parents."

"I wouldn't mind paying that man a visit."

"You'd need to get in line. Donna's husband, Duncan, asked first, and Callum's itching to *talk* to him too."

"So," Logan said, his eyes straying to the door where Agnes had disappeared, "she's used to dealing with her own problems any way she deems fit, and she's desperate to hold on to this job because it's her only chance to shake off being blacklisted." Logan thought about it for a minute and then sighed. "I'd better call my mum and get her to watch the kids tonight. I'm going to be busy stopping Agnes from getting herself into trouble."

"And that right there is why you get paid the big bucks." Lake relaxed back in his seat, taking his coffee with him.

And Logan flipped off his smug English boss.

CHAPTER 7

Logan spent the rest of his day running routine background checks for Benson Security clients. As the information guy in the operation, his job was to dig through databases, investigate trails online, and call leads for preliminary chats before presenting his work to the field agents in a report. To others, it might have sounded like dull work, but it took skill, creative thinking and some serious finesse.

Really, it wasn't unlike the work he'd done as a detective in Glasgow. And, as well as giving him the same training as the rest of the Benson Security staff, Lake gave him jobs out in the field to keep his skills sharp. But, generally, he was home in time for dinner. As was the case that night.

When he'd first moved back to Invertary, a year or so after his wife left him, he'd stayed with his parents while he looked for a house. Only, while he'd been looking, the house that made up the other half of his parents' building went on sale, and he'd jumped at it. Now he lived next door to his parents and had built-in babysitters for his kids. His mum loved it. He wasn't sure what his dad thought, as he spent most of his time in the shed at the bottom of the garden.

"Hello," he called out as he let himself into his parents' house.

He followed the smell of beef stew to the back of the house and the kitchen.

"Dad!" His daughter, Darcy, roller-skated over and wrapped her arms around him. "I got a certificate in school today. For maths. I'm a genius!"

"Well done, you." He squeezed her in a bear hug and kissed the top of her head. She had the same rich brown hair her mother had sported before she'd gone blonde, but she had his hazel eyes. In other words, she was perfect. "Should you be wearing roller skates in the house?"

"I can't wear them outside, Dad. It's dark and cold."

"Maybe take them off until we get home. By the smell of things, Gran has dinner about done anyway." Plus, his half of the duplex came with a concrete-floored garage, where she could roller skate until she exhausted herself.

"Hey, Mum." He leaned down to kiss his mother's cheek.

"I made apple crumble for pudding." Shona McBride smiled up at him. "You look tired."

"It's going to be another long night tonight too." He hung his jacket on the back of one of the chairs at the dining table. "Seeing as I've got a stakeout." However, this stakeout wasn't so much to catch the bad guys, but more to save the good guy from herself. Working for Benson Security was definitely very different from being a cop in Glasgow.

"Oh!" Darcy squealed. "Can I come?"

"No," Logan and his mother said at the same time.

"I never get to do anything fun," Darcy complained as she sat down to take off her skates.

Logan shared a look with his mum, and they both grinned.

"So, you're staking out the hotel?" his mum said with a sly smile. "Does Dougal know?"

"No. And let's keep it that way."

"My lips are sealed."

Yeah, right. As soon as he was out of sight, she'd be on the phone to her knitting cronies. And who knew what trouble they'd cause.

"I'm serious," he said. "No stirring up Knit or Die. No spreading rumors. This is my work. No using it as an excuse to wind up Dougal."

"I wouldn't dare." Although she sounded affronted, he detected a maniacal glint in her eye.

He sighed. He'd done what he could to shut her down, and it was out of his hands now. "What can I do to help?" He shoved up the sleeves of his sweater.

"Nothing. The kids will lay the table. You can go fetch your dad." Her eyes sparkled with mischief as she lowered her voice. "He's watching porn in the shed."

"You can't embarrass me, so you might as well stop trying," he said as he headed for the back door. "I was a cop. I've seen it all."

"Challenge accepted," his mother said as she checked the oven.

Even in her sixties, Shona McBride was still full of energy, looked years younger, and got up to a ton of mischief with her friends from the knitting club. Right now, the bizarre war the women of Knit or Die periodically waged against Dougal and the old men who played dominoes had ended, but it wouldn't take much to start it up again. Both sides were always itching for a fight.

Logan stepped out into the icy wind and jogged down the path to the shed. He didn't knock, but then he knew his dad wasn't really watching porn. You'd have to know how to work a computer for that, or a phone. Something Robert McBride, Rab to his friends, hadn't mastered. Instead, he was bent over his workbench, tying flies for fishing.

"Dinner's ready," Logan said.

His dad grunted as he continued to tie off the fly, winding red silken thread around a serious-looking hook bedecked with feathers. Although Logan hadn't inherited his dad's love of fishing, he had inherited his build. At seventy, his father still had the same lean, muscular build he'd had Logan's whole life. The only difference between them was his father's gray hair and the lines on his face. Which boded well for Logan.

"Are you coming?" Logan said.

"In a minute." When his dad was in the middle of something, there was no hurrying him, or stopping him—he did things at his own pace.

"I'll tell Mum you're coming."

His only reply was another grunt. Logan grinned as he jogged back up the path to the house. He worked with an American guy they called Grunt, because he rarely talked, and Logan had once introduced him to his dad. It had been hysterical. A whole conversation in grunts, snorts and growls. It had been like watching an episode of *Animal Planet*.

"He's coming," he told his mum when he opened the door, grateful the house was warm.

"I'll bet he is." His mum never seemed to get anxious over her husband's antisocial tendencies. If he didn't come in for dinner, she made him a plate for later and got on with her life.

"Hey." Logan ruffled his son's hair as he set the table. "How was school?"

Drew grunted. There were no prizes for guessing who he took after personality-wise.

"I'll take that as you had a good day," Logan said with a smile.

As they settled in at the pine table in the corner of the kitchen, Logan glanced around the room, feeling the tension of the day melt from him at the sense of being home. His mother had decorated the room in lemon and blue, as she liked bright colors and couldn't grasp the concept of neutral decorating. Each room in her house was a different color scheme, and she was always tinkering with it. He wasn't overly fond of the orange living room, but the kitchen was warm and welcoming, with the radiator blasting in the corner and the smell of good food.

As they passed around the dishes of beef stew, roast potatoes, and bread, Darcy elbowed her older brother. "Ask him," she hissed.

Logan wasn't sure whether he should pretend he hadn't heard the order or give in to curiosity. Fortunately, he didn't have to decide because after a scowl at his sister, Drew looked over at him. "Can I go into Fort William on Saturday?"

Their nearest big town was about an hour away, and they often popped over there for the things they couldn't get locally. This was the first time Drew had asked to go alone.

"You want to tell me why?" Logan loaded his plate as he watched his son.

A slow pink blush filled his cheeks. "No reason. Just some kids from school getting together. We thought we might see a movie and, you know, hang out."

"Which kids from school?"

As the kids' secondary school was in Fort William and they bussed there every day, Logan hadn't met all of their friends—yet. But he intended to. He was a hands-on parent, and he liked to get to know the kids they hung out with, even if it meant his house was an open home to their friends. He'd rather they were in his house than roaming around and getting into trouble.

"Just Zander and Harris, and maybe Zander's sister…"

Ah, so there was the reason for the blush. "Zander's twin sister, right?"

"Aye." Drew suddenly found his plate fascinating.

Meanwhile, his sister was bouncing in her seat, bursting to get in on the conversation. Logan shared a look with his mother, who was trying not to grin.

"So, can I go?" Drew said.

"Seeing as I already know Zander and Harris, I don't see why not."

"And Zoe," Darcy blurted out. "Don't forget Zoe. She'll be there too." She grinned at her brother. "Drew wants to be Zoe's boyfriend." The words came out in a delighted rush.

"Do not!" Drew shouted, but his face was now beetroot red.

"Do too." Darcy stabbed the air between them with her finger. "You stare at her all the time, and you go red every time you talk to her. You totally want to be her boyfriend."

It looked like Drew's head was about to explode, so Logan held up his hands to stop them. "Enough, you two. We're having dinner here. And a guy can be friends with a girl without anything going on."

"Exactly," Drew muttered, before stuffing food in his mouth.

Logan's mother gave him a suspiciously sweet smile. "Like you and the new hotel manager?" she said with fake lightness.

Darcy shot to her feet, the excitement clearly too much for her to stay seated. "Does Dad have a girlfriend?" She looked awestruck.

"Sit down," Logan ordered. "No, I don't have a girlfriend. I'm working a job at the hotel, and that means working with the manager."

"The very pretty manager," his meddling mother said. "I heard you were helping her inspect the storeroom last night."

Bloody gossip grapevine. There was no such thing as a secret in Invertary. It had to have been Mrs. Edwards who'd told on him. That woman had already ingratiated herself with the town's gossipmongers.

"Things have been going missing from that cupboard," he said, sounding overly defensive even to his own ears.

Thankfully, his father chose that moment to come in for dinner. He banged through the door, pulled out his chair, and loaded his plate—all without saying a word. Slowly, he seemed to become aware that no one was talking and stopped dishing up potatoes to look at each of them.

"What's going on?" he said.

"Dad's got a girlfriend," Darcy blurted. "He was in a cupboard with her last night." She frowned and looked over at Logan. "Why were you in a cupboard with your girlfriend?"

Drew laughed and reached for his water. "I know why kids my age go into cupboards with girls."

"Why?" Darcy demanded, her eyes wide. "Were you *kissing?*"

"I don't have a girlfriend." Logan gave everyone a firm look. They were just amused. Well, except for his dad, who looked confused. "I was investigating some thefts at the hotel, with the hotel manager."

"And you just had to examine the store cupboard in the middle of the night, in the dark, with the manager..." his wicked mother said.

Darcy gasped. "You *were* kissing in the cupboard!"

"Caught." Drew laughed.

"Why were you in a cupboard?" his dad said. "Why didn't you take this woman on a proper date? In my day, we took them out for dinner. We didn't steal kisses in cupboards."

"It was work," Logan said firmly.

"Oh, I hope you didn't tell her that," his mother said. "Women don't like to hear that sort of thing."

It was official. He'd lost control of the conversation.

"So," Darcy said, "when can we meet her?"

"She isn't my girlfriend," he tried again, but it was pointless. And he wasn't about to humiliate himself by admitting that she'd shut him down cold after the world's most perfect kiss. "This is work. Nothing more. You can get any other ideas out of your head."

"He's seeing her again tonight." His mum stirred further. "They're going on a stakeout together."

"No. We're not. Agnes is up to something, and I'm watching her. There's no *together*." It was like explaining physics to toddlers.

"Agnes?" Darcy said. "Is that her name? It's lovely."

Logan groaned.

"Come on, Dad," Drew said, obviously happy he was no longer the center of attention. "You haven't had a proper girlfriend since Mum left, so it's about time. But we should definitely get a veto. After all, we *are* talking about a possible stepmother here."

Logan glared at him. "Do you want to go to Fort William on Saturday or not?"

"I take it back," Drew said. "It's totally a work relationship. There's nothing to see here. Moving on…"

Logan nodded, satisfied that someone got the message. Then he saw Darcy's excited face.

"I've always wanted a stepmother," she gushed. "I'm sure the movies get it wrong—they can't *all* be evil."

Logan just shook his head as everyone, except his bewildered father, laughed.

CHAPTER 8

It had taken some doing, but Agnes had turned her hotel room into command central. Using her room's TV, the computer screen from her office, her tablet, and her cell phone, she'd managed to send the signal from each of the cameras they'd set up to different screens. Now she could watch every camera view at the same time. Like an evil mastermind. Or a gamer getting ready for a marathon session.

There were plenty of snacks and high caffeine drinks stuffed into the mini-fridge. Blankets were draped over the curtains to ensure that anyone outside the hotel would think she was asleep or her room was empty. She'd placed a rolled-up towel at the bottom of her door, to stop any light leaking out, and stuck a Post-it Note over the spy hole to stop light escaping there. To the world, she was asleep. As she normally would have been at past midnight. But instead, she was holed up in her bat cave, jacked up on caffeine and sugar.

The pub had closed an hour earlier, the staff leaving not long after that. Dougal had been last to go, his dog following close behind. The alarms were set, and the guests were asleep. All she had to do now was wait. Pen poised, ready to note anything suspicious for follow up later, she sat and ate her way through a family-sized bag of Maltesers as she watched the feeds from the security cameras.

It was like watching paint dry.

After fifteen minutes, her eyelids began to droop. She jerked up straight, gave herself a shake, and popped another can of Red Bull.

"Focus," Agnes muttered to herself. "This is important. Your career depends on it. You already have a bad rep in the hotel industry. You don't want to get fired from your first job because your boss suspects you're a thief. Find the real thief. Do a victory dance. Rule the world. You can do this!"

All she needed to do was get into a rhythm. Sitting on the end of the bed, facing the screens on the dresser in front of her, Agnes worked from left to right. The TV showed a split view from the two hall cameras on the ground floor. The halls were empty. Her desktop computer monitor showed another split view of the first-floor hallway and the store cupboard door. Again, nothing. Her tablet showed a view of the hallway outside her room, with, the main guest rooms on the first floor visible on her cell phone. Her eyes flicked back to the TV, and then she went through the whole routine again…and again…and again…and ag…

When a knock at the door jerked her awake, she realized she'd fallen asleep at some point and was now lying on the bed, her pen still clutched in her hand. Bleary-eyed, she sat up, and a glance at the tablet showing the view outside her room made her heart sink—Logan.

"I know you're in there, and I know you aren't asleep. Open up."

How could he know that? He couldn't possibly. It was a bluff.

"Go away. I'm asleep," she called.

"You're watching the security camera feeds. I have the same app, and I can see they're all being accessed, which means you're awake."

A curse on his detective skills. With a grumble, she crossed the room and threw open her door.

"What are you doing here in the middle of the night, anyway? I told you I'd call if anything came up." Was it still the middle of the night? What time was it? How long had she been asleep? Agnes glanced back into the room, but the bedside clock was at the wrong angle so she couldn't see its face, and as there were no windows in the hallway, she couldn't go by the sun either.

As a horrible thought occurred to her, she looked down. Relief flooded her and she smiled. Thank goodness, she wasn't naked. For a second, she thought she'd stripped to sleep, as she usually did, but she was still wearing the yoga pants and camisole she'd donned for her stakeout.

"I take it back," Logan drawled as he watched her. "Looks like you were sleeping on the job after all." He didn't so much push past her as stroll into the room.

"I didn't invite you in." But she did shut the door behind him and put the towel back along the bottom of it.

"I'm not a vampire, so I don't need an invitation to enter. What are you doing with the towel?"

"Blocking out light." Her head was a little foggy, but she was pretty sure he was supposed to be the one experienced in subterfuge.

Agnes walked over and pointed at her bedside alarm clock. "Ha! I was only asleep for fifteen minutes." She flopped into the armchair in the corner of the room. "Stakeouts are the worst. How do people do this? It's mind-numbing."

Logan took off his leather jacket and tossed it over the desk chair. "How long have you been staring at the screens?" he asked as he checked the monitors.

"Years," she groaned.

He cocked an eyebrow.

"Fine, about an hour."

That made him grin. "Amateur. You couldn't even stay awake for more than an hour."

She wasn't about to admit she'd fallen asleep twice in that time. In fact, she would probably still be asleep if he hadn't come knocking. And right now, she wished he hadn't.

Although…

"How about we do this in shifts?" She batted her lashes at him and flashed, what she hoped was, a non-threatening smile. "You watch while I nap, and then I'll watch while you nap."

"How about you come over here and explain exactly what you've set up that makes you so sure someone will try to steal from the hotel tonight?"

"And then naps?" she asked hopefully.

There wasn't much reassurance in his answering grin.

"Fine," she grumbled as she crossed the room to sit on the end of the bed facing the screens. She pointed at room ten, where the Dutch couple had been staying. "The de Jongs checked out this morning, but I didn't have their room prepped for a new arrival. Instead, I spread the word that they were away for the night but would be back tomorrow to pick up their belongings. I made sure to tell housekeeping to keep an eye on the room because there were valuables inside."

"Why housekeeping? They go home mid-afternoon." His eyes were on her and not on the screens.

"Because they chat and I figured they'd get the word out. Meanwhile, I made sure everyone knew about the new delivery of sundries this morning." She'd been proud of that part of her plan—it'd gone like clockwork.

Logan obviously wasn't as impressed as she was. "You think new soap will attract the thief?"

"These soaps are handcrafted using pure goat's milk and organic fragrances. There's a waiting list of boutique hotels wanting to get this range. The only reason we have it is that I've dealt with the company a lot in the past and have a good relationship with them." And because they hadn't heard she'd been blacklisted. But she kept that part to herself. "These toiletries are so good that I even bought extra for my personal use."

"Okay, okay." He held up his hands in surrender. "I get it. This is the gold standard of hotel soap. How did you get them here so fast?"

"I ordered them my first week in the job. Their delivery just happened to coincide with my plan."

"Your plan to trap a thief using soap?"

She ignored him. "I have the de Jong room set up as a trap and a stock cupboard full of top-rate goodies. Now, we just have to wait." She looked up at him. "This is the part I hate. I thought if I had snacks and caffeine, it would be fine. But this is duller than dishwater. I can actually feel my brain atrophy as I sit here. How do cops do this?"

"Generally, they sleep during the day, so they can stay awake at night." He reached for a bag of salted nuts, popped it open and took a handful. "Plus, cops tend to work in pairs, which means they have someone to talk to and keep them awake. Then there's the radio. Never underestimate a good late-night DJ. And there's peeing in a bottle. That kills a good five minutes." The sparkle in his eye said he was messing with her again. At least *one* of them was having fun.

"Peeing in a bottle? I'm guessing your partner was male too. Makes me wonder how you even managed to stretch that to five minutes."

"Too much coffee." He passed the bag of nuts to her.

"What *I'm* wondering is what you thought you'd do with a thief if one turned up. You were going to call the cops, right?"

"What else would I do?" Did he think she was stupid?

"Confront them?"

Well, that answered that—he *did* think she was dumb. "Don't let the blonde hair fool you." She tapped the side of her head. "There's a brain in here."

At this point in the conversation, most men would have backtracked. But Logan wasn't most men. "I asked around about you. Seems you have a hot temper and a violent streak rigged with a hair-trigger. I was worried you'd react without thinking and get hurt."

"Because I'm a woman?"

The idiot nodded. "Well, that, and you're a small woman. Which, let's face it, is a problem if the thief is bigger than you, and from what I can see, most people are bigger than you. It's a disadvantage in an attack."

Oh, that *infamous* hot temper of hers was flaring up for sure. "Did you ever work with women when you were on the force? And what about at Benson Security? I know they have women security specialists. Do you tell all of your female colleagues to step back and let the big, strong man handle the situation?"

"No. They'd kick my arse."

"Exactly."

"But they've been trained. Have you been trained? Do you know how to handle yourself in a fight?"

"What? I have to pass some sort of test to satisfy you that I have the skills to catch a soap thief?"

"I didn't say that."

"No, you just said that I'm tiny, defenseless and incapable of making the decision to call the police rather than tackle a bad guy all on my own."

He seemed to think about that for a second. "This conversation isn't going the way I thought it would. I'm just trying to tell you that I'm here because I was worried about you."

"Because I'm too dumb to stay out of a situation that could hurt me?"

"I *really* didn't say that."

Agnes was done with this conversation. She stood and pushed the chair and coffee table back against the wall to make space beside the bed. Then, hands on the hips of her gray yoga pants, she faced Logan. "Come on, attack me. If you dare."

He shook his head. "I'm not going to hurt you just to prove a point."

"Why? I have no problem hurting you to prove mine."

"Agnes…"

"Don't Agnes me. Get moving." She pointed at the red tartan floor in front of her.

"No. We're not doing this."

"Chicken." She made clucking noises. "Scared of a tiny, wee woman."

"Mature." He heaved a sigh. "Okay. If this will make you see reason, I'll play along." With clear reluctance, he stood in front of her. "I'll try not to hurt you."

"Thanks." Like he had a chance! "Now attack me."

Without warning, he lunged at her, his right hand going for her arm. Agnes grabbed his wrist, yanked him toward her, slammed the heel of her hand into his nose, and released him.

"What the hell?" he barked as he covered his bloody nose. "I think you broke it."

Agnes waited for guilt to set in, but it didn't manifest. "Don't be a baby." She strode through to the bathroom and wet a washcloth for him. "And don't get blood on the bed. It would be murder to get out of those white sheets. Aim for the floor. No one will notice a stain on this carpet."

Logan pressed the cloth to his nose. "I can't believe you did that."

Rolling her eyes at him, she dug out some ice from the mini-fridge. "Here, put this in the cloth. It will help with the swelling."

"What kind of woman pulls her attacker to her?" He took the ice, wrapped it in the cloth and gently pressed it to his nose.

"One who knows how to defend herself."

With a shake of his head, he strode into the bathroom. Agnes sat on the end of the bed watching the screens—where nothing was happening—and finishing the nuts. It was a good job they'd already talked about how pointless a relationship between them would be, because bloodying Logan's nose was probably a deal-breaker on the romance front.

The nuts were gone, and she'd started on the Pringles by the time Logan came out of the bathroom. His nose was swollen and red, but otherwise he didn't seem too upset. Sitting beside her, he took the Pringles out of her hands.

"It isn't broken," he said as he ate one.

"I pulled my punch." Which was true. She totally could have broken his nose if she'd wanted. "I could also have kneed you in the balls while you were whining. I think I should get points for not following through."

"Appreciated." He returned the Pringles. "Where did you learn to fight?"

She shrugged. "I grew up in a rough neighborhood."

In silence, they stared at the screens for a few minutes. Adrenaline had left Agnes wide awake, and now she was a little unsure about how to deal with the man in her room.

"Is it wrong that I'm a tad turned on right now?" Logan said at last, giving her a slow, sexy smile. "That was seriously hot. It makes me want to spar with you some more. Only this time, I won't go easy on you."

She couldn't help her answering smile or the warmth that spread throughout her at his comments. "You still wouldn't stand a chance," she boasted.

"You're a fascinating woman, Agnes Sinclair." He held out his hand for more Pringles and she gave him some.

"If I'd known you were coming, I'd have gotten more snacks."

"Don't worry," he said as he leaned back onto his elbows, his eyes still on the screens. "I hear you know the new code to the kitchen, and Chef's made coffee walnut cake for tomorrow's lunch crowd. You know, it would be easier if we put sensors on the doors. That way, if someone opened them, an alarm would sound on our phones."

"And we could sleep." Relief flooded her. "Do you have sensors at the security shop?"

"Aye." He continued staring at the screen.

Agnes gave him less than a minute before she lost patience. "Are you going to get them or what?"

"It's the middle of the night."

"And you're awake anyway."

With a sigh, he dragged himself off the bed. "You are hard work, Agnes Sinclair," he said, making her feel inordinately proud. Once he'd put his jacket back on, he held out his hand. "Gimme your keys, and I'll be back in ten minutes."

"I'll be waiting," she called after him.

Five minutes after the door closed, Agnes decided her wait would be more comfortable if she lay down. Thirty seconds after that, she was sound asleep.

Agnes' first thought when she woke was that she'd set the heating too high because the room was roasting. Her second thought was that the bed was much harder than she remembered. No, not harder, *firmer*. More muscular. Blinking open bleary eyes, she looked up to find Logan's dark gaze fixed on her.

"For a tiny person, you take up a lot of bed," he said softly.

There was only fog where her brain should be. "I'm five foot ten in my head."

"Good to know," he whispered as he tucked a loose strand of hair behind her ear.

Slowly, she became aware of the reality of her situation. While her legs were still on the mattress, the rest of her was on top of Logan. And it felt good. The heat from his body seeped into her, warming even the coldest parts deep within.

"Why are you in my bed?" Her voice came out as a sleepy rasp.

"Technically, we're *on* the bed, not in it. When I came back after rigging sensors to the doors, you were out cold." Unlike hers, his soft voice sounded low and sexy. Intimate. It made her want to close her eyes again and drift away while listening to him.

"And you just decided to lie down beside me?"

"I *was* watching the monitors, but, about four o'clock, you wrapped yourself around me and pulled me back onto the bed. Then you climbed on top of me, mumbled something about central heating and fell asleep. It seemed rude to move you."

"Huh." Agnes frowned, confused. "Did the thief turn up?" Had she slept through it? Had Logan let her?

"Not yet." His fingertips traced down her cheek to her jaw, making her skin tingle in their wake. He watched their progress, his attention absolute.

She groaned and thumped her forehead on his chest. "We need different plan. I can't spend another night watching security footage, hoping the thief will show."

"Agnes, love, you haven't spent even one night watching the feeds. And there was no *we*. This plan was all your idea. Anyway, now that the doors are rigged, you can sleep until the alarm wakes you." He caressed her hair. "Did you know you sleep curled up like a cute little kitten? And you purr."

Her head shot back up, and she glared at him. "I don't purr." The thought of it was completely outrageous. She was fierce. If she made any noise at all, it would be a roar.

"Well, technically, it's snoring. But it's still adorable." His thumb traced the outline of her lips, building a slow warmth deep inside of her.

"When I'm more awake, I'm going to get you back for that comment."

"I'll make sure to wear protective gear."

That reminded her of his nose. "Is it sore?"

"Just a bit swollen." His eyes sparkled at her. "I have other concerns right now."

"I feel bad about hitting you." No, that wasn't strictly true.

"I mean, I feel I *should* feel bad about hitting you, and I feel guilty that I don't."

A slow, teasing smile curled his lips. "If it helps, you could kiss it better."

One of his hands curved around her shoulder, and she felt the slow caress of his other hand on her back. The blue light from the screens cast his features in soft shadow, but that didn't detract from the sheer maleness of him. In the back of Agnes' sleep-dulled brain, there was a weak reminder that she didn't want to start anything with Logan. That there were complications that could bite them both in the rear. But in that moment, none of those sensible arguments for caution meant very much. As desire seeped into her fog-ridden head, all she could think about was the feeling of Logan's body under hers. And it was wonderful.

She wriggled farther up his chest, putting one hand flat on the bed beside his head. With the other, she cupped his cheek and gently traced the edge of his nose with her thumb. She wasn't sorry she'd hit him. So she couldn't apologize with any honesty, but she found that she didn't like to see him injured. And it made her uncomfortable to think she'd been the cause of it. It was as though she'd suddenly developed a conscience overnight, and it was…unpleasant.

Slowly, Agnes leaned in and pressed a gentle kiss to the tip of his nose. His hands flexed on her body, making her breath hitch as she made little butterfly kisses across the bridge of his nose.

"Better?" she whispered, sounding faintly breathless.

"My cheekbone took a bit of a whack too," he rumbled.

She kissed across his cheekbones, first one, then the other, making sure she didn't miss anything. His hold on her tightened as he pulled her firmly against him.

"We done now?" she asked, when she looked into those dark eyes of his.

"My lips. You smacked them on the way to my nose."

"Poor baby," she whispered. "You really suffered."

"It was terrible," he whispered back. "But I'm sure you kissing them better will help."

"Seems the least I can do." And with that, Agnes brushed her lips against his.

That's all it took. Just one, gentle touch, lips to lips, breathing each other's air, and she was free-falling. The room, the hotel, the ground beneath them, it all faded away. She became lost in the moment. In the feeling of Logan's lips teasing hers. Of hers teasing his. It was a slow, thorough tasting. Kiss, after kiss, after kiss. Each one more drugging than the last.

Her fingers threaded through his hair. His hand clasped her nape. A moan. A sigh. Tongues tangled with groans of need. The world tipped and turned until she was on her back with Logan's weight pressing into her, their legs entwined, their arms enfolding each other. The taste of him took her far away. To a place with fragrant meadows. Where, in the dark nights of summer, the warmth of the day would enclose her as the stars appeared like a blanket overhead. A haven of heady sensuality, just for her. Somewhere she didn't have to think, where she only had to feel. A place where she felt safe.

Until the beeping intruded.

With clear reluctance, Logan broke their kiss. Dark eyes, filled with a stunned need, stared into her soul.

"Damn," he groaned, before pressing his mouth back over hers.

The beeping grew louder, forcing them to separate once again, gasping for breath, hearts racing.

"What is it?" Agnes found the words difficult to form. She wanted to be kissing, not talking.

Logan pressed his forehead to hers. "The sensors on the doors, someone's just triggered one of them."

"Doors?" His weight was delicious, pressing her into the bed. Solid, strong, secure. Sexy. Oh so sexy. Her fingers massaged his shoulders of their own volition. She wanted skin, not cotton, under her touch.

"The trap you set, remember?" His smile was amused, but his eyes held only heat. "The thief," he added.

"The thief?" The angles of his face were fascinating in the cool blue light that filled the room. The light from the monitors. With the security feeds…

"The thief!" The memory was a bucket of cold water over her head.

Agnes shoved his shoulders, and he rolled off her. She scrambled to her knees and crawled to the end of the bed, adrenaline coursing through her. The door to the store cupboard stood open.

"What time is it?" she demanded, feeling far more awake now.

"Almost seven."

"Someone's in the cupboard." She glanced beside her to see Logan sitting on the side of the bed, pulling on his boots.

"Could be the cleaning staff."

"They aren't due for another hour. The only staff in this early are the ones who work in the kitchen."

Logan rounded the bed and came to stand beside her. "Do any of them have keys to that cupboard?"

"Not that I'm aware of."

He ran a hand over her hair and smiled wryly. "Get sorted, and we'll go see who it is. It's either that or I tumble you back onto the bed, and we forget about the thief."

Damn, but that was tempting. She must have spent too long considering her options because Logan chuckled as he took her hand and tugged her from the bed.

"Shoes, and whatever else you think you need. You've got

one minute. I'll watch the monitors to make sure we don't miss them."

Agnes threw a sweater on over her camisole, slid into a pair of flip-flops, and tied her hair back in a messy bun. "Done. And in well under one minute."

"Come on then," Logan said as he opened the door. "Let's surprise your thief."

After one last glance back at the rumpled bed, they jogged out of the room and down the stairs.

* * *

HE WAS GOING to kill the thief, purely on the basis that their timing sucked. Logan's jeans were uncomfortably tight and, with every step he took, he had to fight the urge to take Agnes back to bed. Aye, the thief had to die.

Logan signaled to Agnes to keep behind him. She signaled back in her own unique way—by scowling, then pointing at her nose, then the heel of her hand, then at him. Guess she didn't want to be protected. With a resigned shake of his head, he stepped in front of the open door. And groaned.

"Who the hell are you?" Agnes demanded as she elbowed him out of the way.

Logan looked toward heaven, muttering a desperate prayer for patience before he answered Agnes. "That's Jean. She's a friend of my mother's. They're in the same knitting group, and she shouldn't be in the hotel store cupboard."

"Logan." Jean beamed at him. "What are you doing here? And so early in the morning." Her eyes went from him to Agnes, and her eyebrows shot up. "Oh, are you two a thing? Does your mother know? That was awfully fast—she's only been here a couple of weeks." She smiled at Agnes. "But from what I hear, you sound like an interesting hotel manager.

Very…dedicated…" Her smile froze as she searched for something else to say. "You have nice skin," she added at last.

"Get out of the cupboard." Agnes grabbed Jean's arm and dragged her into the hallway.

Jean held up a canvas tote with the words 'Knit or Die' emblazoned on it. "But I haven't finished collecting my order."

"Oh, you're finished all right." Holding the woman's upper arm, Agnes marched her downstairs toward her office.

"I'll take her," Logan said. "You go get changed. Unless you want to do this in your pajamas."

Agnes glanced down at herself and seemed irritated that she was wearing her sleepwear. "I'll be five minutes. Don't let her escape."

He barely refrained from rolling his eyes. "I think I can handle Jean." The woman was in her sixties and barely topped five feet tall, and even though she'd taken Lake's self-defense class years ago, he was pretty sure he could take her in a fight. None of this he said to Agnes, mainly because he didn't think she'd appreciate it.

With an irritated humph, she ran up the stairs to her room.

"Do you think we could get a cup of tea and some cake while we wait?" Jean said as Logan gestured toward Agnes' office.

"This isn't morning tea, Jean. We just caught you stealing from Dougal."

She gaped at him. "What do you mean stealing? I wasn't stealing anything. We have an arrangement with Dougal."

"We?" Oh crap, he knew where this was going. Forgetting his nose was bruised, he pinched the bridge then winced.

"Aye," Jean said. "Knit or Die. We've had this arrangement for years."

And there it was. "My mum's in on this? Of course, she's in on it. Where there's one of you, there's always more."

"I don't know what you're talking about, but I didn't have any breakfast, and my sugar levels are getting dangerously low." She put out a hand to hold on to the wall. "I feel woozy. There's a good chance I might faint. Who knows how long I'll be out? You might have to take me to the hospital or call the doctor. Wouldn't it just be easier to get me a cup of tea and a slice of cake? Chef always makes a nice cake for morning tea. I expect it's just sitting in there, waiting to be sliced."

"Get in the office," Logan said. "I'll get you some tea after I've called the rest of your coven."

"Thanks." She sat in one of the straight-backed guest chairs. "When this was Dougal's office, he had a sofa in here. But he probably got rid of it because of the bad memories."

Don't ask. Don't ask.

He had to ask. "What bad memories?"

"Well, he wouldn't want to sit at the desk and look at one of the places where we'd made love. He was brokenhearted when I left him. Said those were the best three months of his life."

He shouldn't have asked. "I feel nauseous."

"You're probably hungry."

Logan pinched his nose again and yelped.

"Do you think we should get the tea before you ring your mum?" Jean said. "I'd like to fortify myself before the new manager gets back. I think she might have some anger-management issues. Are you sure you know what you're doing with her?" She rummaged in her tote. "Tell you what, I'll ring the girls and you get the tea. We have a conference call thingie." Before he could stop her, she'd swiped the screen. "I'll put it on speaker. Hello? Hello? Shona, is that you?"

"Aye." His mother's voice came through the phone, followed by the other main members of Knit or Die.

"What's going on?" Heather Donaldson, the mother of Invertary's only cop, said. "Do you realize what time it is?"

"Aye, I'm at the hotel, and Logan's arrested me."

There was a pause before all hell broke loose.

"I didn't arrest you," Logan said over the shouting. "I have no powers of arrest."

"You also don't have any cake. You're still standing there, and I'm still suffering from low blood sugar."

"Jean," his mother shouted, "pay attention. What's going on?"

This could take all day, and Agnes would be back any minute. He snatched the phone from Jean. "This is Logan," he said to the rest of the gang. "I need every member of Knit or Die at the hotel, right now." Then he hung up. He put the phone into his back pocket. "I'll keep this until they get here." Who knew what plans they'd hatch if they could talk to each other.

"Are we getting tea now?"

"I'll run to the kitchen." He pointed at Jean. "Don't move from that spot."

She nodded solemnly. "Maybe you could get Chef to make me an egg sandwich while you're there, with some bacon if he's got it, and maybe a potato scone."

With a shake of his head, Logan shut the office door on Jean and jogged to the kitchen, hoping he'd be back before Agnes found their thief unattended.

CHAPTER 10

Four women sat in a row in Agnes' office, on chairs she'd had to grab from the pub. They were all of retirement age, none of them were happy to be there, and only one wasn't related to a cop or Benson Security employee—their thief, Jean.

Dressed in her gray pantsuit, Agnes wore her hair clasped at her nape and sensible low-heeled work shoes on her feet. Usually, the outfit made her feel in control. But not in this situation. No, this situation was completely out of control and getting worse by the minute, because not only was one of the women Logan's mother, she'd also brought his daughter along.

The preteen sat on the floor beside the door pretending she was too sick for school, while she soaked up everything that was happening. And the sight of her brought reality crashing back down on Agnes—Logan was a father. Just the thought made her take another step to the side, to widen the distance between them. And, of course, Logan noticed her retreat. Not only him, but his mother and daughter too.

The temperature in the room seemed to go up a few degrees.

"What are we waiting for?" Margaret Campbell demanded. Agnes had learned that Margaret was the leader of the knitting group. She was also Lake Benson's mother-in-law.

"Dougal." Agnes wasn't happy about that, but when she'd called to update him on the situation, he'd insisted on being present.

"Do we have to?" Jean complained. "It's awkward between us. I don't think he's ever gotten over me."

"That was years ago," Shona McBride, Logan's mother, said. "Of course, he's over you."

Jean shook her head. "I see it in his eyes every time I'm around him." She lowered her voice conspiratorially. "Unrequited love."

"Piffle." Heather Donaldson, the mother of Matt, Invertary's only cop, rolled her eyes.

"I'm a hard woman to get over." Jean reached for another slice of cake.

Which reminded Agnes. "Why do they have cake?" she asked Logan.

"They were hungry." There was a sparkle in his eyes again. He was amused.

She wasn't. "They're stealing from us, so we're rewarding them with cake?"

"Stealing? Who's stealing?" Margaret shot to her feet, clasping her massive handbag in front of her. "You think we're stealing? I won't stay here to be maligned like this. And you"—she pointed at Logan—"you can explain this to your boss. Lake will hear all about it."

"Sit down, Margaret," Logan said with long suffering. "Lake already knows, and he trusts us to get to the bottom of this."

"You stole something, Gran?" Logan's daughter's eyes widened.

"Of course not." Shona sounded outraged. "And keep quiet, or I'll decide you're well enough to go to school after all."

It was Agnes' turn to roll her eyes. "She isn't sick. She's faking it. Those dark circles and that white complexion are makeup."

"Darcy," Logan rumbled. "Is that true?"

The kid's cheeks flushed red. "I just wanted to meet your new girlfriend. She's the first girlfriend you've had since Mum, and I heard Gran say it must be serious if you're showing this kind of interest. Gran said you live like a monk, although I had to ask my teacher what a monk was, and I'm not sure Gran's right."

"*Gran* sure says a lot of things," Logan drawled as he stared at his mother.

Shona stuck her nose in the air. "In my defense, usually nobody listens."

Logan turned back to his daughter. "You shouldn't have cut school. You should have asked me if you could meet Agnes."

"I did, and you said no."

"So, you thought you'd just take matters into your own hands, because you know better than me?"

"I'm sorry, Dad." Tears sprang to her eyes as she looked at Agnes. "I only wanted to meet the woman who might become my stepmum."

Stepmum? A shudder went through Agnes. Oh, hell no. She was shutting this down. Right now.

"I'm not your dad's girlfriend, so you don't have to worry about me becoming your stepmother." The girl looked weirdly disappointed, which twanged Agnes' hardened heartstrings like someone playing an out-of-tune guitar inside of her. "I will give you some advice though. If you're going to fake dark circles, don't use a shadow with a shimmer. And you might want to enroll in some acting classes. Otherwise, having an ex-cop for a dad will seriously scupper any future cons you run."

"Will you stop encouraging my granddaughter to rebel and explain exactly what I'm supposed to have stolen," Shona demanded.

"It's not encouragement. I'm giving constructive criticism." It was clear that Logan had inherited his even temper from his father. "And she needs it. I was faking illness better than that by the time I was five." To her horror, Darcy looked awestruck. "No." She pointed at the kid. "I'm not teaching you how to do it right."

"I should think not," Shona snapped before scowling at Logan. "You've got two minutes to explain what's going on before I leave."

"I think I can help with that," Dougal said as he made a dramatic entrance. Today's ensemble consisted of purple tartan trousers, a purple shirt, and a green waistcoat. The sight made Agnes feel nauseous.

His dog ran in on his heels and headed straight for Darcy, who started cooing over it.

"Dougal," Jean simpered, batting her eyelashes at him.

His cheeks went red, and he blustered for a second or two. "Jean, it seems you have been stealing from my store cupboard over a period of months, if not years. Empty your bag."

Sharing a look of confusion with her friends, Jean upended her bag over the coffee table in front of them. Several small shampoo and conditioner bottles fell out.

"They stopped me before I got to the soap," she explained to her fellow crooks.

Wasn't anyone taking this seriously? "This is no laughing

matter," Agnes said. "You've been picking the lock and helping yourself to the hotel's sundries. That's a serious offense."

"You picked the lock?" Shona said. "I thought you had a key."

"I forgot it one time. Picking locks hasn't gotten any easier since the time we tried to get into Lake's shop. Even after watching all those YouTube videos on how to do it. Maybe I need better lock picks."

"For goodness' sake," Agnes exploded, swapping out the words she wanted to say in deference to the kid's presence. "You're stealing from us, and you're worried about the quality of your picks?"

"We aren't stealing," Margaret said to Dougal. "We've had an arrangement since you and Jean were an item. Remember, we told you we liked the tiny bottles, and you said that we could help ourselves at cost? We pay every month."

"Aye." Jean held up a plain white envelope. "In cash, because you said charging us would make accounting awkward." She tossed the envelope onto the table, where everyone stared at it for a minute.

"Dougal?" Agnes said at last.

The hotel owner cleared his throat, his face a fluorescent red. "I, um, assumed that arrangement was only in place for the duration of our...dalliance."

When Logan made a strangled noise, Agnes shot him an irritated glance, only to find that he was suddenly fascinated by the books on her shelf.

"But, Dougal," Heather said, "how could you think the arrangement was over when we pay you every month?"

He tugged at that damn waistcoat again, making Agnes want to take a pair of scissors to it. "I haven't received any money since Jean and I separated."

"Saying it like that makes it sound as though I was paying you for services rendered," Jean said with a wink.

Logan coughed and ran a hand down his face.

"Who do you give the money to?" Agnes tried to keep the discussion on track. It was like trying to herd kittens.

The women shared a look. "Why, Bernadette, of course."

Agnes took a deep breath and shouted, "Bernadette, get in here!"

A few seconds later, Bernadette burst through the door. "Yes?" she said, smiling nervously at everyone in the room. With her shoulders up around her ears, she looked like a terrified puppy. And, in a weird twist of fate, both her makeup and the streak of color in her hair matched Dougal's outfit perfectly.

Agnes picked the envelope up off the table. "Does Jean give you an envelope full of money every month?"

"Oh." Bernadette visibly relaxed. "Yes, she does."

"See!" Jean pointed at the receptionist then folded her arms in triumph.

"And what do you do with the envelope?" Agnes said.

"Well." Bernadette looked up as she concentrated on her answer. "Usually, I buy makeup for my tutorial videos, but one month I bought new lighting for my studio. Well, my bedroom, but that's where I shoot my videos. The lights have made a huge difference to the quality of the recording. Everyone said they would, but I wasn't sure until I tried. It's so, so much better now."

"You spent the money?" Jean gaped.

"Well, yeah." Bernadette looked around at everyone. "Wasn't I supposed to spend it? Did you want me to save it? You never said, but I thought what I did with it was up to me."

The women started to argue, but Agnes held up a hand

for silence. "Bernadette, why did you think Jean was giving you cash?"

"I thought it was a tip. Was I wrong?" She twisted her hands in front of her. "I mean, it's okay if we get tips, isn't it? It isn't against the rules or anything. I don't think…"

For a second, you could have heard a fly buzz.

"Why on earth would I give you a tip?" Jean said. "I'm not a hotel guest."

"I thought it was because you appreciated my service."

"What service?"

"You know, when you come in through the hotel lobby and I'm friendly and stuff. And when I help you carry out new bedding and bring back laundry. That sort of thing."

"Wait. What?" Agnes turned back to Jean. "We're doing your laundry?"

"No. Of course not. I just like the sheets here better than mine, so every week I borrow some and bring them back when I pick up new ones."

Margaret groaned, Shona glared, and Heather reached out to smack Jean on the back of the head.

"Dougal never agreed to us borrowing sheets," Heather said.

"I didn't think he'd miss them." Jean looked at Dougal. "Have I left you short?"

"This is unbelievable," Agnes muttered.

"I'm confused," Bernadette said. "It sounds like the money wasn't a tip."

That prompted groans all round.

It was time to take control of the three-ring circus happening in her office. Agnes held up her hands and shouted, "Right, things are going to change, starting now. Hand over your keys." She pointed at Jean. "Anyone else have keys that I don't know about?" There were shakes of heads.

"No more taking toiletries," she told them. "The arrangement you had with Dougal is over."

"Well," Heather said huffily, "I think that's up to Dougal, not you."

Agnes turned to her boss and, for the first time since she'd taken the job at his hotel, she let every bit of her irritation show on her face. She folded her arms, tapped her toe, and dared him to undermine her. Career at stake or not, she'd walk out the damn door if he did. "Dougal?"

He took a step back from her while tugging at the collar of his shirt. "I'm afraid I have to agree with my manager. This situation is making it difficult to keep track of stock."

Agnes nodded her approval. That was the right answer.

"But where will we get our wee shampoos?" Shona said.

"And those mini soaps. I love the mini soaps," Margaret added.

"What about my sheets?" Jean asked.

Agnes narrowed her eyes at all of them. "This hotel isn't your own personal store cupboard. You lot will stop entering the areas that are only intended for staff. If you want access to a room, pay for a night. No more sneaking in early in the morning, and no more giving money to the staff." She glared at Bernadette. "There will be no more tips. We aren't in America. Nobody tips in Scotland."

The receptionist looked crestfallen, but she nodded.

"As for the sheets." She turned to Jean. "You'll have to learn to live without them. Otherwise, you can purchase a set from our supplier and pay for washing them yourself."

"But…" Jean started.

"No," Margaret said. "She's being fair."

"Now." Agnes folded her arms. "Are any of you helping yourselves to anything else in this hotel?"

"No," came the chorus as the women looked shamefaced.

Agnes studied them until they squirmed in their seats.

Stealing jewelry seemed outside the spectrum of what they'd been doing.

"Okay," she said at last. "Then I think we're done here." She turned to Dougal. "Unless you have anything else to add."

"No. I don't think I have. You seem to have everything in hand." He tugged down his waistcoat, making her want to rugby tackle him and remove the damn thing. "I trust you'll explain things properly to Bernadette?"

"You can count on it."

Bernadette looked like she was about to burst into tears, but she held it together, raising Agnes' opinion of her in the process. Maybe there was hope for her yet.

"Sorry about the sheets, Dougal," Jean said.

"And I'm sorry we didn't check the situation over the sundries with you instead of Jean," Margaret said.

"Aye, we should have known better." Shona glared at Jean.

"It's not my fault she pocketed the money." Jean pointed at Bernadette. "If she'd just given the envelope to Dougal, everything would have been fine."

"No, it wouldn't." Agnes held up the envelope. "It's blank. Did you write instructions on any of the envelopes you handed over?"

"I didn't think I needed to," Jean said, and her friends groaned.

"Okay," Dougal boomed. "I think we're done here. I have a pub to run and a council meeting to prepare for. Ladies." He nodded his head at them before striding from the room.

"Do we have to pay for the last two years of supplies?" Margaret asked as she frowned at Jean. "Again?"

Weariness suddenly swamped her. If Dougal wasn't bothered about the missing shampoo, she wasn't going to lose sleep over it either. "No, just stop helping yourselves and we'll call it good."

"I know it's pushing it a bit," Shona said demurely, "but is there any chance we could buy some of the soaps and shampoos? I love the wee bottles. They're great for travel, and we heard you have a new range that you can't get on the internet."

Against her better judgment, Agnes caved on that. "I'll set up a shelf behind the front desk where you can buy bottles of product and bars of soap. You'll pay Bernadette, who will put the money straight into the till." She stared at her receptionist, who nodded fervently.

"Thanks, Agnes," Margaret said. "We appreciate it." She turned to her friends. "Come on, time to go."

As they passed, Margaret stopped in front of her. "You'd make a great member of Knit or Die. We already have a couple of younger women, but they weren't in on Jean's soap caper. You'd fit right in. We need your backbone, and you need some women at your back."

It was hard not to smile at Margaret. "I'm not staying in Invertary long enough to join anything."

"Aye, well, we'll see about that," the woman said. "You don't choose knitting. It chooses you. Come on, ladies." And she herded her friends out of the room, leaving Agnes to wonder what that meant.

Last to leave were Shona and Darcy. The young girl wasn't shy—she came right up to stand in front of Agnes. "I know you aren't my dad's girlfriend, but if you have time to tell me any tips and stuff for getting away with things, that would be awesome."

"Darcy!" Shona snapped.

The girl gave her grandmother a contrite look before winking at Agnes and making a call-me gesture with her hand.

"You do realize I'm standing right here, don't you?" Logan said. "And we're going to talk about all of this tonight when I get home."

"Bummer." Darcy's whole body slumped as she dragged herself from the room, leaving Agnes alone with her father.

"You were no help at all," she told him.

"You didn't need my help. But I do wish you'd asked how much was in the envelope every month because I'd like to know what Bernadette considered a reasonable tip."

"That woman is more work than she's worth."

"Maybe, but I think you're more than capable of sorting her out." He stepped into her space, but Agnes retreated to the other side of her desk.

"You realize we still have the stolen jewelry and booze from the bar to account for," she said, her gaze fixed on the desk. Not on the man who'd been kissing her senseless an hour earlier. "I don't think your mother and her crew were responsible for those."

"Probably not." He folded his arms and considered her. "What's going on now?"

"I don't know what you mean," she lied.

"Aye. You do. One minute you're melting in my arms, the next you're an iceberg. I deserve to know what's happening here."

Sadly, he was right. "I can't do this *thing*." She motioned between them. "You have permanent written all over you, and I'm not staying in Scotland."

"I'm not looking for anything long term."

She gestured toward the door, where his daughter had disappeared seconds earlier. "Little Miss Curiosity says otherwise."

"She misses having a mum, but that doesn't affect us. When I say I'm not looking for long term, I mean that I'm not going to ask something from you that you aren't willing to give. You've made it plain you don't want to stay in Scotland. I respect that. The kids knowing about you doesn't change anything."

Oh, he was fooling himself more than she'd thought. "Yes. It really does. Maybe you should ask Lake to assign someone else to work with me. I think it would be for the best."

"No." He shook his head determinedly. "No. This is bullshit. You're just using this as an excuse to retreat. I don't know why, but I know you are. You might not believe me when I say I'm not looking for something serious, but it's the truth."

He rounded the desk to stand in front of her before putting his hands on her shoulders. And weak as she was, she couldn't move away from him.

"Contrary to what my daughter told you, I've had my fair share of relationships since the divorce. The kids just don't know about them. All of those relationships were casual and, if I'm honest, pretty empty. But I'm used to situations that end." He cupped her cheek, staring into her eyes with such intensity she could see her reflection shining back at her. "Do I think there's the possibility we could have a future together? Aye, I do. I think there's something between us, something that could be special if we let it grow. But I also know that you have different plans for your life."

"Logan," she tried to cut him off before he cracked open her heart with his words.

He shook his head to stop her. "Before we married, my ex-wife told me she didn't think she wanted kids. I thought she was too young to know her own mind, that she'd change it once she saw how good we were together. I was young, stupid, and wrong. It's not a mistake I'll make again. I believe you when you say you're leaving and that you're only here for the year. What I'm asking for is a chance to spend that year with you." He stroked her cheek with his thumb. "Our chemistry is off the charts, we have fun together, and I even appreciate that violent streak of yours. But I've grown up a lot since my divorce, and I won't ask anything of you that you aren't willing to give."

Damn, listening to him offer her everything she wanted was agony. "The kids…"

"Let me worry about my kids. I'm their father. If you want to explore this thing between us, then we'll keep it to ourselves—for however long it lasts. The question is, what do you want?"

CHAPTER 11

'*What do you want?*'

Logan's words tormented Agnes through the rest of the morning and into the afternoon. After he'd finished his speech, he'd given her the gentlest kiss, then told her to call him when she made up her mind.

Men.

They were genetically programmed to know exactly what to say and do to drive women mad. Now, instead of getting on with her work and straightening out Dougal's hotel, she was spending her time thinking about Logan.

It just wasn't fair.

Needing some fresh air, she took her late lunch down to the loch and stared out over the water, her brain replaying Logan's question over and over.

What did she want?

At that moment, it was to be as far away from the hotel industry as possible. Although Agnes knew that wasn't what Logan meant, her job was getting her down. The truth was, and she'd known it from the first day she'd worked in a hotel, she wasn't really a people person. She was more of a behind-the-scenes person. She was good with project management and strategy, which is why she needed to work in a huge hotel, where the guests never dealt directly with the manager. If she was stuck in a tiny boutique hotel, there was a good chance she'd end up the female version of Basil Fawlty. Because, in general, people sucked.

After placing the nylon-covered cushion she'd brought with her on a rock, Agnes sat at the edge of the loch and unwrapped her sandwich. With a heavy gray sky that hung low over the murky waters, the weather matched her mood. Dense clouds shrouded the hills on the opposite side of the loch, and the muted daylight sucked the color out of the landscape. Everything around her was gray and brooding, pressing down until she swayed under the weight of it all.

Even wrapped in a knee-length padded coat, the cold still seeped through to her bones. It brought back memories of her childhood, trying to sleep in icy cold rooms under threadbare blankets, going to bed wearing layers of clothes and still shivering. If she never saw her breath again, it would be too soon. No, staying in Scotland wasn't for her. She needed a position in a nice big hotel, somewhere in the sun, where she could manage from her huge office, far away from every single person in the building.

It was what she'd been working toward since she was fourteen. And now that her sisters were all settled, starting families of their own, happy and in love, it meant she was free to follow her dream. They didn't need her anymore. Although, a small voice in the back of her mind wondered how *she'd* cope without her sisters nearby. Maybe, just maybe, *she* still needed *them*.

As the gentle lapping of the water soothed her frayed nerves, and the sandwich took the edge off the biting tension that consumed her, Agnes had to admit that Invertary had a certain charm. In the summer, she imagined it would even be considered beautiful, with the green rolling hills and the blue loch, the whitewashed houses and the old stone castle. It had everything tourists wanted from a trip to Scotland. And, yet, it struggled to survive.

Young people were leaving in droves, the high school had very recently shut down because of declining numbers and the kids had to bus to Fort William. Shops were closing due to lack of business, and there was an air of stagnancy about the place. In fact, the only thing she was aware of that brought people to town was Josh. Half of the hotel's patrons were there to catch a glimpse of the singer.

It was little wonder Dougal wanted to build a conference center in an attempt to attract people to the town. But Agnes wasn't sure it was the right way to go. Without expanding his hotel, there would be no place for the conference attendees to stay when they came. It seemed like bad planning to her.

As she ate, she pulled out her phone, opened the app she used with her sisters and started a group call. If they were free, they'd answer, if not, she'd try again later. But she wanted to spend a few minutes touching base with them, reassuring herself that they were fine and happy. They'd been living in each other's pockets their whole lives, and it was far too unsettling to be without them. It was as if she were missing three limbs.

The screen changed, and a tiny image of Isobel's dark-haired visage appeared. "Aggie!"

Unexpectedly, Agnes' eyes welled up, and she blinked rapidly to clear them. "Isobel, how are you?"

Before her older sister could answer, Mairi's head appeared in a little window beside her. "Hello! What's going on?"

The last window popped up, showing Donna's smiling face. "I've missed you three," she said.

"Me too," Agnes said, her heart already feeling warmer at

the sight of her sisters. "I'm sitting out by the loch, having lunch, and I thought I'd check in. You're all too far away now."

"Not that far," Donna said. "Just Glasgow." Someone called out behind her, and she turned to wave. "I'm in the studio," she said when she turned back. "I'm working on a set of illustrations for a kids' fantasy book." She practically danced with joy as she spoke, and Agnes melted inside. At last, her gentle sister had found something she loved to do: studying art at the same college her husband lectured at.

"That sounds awesome," Mairi said. "Send us some pictures. I love your drawings. As for us, we just woke up. It's absolutely Baltic here, I'm freezing my backside off. And there's snow. So. Much. Snow. Look!" She turned her phone to show them the view from her hotel window. Mairi was in Montreal, meeting with two of the geek boys who'd signed up for her dating agency and recruiting more talent. Her matchmaking business had taken off, and she was having a blast with it.

"I'm getting cold just looking at that," Isobel said. "It's raining here in London, and everyone's in a bad mood because of it. Or, it could be because they're working on a tough case right now. Who knows? All I know is everybody's grumpy."

"It's cold here too," Agnes said. "And damp. And gray." She swung the phone around so they could see the loch.

"But pretty," Donna said.

"Yeah." Agnes sighed. "It's pretty."

The sigh wasn't loud or heavy, but it was enough to make all of her sisters focus on her.

"What's wrong?" Isobel demanded.

"Who do I have to hurt?" Mairi said. "I can be on a flight within the hour. It's only seven hours between here and Glasgow. I can be with you in about twelve."

"You look sad, Aggie," Donna said, her brow furrowed with worry. "You never look sad. Do you hate it there? Do you want to come live in Glasgow with Duncan and me?"

Her smile trembled. "I love you three, and I miss you. I guess it's just that I'm used to having you around."

"Oh." Donna softened. "I never thought of that. You're usually so strong all the time. Now I feel bad that we're all getting on with our lives, with our men, and you're doing a job you don't really want to do, with no one beside you. I can come to Invertary as soon as this term ends. I'm so sorry you're there on your own. I'd hate that too."

"It's fine," she reassured her soft-hearted sister. "Honestly, none of you need to rush to my side. I only wanted to see your faces."

"Callum has other connections," Isobel said. "He can ask around and find you a job in a different hotel if that's what you want. Maybe one in London, near us."

"No, no, it's fine. It's just"—Agnes heaved a sigh—"there are days when I wonder what I'm doing."

There was silence for a second before Isobel answered. "You can do anything you put your mind to, Aggie. You're the strongest and smartest of all of us. None of us would have made it this far if it hadn't been for you. Don't let a bad day get you down."

That made her swallow hard. "I'm having second thoughts about being in the hotel business," she confessed. "I don't really like people."

The phone erupted with laughter.

"We know," Mairi said with a huge grin.

"But you're good at organizing them," Donna said.

"That's why you're a manager," Isobel added.

"Look, it's early days," Donna said. "You've only been there a few weeks. Maybe once you get to know some people, it won't seem so hard."

"Don't mind me," Agnes said. "I'm feeling lonely today, that's all this is." Especially seeing as she'd tried to end things with Logan. Again. Why did the one man she'd been attracted to in years have to come with so much baggage? And why, oh why, did he live in the middle of bloody Scotland?

"You do know that you don't have to stay in the hotel industry if you hate it, don't you?" Isobel asked.

Agnes barked a mirthless laugh. "I spent ten years studying for this, and more years than that getting experience in hotels. It would be insane to walk away now, and a waste of all the support you guys gave me while I studied. You scrimped and saved to put me through college. I can't throw that back in your faces by walking away."

"Is that really what you think?" Mairi gaped. "I wish I was there right now to smack some sense into you. That's the dumbest thing I've heard in ages. Why would you changing careers upset us? You have a degree. You worked hard for it. Lots of people have degrees and never work in the area they studied. Look at philosophy majors, most of them work in McDonald's."

Donna nodded. "We want you to be happy—we don't care what job you do."

"You could never disappoint us," Isobel said. "Never. Don't even think it."

Agnes' throat tightened. Things were getting far too soppy for her liking. "Anyway, forget that. Tell me how the baby bump is going," she ordered Isobel, who promptly angled her phone camera so they could see her belly.

"Big as a house," she said cheerfully.

"And happy," Donna added.

"And happy," Isobel confirmed.

"I'm so pleased for you," Agnes said. "For all of you. I love seeing you all looking so content."

"You'll get there too," Donna said.

"I know." She took a deep breath and sat up straighter. "I'd better get back to it. Love you." After they'd finished telling her the same, their images blinked out, leaving her alone again. And then a new call came in.

Her big sister.

"Are you okay?" Agnes said as soon as her sister's image appeared on her screen.

"That's what I'm calling to ask you. I know you'll tell me things you won't tell the other two, so I wanted to give you the chance in case there was something else you wanted to talk about. There is, isn't there?"

Isobel was right. Although Agnes loved all her sisters equally, there was a special bond between her and Isobel. Probably because they'd spent those years alone together, trying to bring up Isobel's son, Jack, with no help from anyone. They'd been tough years. There had been times when she'd thought they wouldn't make it.

After a fortifying breath, she told her, "I met a man."

"Is he a good one?"

"I think so." She looked out over the loch before returning her attention to the screen. "You met him too when he went to the London office. Do you remember Logan McBride?"

"Oh." Isobel nodded solemnly. "He *is* a good one."

"I told him I'm going away when I've done a year with Dougal, that I plan to apply for jobs in other countries."

"And he was okay with that?"

"He said he's happy to take what time he can get."

"Well, that's good, isn't it? I mean, if you don't want anything serious."

And that was the problem. She wasn't sure a relationship with Logan could be anything but serious. "He has kids, Isobel. Two. A boy and a girl, fourteen and twelve. I met the girl today—she's cute and funny. She reminds me a lot of her dad."

"Oh, honey, I'm so sorry." Isobel reached out to touch the screen, as though she could touch her sister. "I know how hard it was for you growing up, looking after all of us when you were only a kid yourself. You gave up a lot to take care of us when I was so busy with Jack. I know you feel you want to have a break from responsibility, but Agnes, was it really all so bad?"

"No!" The answer was instant—she didn't even need to think about it. "I love you guys to infinity. Hell, I'd die for you, no questions asked. It's just that I have plans now. Things I've dreamed about doing since we were kids." Like getting out of Scotland and getting away from a life that was one long struggle to survive.

"You know your plans can change, don't you? Nobody would hold it against you if they did. And, on the flip side, no one will think you're selfish if you hold on to those plans and see them through. You deserve to have the life you want, Aggie. There's no need to feel guilty about it. You've earned it." Isobel bit her bottom lip for a second before continuing. "Why don't you take him up on his offer? Why don't you spend the year with him, with no expectations for the future?"

Her chest tightened and her eyes stung. "I'm scared I'll fall in love with him, Isobel."

"Oh, honey, our parents really stuffed us up, didn't they?"

Agnes nodded because her throat was too tight to answer.

"Not all men stop you from following your dreams," Isobel said softly. "Not all men press you down until there's nothing left of you."

"If I fall in love with him, I'll have to stay here."

"No." Isobel shook her head. "But you'd have to give him up to go. You know how this works. You can't have everything in life; it's all about negotiation and compromise. We learned that young. You're smart, Aggie, and you've got time to think things through. Just make sure the dreams you're following now are the ones you want as an adult, not the desperate dreams you had as a kid. And remember, whatever you do, whichever way you go, you'll always have us at your back."

"Even if I'm half a world away?"

"Even then."

"Thanks, sis." Agnes took a deep breath. "I have to get back to work."

"Call anytime," Isobel said. "I'm just sitting around incubating anyway."

"Love you," they both called out, and her phone went blank.

Agnes spent a few minutes staring out across the loch as the bitter chill from the wind ate right through her bones. As far back as she could remember, she'd always been the strong one. But, at that moment, she wouldn't have minded if Logan had been there so he could hold her for a while. Sometimes she ached for someone who didn't mind being strong for her, now and then, when she needed it. But Logan was a temptation she couldn't afford to succumb to. No matter how hard he was to resist.

After clearing up her things, she headed back to work. And, still, that one question repeated in her head: *What do you want?'*

CHAPTER 12

"I don't understand women," Logan said to his son's football coach as they stood together on the sidelines during practice.

It had been a day since he'd told Agnes to call if she wanted him. She'd emailed Lake about thefts at the hotel, but hadn't reached out to him. If he hadn't been getting updates and random photos from Bernadette, he would have worried she'd skipped town.

"What?" the coach said.

"I said, I don't understand women."

Not many junior teams could boast an ex-premier league footballer as their coach, but Flynn Boyle had grown up in Invertary and, now that he was home, he wanted to give something back. Of course, most folk would say all the animals he rescued was giving back enough. Well, okay, only his wife said that, but she was the one overrun by them. Flynn was studying to become a veterinarian and was a magnet for other people's unwanted pets. And injured wild animals. And, well, just any animal that wanted a free feed.

"What's to understand?" Flynn said, his gaze on the field. "You tell them they're pretty, give them chocolate, make a fuss when they do stuff, and keep them sexed up. It's harder to look after a goat."

"Why am I even talking to you about this?"

"Uh, because the only other guy in Invertary with as much experience with women as I have is Josh, and you don't want to take advice from a guy who asked his manager to find him a wife."

He had a point. "I didn't ask you for advice. We're just talking."

"About your women problems."

"It's what guys do."

"Since when? We deal with our women problems the same way we deal with everything else—a six-pack of beer, pizza, and a football game. After you've shouted at the idiots on the field for ninety minutes, everything's fine again. Do you want to go watch a game?"

"No." Well… "Depends on who's playing."

Flynn grinned as he slapped Logan on the back. "Congratulations, you still have your balls."

They watched the practice play out in front of them for a few minutes, interrupted now and then by Flynn shouting orders at random players and sometimes at the referee. Seeing as the ref was his nine-year-old daughter, she often shouted back. Neither Logan nor the players questioned having such a young referee. It was well known that Katy Boyle knew more about football than everyone in Invertary, except her dad.

"I thought she'd have called by now," Logan said, because he couldn't leave the topic alone. No, he just had to keep picking at the scab until it bled.

"Maybe she's busy," Flynn said.

"There have been more jewelry thefts at the hotel, just cheap plastic stuff, but she didn't even call me about those."

"See? Busy. Dealing with thieves and Dougal."

"She isn't busy. She's avoiding me and I don't understand why. We have explosive chemistry. The kind that doesn't come along every day. So what if I have kids? They're mine to worry about. I've told her we could keep it on the down-low. I've told her we could have any kind of relationship she wants. I don't see what the problem is."

"Sorry, you lost me there for a minute," Flynn said. "I was too busy watching that tackle your Drew made—the boy has skills. What were we talking about? Oh, aye, you want sex and Agnes doesn't. Move on. Don't waste your time."

Logan frowned at him. "Is that what you did when Abby had second thoughts about your relationship?"

"You have to actually be *in* a relationship to have second thoughts about it," Flynn said. "A couple of snogging sessions does not a relationship make." He grinned. "That sounded like Yoda. He was wise. You should listen to him. I mean, me." He took a deep breath and shouted, "Robby, pass the bloody ball."

"She's driving me crazy." Logan stamped his feet to get some warmth into them. The football fields were beside the loch, on the edge of town and, for some reason, it always seemed colder there than anywhere else in Invertary.

"They're designed to do that," Flynn said.

"The first woman I've been seriously interested in since my ex-wife, and she's as skittish as a horse who doesn't like being ridden."

Flynn turned to look at him, his overgrown hair flopping into his eyes. "You really need to work on your similes."

"Should footballers even use words like simile? And you know what I mean anyway," Logan grumbled.

"Aye, you're horny, and Agnes finds you painfully resistible."

"That's it. I'm going to talk to Josh—he has to be better

than this." He turned to stalk off, but Flynn grabbed his jacket and yanked him back.

"I'll be serious," he said.

"Is that even possible?"

"Sadly, aye." Flynn frowned at the field. "Wait a minute. Ref," he shouted, "that was a foul."

"No, it wasn't." Katy put her hands on the hips of her luminous pink strip and glared at her dad.

"It was a total foul," Flynn argued.

"I'm the referee," Katy shouted, "and you're the coach. You let me do my job, and I'll let you do yours."

"I'm pulling you as referee if you don't call all the fouls."

"And I'll tell Mum you're hiding orphaned baby mice in the garage."

"Crap," Flynn muttered. "Didn't think she knew about those. Fine," he shouted, "but I'm watching you."

She tossed her hair at him and blew her whistle to start the game again.

"Look," Flynn said once the game resumed. "You don't need advice. You're just looking for reassurance. But I can't give you that because the only person who can guess what a woman will do is the woman herself. All I can say is that if you're in this for the long game, then you need a strategy. Don't make it up as you go. Nobody ever won the league without a strategy. Utilize your best players, work as a team, and take the ball home." He slapped Logan on the shoulder.

"Are we still talking about Agnes?" Logan was genuinely confused.

"Aye." Flynn gave him a look that said he thought Logan was dumber than dirt. "Use the resources you have around you to help Agnes make the right decision. Find out what she wants and give it to her. Support her, even when her ideas seem nuts. Get the town working on your side. Play for the cup, not just the match."

Logan's mind raced with all the things he could do to remind Agnes he was there and waiting for her call. He'd spend the evening planning, and then put it straight into effect in the morning. It wasn't like he wanted to shove her into a decision—he'd been serious when he said he'd respect whatever she wanted to do, but it wouldn't hurt to keep himself at the forefront of her mind.

"I can't believe I'm saying this," he said, "but that actually helps."

"Don't sound so surprised. Just because I don't want to talk about this crap, doesn't mean I don't know what I'm talking about when I do. And you can tell Josh that." He took a deep breath. "Robby, pass the damn ball. That's the last time I'm telling you."

* * *

Forty-eight hours. Two sleepless nights. That's how long Agnes' brain had been stuck on one continuously repeating question: *'What do you want?'*

She pushed back her chair and rested her forehead on her desk, when what she really wanted to do was bang it against the wood—repeatedly. She couldn't go on like this. All she thought about was Logan. Memories of his kisses kept her awake at night, making her body burn to the point where her skin was so sensitive even the sheets rasped. Why did he have to be such a good kisser? Why couldn't he have been one of those sloppy, wet kissers? Or one of those guys who thought shoving their tongue down your throat made them irresistible?

And his body? His body should be outlawed. All those firm, lean muscles. His thighs! Sweet heavens above, those thighs. And that backside of his. He had the perfect bubble butt. But it was his eyes that really drove her insane. Those long lashes, the way the color changed from gold to the deepest chocolate…

She groaned and thumped the desk with her fists. "This isn't fair," she whined. "Nobody could hold out against this."

A knock at her door made her head jerk up. One of the waitresses stood in the doorway, a tray in her hand.

"Um, I'm just delivering your breakfast." Ruby was very young and obviously scared out of her mind at being the one sent to deal with the manager.

Agnes sat up straight. "I didn't order any breakfast." In fact, she hadn't even had time to grab a muffin before the calls started coming in about one problem or another.

"We know." Ruby hesitantly entered the room to put the white-linen-covered tray on the desk. "Chef found a note this morning."

Agnes waited a second, but further information was not forthcoming. "What did the note say?"

"Oh, that we're to make sure to feed you every few hours, or you become hangry." Ruby looked ready to bolt, but Agnes pinned her with a well-practiced stare.

"I don't get hangry," she snapped, watching as Ruby took two steps back.

"Okay," the girl said slowly, and Agnes got the distinct impression she was being humored.

"Was the note signed?" she demanded.

Ruby shook her head. "But Chef thought better safe than sorry, so enjoy." With that, she turned and practically ran from the office. "Someone will be over with your lunch," she called, and then Agnes thought she heard her mutter, "Please not me."

Everybody was so sensitive these days.

Agnes slid the tray toward herself and removed the napkin. An assortment of Danish pastries sat on a white plate beside a cup and saucer, milk jug and sugar bowl, and a French press filled with glorious black coffee.

"Bloody Logan," she muttered. It had to have been his idea, and she wasn't sure what to do about it other than ignore that he was behind it.

In the meantime, the coffee was calling to her. Eyes closing at the first glorious sip, she inhaled deeply. That was better. After two pastries that melted in her mouth, she had to admit she felt more human. Okay, so maybe there was something to this hangry thing after all.

Maybe.

* * *

MID-MORNING, after doing a walk-through of the hotel to make sure everything was running smoothly, Agnes returned to her office. Only to stop dead as she entered.

She could have sworn she smelled Logan's new deodorant.

Sniffing, she walked around the room. There was no sign of him or the source of the smell anywhere.

"Bernadette?" she shouted, and the receptionist came scurrying in. "Did you let someone into my office while I was gone?"

"No. Nobody's come into the hotel since you went walkabout."

"Then why does it smell like the ocean in here?"

"Eh." Bernadette looked confused. "It smells normal to me."

No help at all. "Go do something." She ushered the young woman out of her office and closed the door behind her.

It had to be in her head, but she was sure she could smell Logan. She'd know that scent anywhere. And being surrounded by it was driving her crazy. It brought back memories of them wrapped around each other in her bed, exchanging kiss after kiss after kiss while she breathed him in.

Damn it.

He'd gotten into her office somehow. She knew it.

Agnes threw the windows wide open and sat down to work. Ten minutes later, her fingers were ice and she couldn't stop her teeth from chattering. But the smell hadn't receded. After closing her windows again, she cranked up the heating and grabbed her padded coat from the stand behind the door. She needed to escape the scent, give it time to disperse.

"I'm going up the street to buy wrapping paper for the raffle prizes," she told Bernadette.

Who inexplicably held up her phone and snapped Agnes' picture.

* * *

EVERY SHOP AGNES passed on the way to the newsagent had posters taped to their windows that hadn't been there the day before. Apparently, the community center had decided to hold a last-minute movie night that evening, and they'd picked two romcoms for the event: *Friends with Benefits* and *No Strings Attached.*

Just when she was trying to get those concepts out of her head, she found herself confronted with them at every turn. This town was crazy. It was only a few weeks to Christmas, and they'd decided to show two very similar romcoms instead of a holiday-themed movie.

Agnes glared at the posters as she let herself into the newsagent, the only place in town where you could buy wrapping paper.

"Are you going to the movies tonight?" Maggie, one of the

aging owners, asked when Agnes put the paper on the counter. Although she'd only been in town a few weeks, Agnes already knew most of the shopkeepers by name. Invertary was just that small.

"Uh, no."

"Oh, but you should," Maggie gushed. "I hear tell that you see Justin Timberlake's backside! I'm not sure how much of Ashton Kutcher you see in his movie, but we can compare. After we've watched both, there's going to be a comparison discussion over eggnog. It sounds like fun."

"Sorry, I'll have to pass. I have things to do." Like sitting alone in her room, staring at the tartan carpet and questioning her life choices.

"Oh, that's a shame," Maggie said. "When Logan put up the posters, he mentioned that you might enjoy the movies, and he said it would be a good way for you to meet some of the locals."

She did *not* just say Logan's name… "Who?"

"Logan," Maggie said. "From Benson Security. I thought you knew him. It certainly sounded like you did." She placed her hand on her chest. "Did I make a mistake?"

"No, not at all. I do know Logan." And she was possibly going to kill him. "I'd better get back to the hotel. Enjoy your movies tonight."

On her way out the door, Agnes grabbed a poster and took the damn thing with her as evidence. Once she'd calmed down, she planned to shove it up Logan's backside.

* * *

LOGAN HADN'T BEEN into the Benson Security office this morning. And none of the amused staff knew where he'd gone.

Typical.

There was nothing to do except go back to the office that smelled like the man who was driving her nuts.

She'd managed to miss lunch by being out of the office, but her luck didn't hold out when dinnertime came around. Although, by the time the tray appeared on her desk, she realized she was actually quite hungry. Agnes might even have appreciated having the food delivered if it hadn't been for the ocean-freaking-breeze smell permeating her office.

Staring down at the linen-covered tray, she wondered what to do about the man who seemed determined to remind her of him at every turn. His scent filled her office, his proposition was plastered all over town, and his care was in the meal sitting in front of her at that very minute. He was trying to wear her down.

The sneaky, sneaky man.

But if he thought she'd crumble that easily, then he didn't know her at all. Agnes could resist this temptation. She had a backbone of steel. Logan had no idea what he was up against.

Agnes pulled the tray toward herself, whisked off the napkin, and gaped. It was the exact meal they'd had at the spa. There was no way the hotel kitchen had made this. No, this meal had been ferried in from the only other restaurant in town. As she sat staring down at it, there was a flash, and she looked up to find Bernadette aiming her phone at her.

"What are you doing?" Agnes demanded.

"Nothing," she said. "I was just wondering if you're going to the movies at the community center tonight."

"No! And close the damn door."

As her office door shut quietly, Agnes massaged the ache in her temples and groaned. Her phone lay on the desk in front of her, tempting her to just call Logan and tell him she was giving in. But, no, she could resist his onslaught. She was made of iron.

After switching off her phone, she dug into the meal, all

the while trying not to breathe in Logan's scent.

* * *

IT WAS ALMOST nine before Agnes finished up in her office. Dragging her tired body up the stairs to her room, she longed for a hot bath, some chocolate, and at least fourteen hours sleep.

Instead, her room had only a shower. And she had to be back at her desk by seven in the morning. At least she still had a bar of chocolate in her fridge. Chocolate helped everything. She opened her door, stepped into her room, and stopped.

Folded on the end of her bed was a massive, plush wine-colored blanket, an electrical cord wound in a circle on top. Agnes had seen those blankets in Invertary's gift shop and had longed for one, but it'd been just out of her price range—until her wages came in.

Now here it was.

She ran her fingers over the sensual material, already eager to plug in the blanket, switch it on and wrap herself in its warmth.

A piece of folded paper sat beside it on the bed. Agnes picked up the note and read it.

I didn't want you to be cold.

Agnes sat on the edge of her bed, pulled out her phone and dialed Logan.

She'd been wrong. There was no fighting this. This kind of temptation was too much to resist. All she could hope for now was that he was so terrible in bed it put her off him for life.

The call went straight to voicemail, so she left a message. Just three small words before she hung up.

"I want you."

CHAPTER 13

Logan dried his hands, shut the dishwasher and reached for his phone. He'd been elbow deep in water so had let the caller leave a message. With a swipe of his screen, he accessed his voicemail and promptly lost the ability to breathe, because the message was from Agnes. And all she'd said was, *'I want you.'*

Damn.

He ran a hand down his face as his stomach filled with butterflies and his heart raced. All at once, he was a teenage boy again, nervous before his first date. Hanging his head, he muttered some curses under his breath. That woman was twisting him inside out.

"Who was on the phone?" Drew said as he sauntered into the kitchen.

Fighting to get his reaction under control, Logan turned to face his son. "I have to go out. I'm needed at the hotel, and I could be gone all night. Go next door and get your gran for me, will you?"

"You do know I'm old enough to look after Darcy, right?" Drew said, but he was already heading for the door.

"Not overnight you aren't." He didn't care how many bolts they had on the door, or how sensible his kids could be, they weren't spending the night alone.

He found his daughter lying upside down on the sofa, reading a book. He crouched beside her. "I'm going out. Gran's coming over, and she'll put you to bed, okay?"

There were no arguments about her being too old for anyone to put to bed. She just said, "'kay. Night, Dad." And carried on reading.

With a smile, Logan kissed her forehead before getting ready to go out.

Her knitting under her arm, his mother appeared as he pulled on his jacket. "Work?" she asked as he kissed her on the cheek.

He wouldn't lie to his family, but that didn't mean he had to spill his guts to them either. "Let's just say something came up."

She stared at him, and he felt exactly the same as he had when he was a kid and tried to sneak things past her. He'd never managed it. Not once. She had a built-in radar for bullshit.

"Does this *something* have anything to do with a certain hotel manager?"

"I know what I'm doing," he told her. And he was also old enough to do it without his mother's input.

"I hope so," she muttered. "Be sure to tell her that if she breaks you, she buys you." With that, she headed into the living room.

"Night," Logan shouted as he opened the door. "See you all tomorrow."

There were grunts for replies. Good to know they'd miss him.

Sleet hit the car windshield as he drove through town, telling him that, just like Agnes, the weather couldn't make up its mind either. Instead of rain or snow, they were getting both.

Clenching and unclenching his hands on the steering wheel, Logan negotiated the narrow old roads down to the loch. He shouldn't jump to conclusions over Agnes' call. Just because she'd said she wanted him, didn't mean she wanted to get physical with him. She probably meant she wanted to talk to him. Aye, that was probably all she meant.

He shifted in his seat, adjusting himself in his jeans to get more comfortable. Why was it taking so long to get there? You could drive right across the whole of Invertary in fifteen minutes, yet this trip was taking a lifetime.

"I want you," she'd said. Damn it to hell. He wished she'd been more specific. What kind of want were they talking about exactly? Friends? Friends with benefits? Just benefits? Could he be a booty call for her if that's all she wanted? *Hell, yes!*

At last, the pub came into sight, its walls glowing yellow under the uplighting. Logan parked behind it and was out of his car in two seconds flat. They would have locked the hotel doors by now, with only guests having a code to open them, so he'd have to go through the pub. His stomach sank. The last thing he needed was somebody stopping him to chat.

Keeping his head down, Logan prayed no one would notice him as he aimed straight for the interior entrance to the hotel. Of course, he wasn't that lucky.

"Logan," Dougal boomed. "What can I get you?"

There weren't enough curse words in the world for his reply. "Nothing. I'm just cutting through. I have a meeting with Agnes."

Dougal's bushy white eyebrows shot up. "At this time of night?"

"It's barely half past nine," Logan pointed out, still walking toward the hallway that led to the hotel.

"It must be important if she called you in this late in the day," Dougal said. "I'd better come with you."

"No!" Logan almost tripped over a stool. "No need for you to leave the bar. I can handle this."

"Not at all," Dougal said before turning to one of his staff. "Grace, watch the bar. I need to have a word with my manager."

Fuck. Fuck. Damn. Hell. Shit. Crap.

Taking a deep breath, he pulled out his phone. "I'll send Agnes a text to ask where we're meeting."

"I expect she'll be in her office if she called you in," Dougal said as he came around the bar.

Logan shot off a text: *Dougal thinks we have a meeting. He's coming with me.*

He received no reply. Nothing. Now what?

"As you know," Dougal said as they headed into the hotel, "we've had a few more thefts this past week, but nothing on the level of Mrs. Edwards' ring. I don't understand it myself —it's as though the thief can't tell the difference between a diamond and cheap glitter."

Logan glanced at his phone. No message. He quickly typed another: *Dougal is with me!!!!*

"Everything all right?" Dougal said.

"Absolutely." The phone was a burning coal in his hand, his jeans were strangling the erection of the century, and Santa was cockblocking him. But apart from that, everything was just hunky-dory.

"That's strange," Dougal boomed as they rounded the corner to Agnes' office. "The lights aren't on. She can't be in there. Are you sure you're meeting her tonight?"

"Pretty sure," Logan said, checking his phone again. Still nothing.

"You don't think she's working in her room again, do you?" Dougal frowned. "I've told her to stop doing that. I don't expect her to work in her sleep. She needs time off, the same as everybody else. That girl just doesn't take care of herself. Come on. We might as well go see."

"I don't think it's wise to call her a girl. She might take offense at that, seeing as she's a full-grown woman."

"She's a girl to me," Dougal huffed. "I'm old enough to be her grandfather."

"She's thirty-two."

"Okay, then a late-in-life father."

Logan shook his head—this conversation wasn't the one they needed to have. He'd gone off track. "I can deal with this on my own," he said. "I expect you want to get back to the bar, anyway."

"Nonsense, it's no trouble." Dougal started up the stairs. "After all, this is my hotel, and I like to keep abreast of everything that goes on in it."

"A breast?" Logan was thirteen again, blushing at words with even the vaguest sexual connotation.

"Don't tell me you don't know what abreast is?"

This was *not* happening! Aye, he knew what a breast was, and he'd been hoping to get his hands on a couple until Dougal butted in.

"It means keeping up-to-date on a situation," Dougal said with disgust. "Young people today, you're so busy texting, you've forgotten real words. When I was your age, I had an amazing vocabulary. Still do, mind you."

"I know what abreast means, Dougal." Logan shot off another text as he spoke: *URGENT Dougal and I are outside your door.* They weren't, not yet, but they were damn close.

"Then why did you ask about it?" Dougal huffed.

Still no reply from Agnes. All Logan could do was hope she checked her phone before opening the door. Otherwise, this could go south pretty fast, and any plans she had of keeping things between them off the town's radar would be gone.

"Good," Dougal said, "there's light coming from under the door, so she must be in."

Before Logan could come up with anything else to derail Dougal, the hotel owner thumped Agnes' door. For a second, Logan thought he might faint from the stress of the situation, but then the door swung open, and Agnes beamed at both of them.

"Good, you're both here," she said as though she'd been expecting them. "That saves me the trouble of updating you separately. Come on in."

* * *

AGNES HAD BEEN in the shower, shaving her legs, while Logan was sending her desperate messages. She'd barely had time to throw on some clothes, and even then, not all of them, as she had nothing on under her buttoned suit jacket, when there was a knock at the door. After twisting her wet hair into a knot and clipping it in place, she slipped her damp feet into her shoes, kicked her bra under the bed and opened the door, all the while praying that this wasn't happening.

Bloody Dougal. He should just go back to running his own hotel. It would be more efficient than poking his nose into everything she did.

Not that this get-together was about the hotel. No, this one should have been about her and Logan. Who was currently eating her up with his eyes while Dougal waited for a nonexistent report.

"What's this all about then?" Dougal boomed.

"Well." There was nothing she could do but start talking in the hope that something would come to her. "I was going over the list of stolen items, and I found a..."

What? What the hell had she found?

Logan cleared his throat. "Is this about that pattern you mentioned?"

"Yes, yes, the pattern!" *What pattern?* "Perhaps you could explain about the pattern while I switch off the monitors. They're very distracting."

That's when she realized the monitors weren't on. And that Dougal didn't know about the cameras. For a second, she just stood there, frozen midstride, completely at a loss as to what to do next.

"What are you talking about?" Dougal boomed again. "And why do you have so many screens in your room anyway?"

"About that pattern," Logan said loudly, attempting to save her. "Agnes mentioned that all of the items have gone missing during daytime hours. So we can definitely rule out night people. I mean people at night. As in, hotel guests."

Agnes bugged her eyes at him. *That* was the best he could do?

Judging by the look on Dougal's face, he was about as impressed as she was with Logan's explanation. But there was nothing she could do now but go with it.

"Yes." She nodded solemnly. "It means the thief has to be someone who has access to the place during the day. I think we can rule out guests because, as Logan pointed out, they would be better off stealing at night." *Holy crap, that sounded worse.* "Also, I noticed all of the stolen jewelry was shiny. And small. So that means we're looking for someone who likes small shiny things." *Damn, she was dying here.* She shot Logan a desperate look, but he just stared at her in bewilderment. "Isn't that right, Logan?" she prodded.

"Aye, that's right." He cleared his throat. "And didn't you mention that you thought the thief must be keeping everything because nothing had turned up in any pawnshops or online sales sites?"

"Yes!" She pointed at him. "That too."

"That's it?" Dougal sounded incredulous. "This is why you called Logan all the way down here? I have to say that I'd expect more from my manager." He looked like he was gearing up to give a lecture on how to run a hotel properly, possibly including how she wasn't cut out for management. Yeah, he had the look of a man who was wondering why he'd hired his staff.

She had to salvage this situation. And fast. "Of course, that isn't everything. I could have told him that in an email. There's also the…"

The what? What was there? A missing plastic bracelet? Still no sign of the diamond ring?

Her eyes came to rest on the screens, and her shoulders slumped. It was a dumb idea, but she'd run out of options. "There's also the new security cameras I've installed."

"Cameras?" Dougal shouted, his head turning red with outrage.

"Fantastic idea." Logan slapped Dougal on his back. "Don't you agree? I told Agnes the best way to deal with this situation was to set up cameras. Of course, she wasn't keen on the idea, kept going on about guest privacy, but you and I both know that guest security is also important."

Dougal didn't look convinced, but he'd stopped blustering.

"I know you don't want a permanent system," Agnes said. "I just got the cheapest stick-up cameras. That way, we can take them down as soon as we've found the thief. Also, I only put up half a dozen and, to ensure guest privacy isn't invaded by anyone else on the staff, I plan to monitor them myself."

"That's going above and beyond," Logan said. "When do

you sleep? Dougal was just telling me that he thought you worked too hard. Isn't that right, Dougal?"

"Well, aye, but I didn't think she'd be watching cameras all night long."

Logan clapped him on the shoulder. "It's hard to find staff this dedicated. You're a lucky man."

It was all Agnes could do not to roll her eyes. At least now it was clear where Darcy got her gift for acting, because her father was seriously bad at it too.

Dougal opened and shut his mouth a few times before he spoke. "I agree. The cameras are a good idea in this instance, but, rather than having my manager watch them, maybe Benson Security could take that on board. It would free up Agnes' time for more important things."

"That's a fantastic idea," Logan said.

"Why didn't I think of that?" Agnes said.

They both smiled at Dougal.

"What I still don't understand—" Dougal started to say.

But desperate to head off any other lines of inquiry she didn't have answers for, Agnes cut him off. "Wait, let me show you the camera feeds." She switched on all the monitors. And there, in the hallway outside the kitchen door, was Dougal's pup peeing on the skirting board.

"Arnold!" Dougal shouted. As though the dog could hear him from the second floor.

Agnes had never loved a dog more in her life than she loved that peeing, farting ball of fur right then.

"I need to deal with this," Dougal said. "I've talked to him about doing his toilet outside. This is not on. Not on at all. Good work, Agnes. I expect we'll get to the bottom of these thefts in no time. Come on, Logan. I'll walk you out."

As Dougal strode toward the door, Logan held up his hands and shrugged.

Agnes dug in her pocket, grabbed her room key with its

security fob for the main door, and thrust out her hand to Logan. "Thank you for coming out so late. I appreciate it."

He took her hand in his, palming the key as he did so. Shivers went right through her body as his eyes darkened. "It's no trouble at all. Call me tomorrow if you find anything."

"Will do."

And then he turned around to join her boss, who waited impatiently in the hallway.

"Don't stay up too late," Dougal said. "We've got a busy few days ahead of us."

Agnes said nothing, she just cast one last glance at Logan, and shut the door.

CHAPTER 14

Agnes' key burned in Logan's hand, branding him. All he could think about was getting straight back up to the room without Dougal in tow. How he managed to carry on a polite conversation while they walked down the stairs, he'd never know.

"Do you want a drink before you go?" Dougal said when they reached the lobby.

"No, thanks, I think I'll just head to bed." Hopefully, not his.

"Have a good night then." Dougal hurried off toward the kitchen.

Logan didn't even pretend to walk toward the door; he just turned and ran back up the stairs, taking them two at a time. His hand shook as he inserted the key in the lock, and he had to take a few steadying breaths before opening the door.

Agnes stood at the end of her bed, watching him. She'd turned off the overhead lights, leaving only the lamp on. Her cheeks were flushed and her eyes dark. When her tongue peeked out to wet her lips, he almost groaned.

"I turned out the lights in case Dougal came back," she said, sounding husky. "You should lock the door."

His breath caught as he did just that. "Are we here to talk about your decision?" If she said yes, he thought he might burst into tears.

She shook her head slowly, her eyes still on his.

There were words to say, but none of them came to mind in that moment. They stood there, just a few feet apart, staring at each other forever, until the world reduced to only the two of them. He was aware of everything about her—the way the light picked up the highlights in her hair, the golden sheen of her skin, the rise and fall of her chest with each breath she took. Every curve, every angle, every outline, all of it, was burned into his brain for all time.

Anticipation grew in the air between them. A living, breathing entity that drowned out everything else until there was only Agnes and Logan. And then, anticipation morphed into desperate need, and they moved. Rushing toward one another in an unspoken agreement. They met halfway, slamming into each other—bodies, hands, mouths.

They kissed with a ferocity he'd never experienced, and a silent roar erupted straight from his soul—*Yes!* He needed this. Needed *her.* His sweater lifted and soft hands caressed his back as their mouths fed from each other in a desperate frenzy. Tasting. Teasing. Swallowing the mewls of need, the grunts of brutal desire.

Agnes tugged at his sweater, and he broke their kiss long enough to pull it off. She sighed as her hands explored his naked chest, and Logan captured the end of the sigh with his mouth. She tasted of coffee and chocolate, of wicked desires and uncontrolled need. She tasted as though she'd been designed just for him. His special addiction.

Without breaking the kiss, not sure he could anyway, he slid a hand between them to unbutton her jacket. The edges parted, and he met…skin. Warm, smooth, perfect skin. His hand stroked up to cup a heavy breast. Damn, she was perfection. Spilling over his hold, a solid weight of soft flesh in his hand.

She pushed into him, and he rasped his thumb over her taut nipple. A shiver. A moan. She liked that. He did it again and her kiss become more frenetic. He teased the underside of her breast as she swayed in his arms. His Agnes was sensitive, and he loved it. He wanted to spend hours caressing her, teasing her, driving her out of her too-busy mind, making her fly for him.

They tore at each other's clothes, casting them off in a whirlwind of desperation, until at last they were skin to skin, and their touches slowed. He wanted to know every inch of her. Every detail. He wanted to discover all of her secrets and use them for her pleasure. His head spinning, he felt drugged. But through it all, Agnes was the eye of the storm that engulfed them. An oasis of peace. Paradise in his arms.

Slowly, Logan backed her to the bed and lowered her gently. Pools of emerald green gazed up at him. But still, they didn't speak. Not with words. The cool cotton sheets a sensual delight against his burning skin, he leaned over her, supporting his weight with his arms as he started the slow exploration of Agnes Sinclair.

He was her servant. His only wish to please and to learn her desires. A tongue twirled around the shell of her ear made her gasp and cling to him. A nip to her lobe educed a moan. His mouth on her breast caused her to arch off the bed, her fingers tangled tight in his hair. So he lingered. Sucking. Nipping. Tasting. Until she writhed against him. Lost in him. Just as he was in her.

Touching kisses to her soft, round stomach, he wriggled lower, wedging his shoulders between her thighs. Everywhere he touched, he found satin pillows of flesh that made his mouth water. She was Venus. And he was happy to worship her.

As the heady fragrance of her sex tantalized him, Logan couldn't resist tasting her any longer. Taking his time, he lavished long, slow, intimate kisses on her that made her heels dig into his back and her fingers tighten in his hair. Attuned to her now, aware of every hitch in her breath, every desperate little sound escaping her lips, he could instantly tell if she enjoyed what he was doing, or if he had to try something else.

As he teased her little nub of nerves with the tip of his tongue, he slid a finger into her wet depths. A gasp before she held her breath. Her hips lifting from the bed, she tightened on his finger, her little nub grew hard, and she exploded with a wail of pure delight.

Was there any better feeling in the world than making a woman orgasm? If there was, he hadn't experienced it. And watching Agnes come apart was something he knew he'd never get enough of.

Slowly, he kissed his way up her body, lingering at her breasts before burying his face in her neck and teasing with his teeth. Her legs widened, welcoming him as she pulled him to her. He wanted to be inside of her more than anything else, but in his haste to get to her, he'd forgotten one thing—protection.

"I don't have a condom," he said against her throat. "I'll go get some and come back." His confession was agony, and his dick would probably snap in two when he tried to force it back in his jeans, but it had to be done.

Clasping his face, she forced him to look at her. Her eyes were glazed, her cheeks flushed, and her lips swollen. So beautiful, it made it hard to breathe.

"I'm on the pill," she whispered.

His heart actually missed a beat. "I haven't had sex without a condom since my wife."

She stared into his eyes for a moment, assessing him, reading something there that only she understood. "Don't go," she whispered. "I want you now."

"Are you sure?"

She didn't answer him with words. Instead, she pulled his head down and kissed him, slowly, deeply, determinedly. Logan didn't ask her again—his Agnes knew her own mind. Slowly, he slid a hand between them to help guide himself into her.

His head fell back at the sensation of her wet heat surrounding him. He groaned to the ceiling as he slowly, deliberately pressed deeper. Tighter than a fist, she grasped him and pulled him further into her.

A small squeak brought his head jerking back down, assessing if she was okay, ensuring he hadn't hurt her in any way. He wanted only pleasure for his Agnes. But rather than pain, he saw ecstasy. Her mouth was open, her head angled back—she was glorious. Her eyes burned into his as she grasped his backside and tugged him closer.

And Logan took that as his cue. He surged deep inside of her, joining them completely. Listening to their moans mingle in the air around them, he breathed deep of their combined scent—sweetness and spice. He stilled, arms taut, holding his weight as he hovered above her, making the moment last so he would never forget a second of it. He shifted his weight to one arm so he could cup her cheek with the other, leaning in to take her mouth in a long, sensual kiss. Then slowly, deliberately, his hips began to move as his lips stole the gasps and moans he elicited from Agnes. It was an excruciating pleasure.

"Faster, please," she begged against his mouth, her voice breathless and needy.

He didn't hesitate to give her what she wanted, holding her gaze as he did so, never once letting her look away. Wanting to see *all* of *her* as they soared together.

His.

She was his.

For now, anyway.

With each surge inside her, Logan lost a little more of himself to the woman in his arms. Together, their breathing became more labored. Together, they clung to each other. Together, they pushed each other higher. Until, with one glorious thrust, his body tightened, his blood boiled and his thoughts turned to white noise. Nothing existed but Agnes. And together, they broke apart in each other's arms.

CHAPTER 15

The weight of Logan's body pressed Agnes deep into the bed, and she clung to him like an anchor in a storm as the room whirled around them. All she could hear was their heavy breathing and the rapid beating of her heart. Her body was boneless and, for the first time in years, her brain had fallen silent. It was blissful.

Her hands gently caressed his back, his shoulders, his arms, as she floated on a cloud of peace. He started to move away from her, but she held him tight.

"Stay," she groggily ordered.

"I'm too heavy for you," he protested.

"Stay." She made it a command.

He settled in over her, giving her his weight, making her feel secure. She lay there, riding the high of their lovemaking and delighting in her completely relaxed state of body and mind.

Until the buzz began to fade and reality encroached.

As much as she fought it off, it still destroyed her languid peace, and her body tensed.

Logan lifted his head. "What's wrong?"

Of course, he'd noticed. He was lying on top of her after the best sex she'd ever had. The realization sent a spike of panic through her veins. This wasn't right. This wasn't how it was supposed to be. She shoved at his shoulders, and he instantly moved from her.

"Agnes, tell me what's wrong." His voice was steady, in control, a lifeline if she wanted to reach for it.

But it was too late—she was already drowning. As she scrambled from the bed, she picked up her suit jacket and held it in front of her, covering what she could.

"You need to leave," she said. "Now."

The tears were already nipping at her eyes, but she wouldn't cry in front of him. She *never* cried in front of anyone. Ever.

Logan's gaze never left hers as he shuffled to sit on the edge of the bed, indifferent to his nudity, only concern showing on his face.

"Tell me what's going on," he said in the same tone people used with scared animals. "Did I hurt you?"

Had he hurt her? Hell, yes, he'd hurt her. Agnes wasn't sure she'd ever get over the wounds he'd inflicted.

"It was supposed to be terrible," she wailed.

Logan was clearly confused. "You wanted *bad* sex? Agnes, love, you need to help me out here, I don't understand what you mean."

She paced the room, ranting while she did so and clutching the jacket in front of her, only belatedly realizing her backside was still bare. Oh, to hell with it. He'd seen it all anyway.

"I thought we'd have sex and get it out of our systems. I hoped it would be a letdown, and then I'd be able to shrug it off and move on. But no, you had to ruin everything. You had to make it good. Not just good. Phenomenal. I can't believe you did this to me!"

"Uh, you aren't making any sense." He stood in front of her, getting in the way of her pacing and tempting her with his far-too-sexy body. "Why don't you calm down for a minute, and we'll talk this through?"

And just like that, he didn't look quite so sexy. "*Never* tell a woman to calm down." She pointed to the door. "It's time for you to go. Get your stuff and leave."

"You're kicking me out because the sex was great?" He stared at her as though she'd lost her mind.

"Out." Agnes dropped the useless jacket, gathered his clothes and shoes, and thrust them into his arms. She pushed him toward the door, threw it wide, and shoved him out.

Logan didn't resist, so he ended up standing in the hallway, stark naked, holding his clothes and gaping at her. "Agnes, be reasonable. If it's that important to you, we can do it again, and I'll make sure it's crap this time."

"It's too late now," she said and slammed the door in his face before bursting into tears.

Nothing was going right. Nothing. First, all of her sisters had moved on with their lives without her. Then, after being blacklisted, she'd ended up working in a hotel where the owner didn't really want her. Now, she'd had the most amazing sex of her life with a man who had *permanent* written all over him. Every single thing Logan did made it harder to walk away, even when staying meant giving up everything else. It was too much.

Sniffing and sobbing, she dragged herself into the shower.

She just couldn't catch a break.

* * *

LOGAN STARED AT THE DOOR, listening to Agnes cry and feeling helpless to do anything about it. He should have been in there with her, holding her while she wept, and trying to understand what she meant. Because having great sex wasn't a reason to end a relationship. It made no sense. She should have been happy. Hell, he'd been ecstatic until she'd lost the plot on him.

Slowly, he became aware of his surroundings and the fact he wasn't alone in them. His heart sinking, he peered over his shoulder to find four of the guests staring at him open-mouthed.

Mrs. Edwards gave him a cheeky smile. "I have to say, Logan, you have very tasty buttocks."

Logan started to turn but immediately stopped when he realized that would only make the situation worse. Instead, he put on his best cop voice and said, "Nothing to see here. Go back to your rooms. Everything's under control."

"Oh," Mrs. Edwards said, her eyes still on his backside, "I wouldn't call that nothing."

"Are you harassing the manager?" an elderly man demanded.

"I think he was definitely doing *something* with the manager," a young Australian woman said with a grin. "But I don't think you'd call it harassment."

The older guy's face turned a deep purple. "Well, you can't hang around in the corridors naked. That isn't right."

Logan was getting a crick in his neck from watching them over his shoulder, so he dropped his shoes, covered his junk with his scrunched-up clothes, and turned.

Mrs. Edwards sighed. "I don't think I've seen muscles like that in real life since I was a teen."

Another young woman looked over at Mrs. Edwards. "Mr. Edwards didn't have a six-pack?"

"You mean the muscles?" Mrs. Edwards pointed at him. "Heavens no. If that's a six-pack, then my dear husband had a keg."

"As much as I love being objectified," Logan said, "it's time for all of you to go back to your rooms so I can get dressed and get out of here."

"I think I should call the police." The old man glared at him while tugging his burgundy-colored dressing gown tight. By the look in his eye, any second now he was going to shove up his sleeves and challenge Logan to 'fisticuffs.'

"He'll be gone by the time the police get here," one of the young women said with a wicked smile. "We should take his photo—in case they need it to track him."

"Do not take my photo," Logan barked the order, but it was too late. The Australian girls were already snapping away.

"We don't need photos," Mrs. Edwards said. "I know who he is. He's Logan, and he works for Benson Security."

"Better safe than sorry," said one of the Aussies, showing the screen to the older woman.

"I see what you mean." She flushed. "I'm going to need copies of those. Perhaps Logan could turn around again so we can capture the full view."

The three women stared at him expectantly, as though it was perfectly normal for them to ask him to flash his arse for a photo.

"Leave. Now." He pointed to the stairs.

Only the old guy moved. "I'm fetching Dougal," he said, before heading down the stairs.

Great. Agnes would kill him if they roped Dougal into this. He appealed to Mrs. Edwards, "It could affect Agnes' job if he involves Dougal."

"I'll stop him…for a price," the evil woman said.

Hanging his head, Logan did the only thing he could—he turned and let the women take photos of his backside. "If any of these end up on the internet, I'm pressing charges," he threatened.

But it was an empty threat, and they all knew it.

"Are you done?" he demanded. "Somebody needs to stop the old guy while I get dressed. Without an audience," he stressed.

"Breanna," Mrs. Edwards said, "run downstairs and stop Mr. Thompson. Tell him it's all under control and there's cake in my room."

"This is the best holiday ever," the young woman said as she disappeared down the stairs. "Scotland rocks."

Logan stared at the two remaining women. This was not how he'd expected the evening to end.

"We're going now," Mrs. Edwards said. "You really do have the most delicious heinie. Makes me wish I was ten years younger."

And with that, they were gone. Leaving Logan to throw on his clothes as he wondered what the hell just happened.

CHAPTER 16

"Agnes," a deep voice snapped. "Are you sick?"

"I was just thinking," she said, jerking upright.

Damn, she'd fallen asleep at her desk. She was exhausted. Out of sorts. And all because she'd spent every night since she'd kicked Logan out, lying awake and thinking about him. Then she'd spent her days avoiding him. It was draining. And to add insult to injury, she kept bursting into tears. Thankfully, none of her episodes had been in public, but she'd still morphed into something she didn't recognize, and it was all Logan's fault. She'd never been this confused over a man. Next thing she knew, she'd be crying because she broke a nail.

She tugged down her suit jacket, her hands stilling mid-motion. It had started—she was turning into her boss.

"Thinking?" Dougal boomed. "With your head on the desk and your eyes shut?"

"It's my zen place." She reached up to straighten her ponytail and found half her hair wasn't even in it. Had she started the day like that? This was humiliating. Usually immaculate in her appearance, she prided herself in being a businesswoman ready for a day at work. Today, she was a mess. All because of Logan. Damn, sexy, irresistible, annoying man. "What can I do for you?" she asked her boss, trying to sound her usual professional self as she continued to fix her hair.

"The Christmas market starts the day after tomorrow, and it's our busiest time of the year."

He wasn't telling her anything she didn't already know. "I'm aware of when the market starts. I also know the hotel is booked solid from tomorrow, and the town will get busy tomorrow afternoon." That's why they'd booked in a band for Friday night.

"Aye, well, I wanted to make sure you had everything ready."

"Yes, everything's ready."

Dougal frowned as though he didn't quite believe her. Although, she had to admit, finding her asleep probably didn't help to instill confidence.

"What about the band? Did you liaise with them? Do they have everything they need for tomorrow night?"

"They're all set for tomorrow, and they're looking forward to it." They'd booked a local folk band to perform Christmas songs. It wasn't as though U2 was coming. The band's main concern was that they'd get their drinks for free.

"What about the karaoke for Saturday night? Is that ready?"

Agnes stared at him, wondering if it was a trick question. There was a stage in the corner of the pub, and the karaoke machine had been loaded with Christmas songs. What else was there to do?

"Yes," she said. "It's all under control."

"Did you do a sound check and make sure the microphone is working properly, like I asked?"

"The mic is great. The speakers are working at peak

performance. It's all completely fine." She slid her hands into her lap and dug her nails into her palms. To stop herself from screaming.

"Good, good." Dougal stroked his Santa beard. "And the kitchen hasn't had any trouble with the menu?"

Why was he asking her this? He must have passed the kitchen on the way to her office.

"No," she said, keeping her voice even. "No trouble. They've got the special festive finger food ready to go, and I've had Bernadette print up some menus for the bar. We'll roll them out tomorrow afternoon."

"What about the prizes for the raffle?"

"All wrapped and numbered."

"Did you remember to appoint someone to handle the raffle table?"

"Bernadette's going to do it."

As she spoke, Dougal's brow became increasingly furrowed. Any minute now, his eyes would disappear under his bushy white eyebrows, never to be seen again.

"The Christmas trees in the pub and the hotel lobby need more sparkly lights," he said.

"Okay." If she dug her nails any deeper into her palms, they'd poke out around her knuckles.

"Shouldn't you be taking notes?"

Honestly, would he even notice if she screamed? "I think I can remember sparkly lights."

"Aye, well, we'll see." Dougal tugged down his damn waistcoat, which was a pink tartan today. Where did he get these things? Did he have a bunch of elves secreted in the basement making them for him?

"We've got a staff meeting tomorrow morning, after breakfast. We'll hand out the Christmas hats and jumpers then so the staff can wear them for the rest of the day," he said.

Agnes froze. *Jumpers?*

"Agnes, did you hear me?" He looked like a shark who'd scented blood in the water. "You do have the items we need, don't you?"

Clearing her throat, she pointed to the box in the corner of her office that contained the Christmas hats. "Of course," she said. "It's all under control."

Only it wasn't, because there were no Christmas jumpers. In fact, this was the first time Dougal had even mentioned them. Hats and headbands, yes. Tinsel and Christmas music, yes. Freaking Christmas jumpers? No!

"Okay, then." He paused long enough to make her wonder if he'd fallen asleep on his feet. "Good job," he said at last.

She bet that stuck in his throat. "Thanks."

"I'll go check the bar. We're doing a stocktake to establish exactly how much liquor has gone missing over the past year."

"Once you have more information, hopefully we can narrow down who's been stealing. On the subject of the thefts, I just had an email from Benson Security." She didn't mention Logan, because the email had come from Lake—and she was trying not to think about Logan. That only led to crying like a baby. "The background checks are back and the staff were cleared, meaning they're no longer on the suspect list."

"As I expected." Dougal turned toward the door. "Don't forget the Christmas napkins," he said before leaving.

When Bernadette popped her head around the door a minute later, Agnes hadn't moved.

"I'm about to finish for the day," the receptionist said. "Do you need anything?"

"You don't happen to have twenty-three Christmas jumpers I could borrow, do you? Dougal needs them for the morning."

"Eh, no. I don't even have one."

"Never mind, I'll think of something." It was late on Thursday afternoon. She'd spent the day dealing with one stupid crisis after another, on barely any sleep. And now, an hour before the shops close, her boss tells her he wants Christmas jumpers for everyone to wear the following morning. It actually seemed kind of funny that her career would end because she couldn't get Christmas jumpers in time.

"Well, if that's all?" Bernadette said, backing up. "I'll leave you to it."

And then she closed the door behind her.

There was nothing Agnes could do but put her head back on the desk and groan.

Where was she going to find Christmas jumpers now?

CHAPTER 17

When Logan opened his door at eight o'clock on Thursday evening, he wasn't expecting to find Agnes standing there.

"I know things are over between us," she said, "but I need…help."

That last word seemed to stick in her throat some. Logan folded his arms and leaned against the doorjamb. This, he had to hear, but, first, there was another little matter that needed clearing up. "Things aren't over between us. I was trying to give you some space. You seemed to need it."

If glares could kill, he'd have been dead on his doorstep. "I kicked you out. That implies things are over."

"You freaked out because the sex was"—he formed air quotes around his next words—"too good."

"I didn't freak out. I told you clearly that this thing between us has no future and, therefore, can't continue."

"Say what you like, but we both know there was definite freaking out involved." Logan folded his arms again.

She'd added teeth gritting to her glaring now. "Let's leave that for now and deal with the reason I'm here."

"That reason being that you need…?" He arched an eyebrow.

"Help." Agnes forced the word through clenched teeth.

"Was that so hard to say? I've seen criminals have less trouble confessing their guilt."

"Will you help me or not?"

Logan threw the door wide. "Aye, seeing as you asked so nicely, I'll help. Come on in."

"Wait." She pointed behind her. "I need to get stuff out of the car."

"Since when do you have a car?"

"Since I had to hire one to get to and from Fort William this evening." She turned and stomped back to the car. Which, by the looks of it, was one of the Davidson brothers' old bangers that they rented out for extra cash. He was surprised the wreck had made it to Fort William and back.

Curious, he followed her to the boot, which she opened by thumping it with her fists.

"Don't say anything," Agnes threatened.

"I wouldn't dare." But nothing could stop him grinning.

Once it creaked open, she took out a couple of huge carrier bags and thrust them at him, then delved inside for more. In the end, they both carried several bags each into his house. Logan led her past the living room and into the kitchen, where Drew sat at the table doing homework with his headphones on.

It wasn't until they'd dumped the bags beside him that he looked up. He did a double take when he spotted Agnes, then shot out of his chair, pulling his headphones off as he stood.

"This is Agnes," Logan said. "She *isn't* my girlfriend. This is Drew. He *is* my son."

"Hi, Drew," Agnes said before turning to Logan. "Was that description really necessary?"

"I know how much you like things to be clear between us." He took the kettle to the sink and filled it.

"Uh, should I leave you two alone?" Drew asked, his eyes darting between them.

"No," Logan and Agnes said at the same time.

While Agnes took off her coat and hung it on the back of one of the dining chairs, Drew inched toward the bags.

"What's all this?"

"This is a problem I have," Agnes said on a sigh. "Dougal came into my office late this afternoon and told me that every staff member has to have a Christmas jumper to wear this weekend." She snorted. "First I'd heard of it. Anyway, I hadn't bought any, so I rushed through to Fort William to see what they had—after renting the car from hell to do it—and they'd sold out. All I managed to get was these." She tipped the contents of one of her bags onto the table and held up several plain sweatshirts in assorted colors.

"They don't look very Christmassy," Drew said helpfully.

"Thanks, that's exactly the kind of thing my nephew would have said." Agnes made the sign of the cross—incorrectly. "May he rest in peace."

"Oh." Drew looked panicked.

"Ignore her. She's being sarcastic. Her nephew, Jack, is very much alive." Logan placed a mug of black coffee in front of the monster, making sure it had two sugars, just the way she liked it. He rummaged in the pantry and came out with a packet of chocolate biscuits that he also put beside her. "Eat. Drink. Have you had dinner?"

"I grabbed a burger." She reached for the coffee, took a sip, then closed her eyes with a sigh.

Damn, she was gorgeous. Logan tore his eyes from her to find his son staring at him. Great, so much for keeping things on the down-low.

"What's going on?" Darcy said as she came into the

kitchen, her ever-present book tucked under her arm. "Agnes!" To Agnes' obvious shock, Darcy threw her arms around her and hugged her tight. "Don't worry. I know you won't be my stepmum, but I still like you." She released Agnes just as fast as she'd grabbed her and looked down at the table. "Why do you have so many sweatshirts?"

Agnes still seemed to be suffering shock from the hug attack, but she shook it off to answer. "I was telling Drew and your dad that I need to make these look Christmassy by tomorrow morning. I got stuff that might help." She grabbed another bag and tipped it onto the table. Glue, tinsel, stickers, and lights fell out. "I was hoping you guys could help me stick this stuff to the sweatshirts and make them look good."

It was Darcy who spoke, and she did it gently, putting a hand on Agnes' arm to comfort her while she broke the bad news. "Agnes, most of that stuff isn't going to stick to a sweatshirt. The glue's the wrong kind to make it stick. And the lights need a socket."

Desperation flashed in Agnes' eyes. "I have needles and thread too. And some stickers. Oh, and fabric pens. Something has to work, right?" She lifted a gray sweatshirt. "I don't have an artistic bone in my body, and I've got twenty-three of these to decorate before the morning."

Logan shared a look of understanding with his kids. "Drew, set up the folding table in the living room. Darcy, run and get your gran. Agnes, get everything out of the bags and sort it so we can see what we've got."

She blinked at him. "So, you'll help?"

"Aye, of course we'll help."

"Craft project," Darcy shouted and then clapped her hands.

Agnes looked at them in utter awe before doing as she was told, laying everything out in an orderly manner over the table and eating her way through the chocolate biscuits while she did so. A few minutes later, Darcy and Logan's mother let themselves into the house and joined them in the kitchen.

"What's this about Dougal needing last-minute Christmas jumpers?" his mum asked, with a look on her face that told him she was ready to give someone a piece of her mind.

"He says he needs them for tomorrow morning and that everyone at work has to wear one. I honestly don't remember him mentioning this before, but that's not the point, so I went to Fort William and got the only sweatshirts left in town," Agnes said. "And everything I could think of to decorate them."

His mother, who was wearing red leggings and a knee-length purple jumper with white pompoms all over it, surveyed Agnes' haul. "This won't do at all. You haven't done much crafting, have you, Agnes?"

"I made a teapot in ceramics class when I was thirteen," Agnes said. "It ended up as an ashtray."

His mum pursed her lips in disgust. "Before you leave this town, the women and I are going to make sure you have some skills under your belt for your future. That way, you won't get into a mess like this again."

Agnes opened her mouth, most likely to complain, but his mum held up a hand as she took out her phone.

"Margaret?" she said once she'd tapped the screen. "We have a couple of dozen blank sweatshirts that need to scream Christmas by tomorrow morning. Dougal has put our girl on the spot, and we can't let her lose a round to that old fart. Raid your shop and bring what we need. All Agnes has is tinsel and glue sticks." She paused. "Aye, clueless. We can't let this go on—we need to take her in hand." Another pause. "I'll call the others, but bring everything you can think of. Dougal's going to get the best damn Christmas jumpers on the planet. And he can take them and shove them right up—"

"Okay!" Logan took the phone from her hand and ended the call.

"I don't understand why you're so upset about this," Agnes said. "I don't think Dougal did it intentionally. There's also the possibility he told me about the jumpers and I forgot."

Logan chuckled, attracting an irritated glance from his mother. But he couldn't help it—that was funny. He'd seen how Agnes worked, and she forgot nothing.

His mum's eyes narrowed. "Did you forget, or did he spring them on you last minute to see what you'd do? From what I hear, he regrets hiring a manager, even for the year. It's driving him nuts to give over control of his baby." She hesitated before adding, "I mean the hotel, not the dog."

"Then why doesn't he fire me? It would be a whole lot less hassle for both of us." Logan thought he saw relief flash in Agnes' eyes.

"And upset Lake Benson and Callum McKay? I don't think so. No, he's playing dirty. And he should know better." His mother's eyes blazed as she looked at Agnes. "We were talking about you in the pub the other night, the Knit or Die women and me, and we were saying how we planned on making you a member whether you wanted to become one or not. A girl like you needs a posse at her back while she stirs things up around here."

Darcy giggled, while Agnes gaped at his mother. "Whether I want it or not?"

Her question had no impact on his mother, who was on a roll. "That old fart must have heard us, but he still had the audacity to pull a stunt like this. Well, he's no' picking on one of ours. This is war." She shoved up her sleeves in a clear sign she was ready to fight, only her jumper wouldn't cooperate, and the sleeves fell again. She shoved them back up. They fell. Now, she was irritated, but it seemed she wouldn't let the jumper win any more than she'd let Dougal win.

Logan caught Drew's eye, and they grinned at each other. The women of Knit or Die had been looking for a reason to start up their war with Dougal again, and Agnes had handed it to them on a plate.

"I don't understand," Agnes said again.

"What's to understand?" his mother asked, still fighting with her sleeves. "You're one of ours." At last, she got the sleeves to stay up, and she grinned triumphantly before patting Agnes on the shoulder. "Don't worry. We've got your back. Now, give me that phone, Logan, so I can call the others."

"But, I'm not a member of Knit or Die," Agnes protested.

"You don't choose knitting," his mum said solemnly. "It chooses you."

Really, there was nothing anyone could say to that.

* * *

THERE WERE two sewing machines set up on Logan's kitchen table, one operated by Heather, the other by Jean. They were attaching applique shapes, cut from fabric Margaret had brought from her craft shop, to the front of sweatshirts. Around the long folding table Drew had put up in the center of the living room, Shona, Margaret, and Darcy sat finishing off the sweatshirts the women in the kitchen had already done. They added detailed embellishments with an assortment of crafty things that Agnes had a hard time identifying. The only thing they'd used that she'd bought was the tinsel.

Logan and Drew were in charge of the fabric markers. It was their job to add witty slogans to the sweatshirts once everything else had been done. After reading some of their efforts, Agnes wasn't sure they were the right people for the job. Meanwhile, after much discussion about Agnes' craft skills, she'd been tasked with making tea.

She'd never felt more useless in her life.

"Do you need help with the tea?" Logan asked as he came into the kitchen.

"Aye, because it's sooooooo hard." She rolled her eyes at him.

She liked his house—it wasn't cluttered, but it wasn't minimalist either. It was just...homey. The walls were a warm cream, the floor a polished wood, the kitchen appliances were white and, in general, the furniture looked sturdy. The living room sofa—an oversized, overstuffed monstrosity—made her want to curl up in the corner of it and sleep in front of the fire. The house was a lot like the man, she decided—uncomplicated, warm and inviting, with some interesting quirks. It was a house that beckoned you in and invited you to stay for a while.

Bloody Logan. Even his house was seducing her.

"How did I become a member of a knitting club when I can't knit and I never applied for membership?" Agnes glanced at the two women at the table, but they couldn't hear her over the hum of the sewing machines.

"Apparently, knitting chose you." Logan's grin was wide.

"How does that work, exactly? Do they don robes and sneak down to their basement to light candles and chant to a big ball of wool?"

"With this lot, I wouldn't be surprised."

"Is there some sort of initiation for new members?" Not that she considered herself a new member. She just wanted to be prepared for whatever was coming her way.

"Aye, you strip naked, wrap yourself in wool and run down the high street shouting, 'You can take our lives, but you will never take our knitting.'"

As usual, Logan was having far too much fun at her expense. "How do you get out of the group?"

"You don't. Once you're in, you're in for life. It's like the Mafia."

"You really are no help at all." She smacked his chest. He caught her hand and held it against him, making her want to sink deep inside the man and never leave.

"I'm glad you came to me for help with this," he said, his voice a low, rumbling sound she could feel right through her body.

"It wasn't like I had much choice." The only people she knew in Invertary were ones she worked with—and Logan. Who she also technically worked with…

"You had a choice," he said softly. "You could have confronted Dougal and told him he'd never asked for jumpers. Or you could have called your sister in Glasgow and had her drive up with some. The shops there are open all the time, and she would have done it in a second."

Agnes didn't have an answer for him. He was right, and she didn't want to look too closely at why she'd chosen Logan.

"Oh, for goodness' sake," Heather said, making Agnes realize the sewing machines had fallen silent. For how long, she didn't know. "Will you two stop making googly eyes at one another long enough to get me a cup of tea? I'm parched over here."

Agnes snatched her hand from Logan's clasp. "There's nothing going on here."

"Aye," Jean said with a mischievous smile. "And I'm sure there was nothing going on at the hotel the other night either when they caught Logan streaking in the halls."

Logan folded his arms. "I wasn't streaking. I was…"

Yeah, there was no logical explanation for being caught

naked in a hallway. At that moment, Agnes felt a little sorry she'd shoved him out the door—but only a little.

"Flashing your backside to the world," Heather said. "We know. It was all over Facebook before they banned it for being too…what's the word?"

"Sexy?" Jean said.

"Salacious," Heather said with a nod.

Agnes covered her mouth with her hands as she looked up at Logan.

"You seriously owe me," he told her. "If the guys at work see it, they're never going to let me live it down."

"Oh, they'll have seen them," Heather said. "It was my Megan who sent the photos to me, and she's in Bahrain, I think, being a bodyguard to some princess or other. I still don't like the thought of Megan with a gun, but she's happy. And she says to tell you that you've aged well."

"Aged well, my backside. I'm only thirty-eight."

"Yes." Heather nodded. "It's your backside that's aged well."

As the women giggled, Logan cast Agnes an exasperated glance.

"I'm sorry?" she said, but it didn't sound convincing, even to her ears. "To be fair, it is a very nice backside. A really cute little bubble butt." She held up her hands to show him what she meant.

"Oh, I am totally getting you back for that crack," he promised.

"Crack!" Jean said, then howled with laughter.

"It's like dealing with teenagers." Logan shook his head before pushing away from the counter. "I was going to help you with the tea, but you're on your own now for that bubble butt crack."

"Men," Jean said. "They're so sensitive."

And then all the women burst out laughing.

CHAPTER 18

"Should we wake them?" a voice whispered, stirring Agnes from a deep sleep.

"Naw, let them sleep," a slightly deeper male voice whispered back. "We should definitely take some photos though —they might come in handy later."

"Good idea."

Agnes wasn't sure where she was, or how she'd gotten there, but it felt great. She was warm, and secure, and... happy. Well, apart from the whispering voices that irritated the edge of her consciousness.

"They look so cute together," the female voice said. "Is it normal to sleep like that when you aren't boyfriend and girlfriend?"

"How would I know?" The male's voice turned gruff.

"I'm only asking. And I figured you'd know because you totally want Zoe to be your girlfriend. Oh, Zoe, my Zoe, I love you, Zoe." She heard kissing noises.

"Stop it." The other voice grew louder. "Seriously, quit it, or you'll regret it."

Agnes knew that voice. She struggled out of the depths of

sleep, trying to remember. Oh, yeah, it was Drew, Logan's son. She started to smile and froze. Her eyes shot open, and she was confronted by the sight of Drew putting his sister into a choke hold.

"What the hell?" Her voice sounded like rough sandpaper on wood.

A deep groan came from behind her. "Go back to sleep." And an arm tightened around her waist.

Logan. She'd been asleep with Logan. In the same room as his kids? This didn't make sense. Where was the caffeine? She needed it—badly.

"Oh, good, you're awake," Darcy said as Drew released her. "We have to go to school, but we wanted to say goodbye first."

Agnes barely heard her. She was too busy looking around the room. She was in Logan's living room, on the sofa—spooning with Logan. With a groan, she shoved his arm away and tried to climb off the sofa. But the damn thing wouldn't let her go. Her legs kicked uselessly in the air as she fought for the momentum to get up.

"What are you doing?" Logan grumbled.

"I don't know," Drew said. "But it's entertaining."

"She's stuck. I saw a tortoise do that once when it was upside down on its shell. Its wee legs were too tiny to get to back up the right way," Darcy said helpfully as she took pity on Agnes and offered a hand to get her up.

Agnes grasped it like a lifeline. Standing beside the kids, she checked what she was wearing—still the suit she'd arrived in last night. Thank goodness!

"This is not what it looks like," she said to them as she finger-combed her hair.

"It looked like you and Dad were cuddling," Darcy said, her innocent, wide-eyed look not fooling anyone.

"What's going on?" Logan propped himself up on an

elbow. Thankfully, he was wearing a T-shirt under the blanket that had covered them.

"We're going to school," Drew said.

"And you're cuddling on the sofa with Agnes," Darcy added with a delighted smile. "Why are you on the sofa?"

Now that was an excellent question. Agnes watched as Logan ran a hand through his hair. "Because Heather and Jean crashed in my bed, saying it was too late to go home. Margaret went next door with Gran. And the only place left to sleep was here."

"With Agnes," Darcy pointed out cheerfully.

"It's all perfectly innocent." Agnes tried for her 'don't mess with me' tone but couldn't quite pull it off. "Obviously, we had to share."

"Or," Drew said with a grin, "he could have slept on the pullout bed in my room."

"There's a pullout?" Agnes screeched at Logan, who shrugged and smiled.

"Does this mean you're his girlfriend now?" Darcy asked.

"No. No, it just means we slept together." Oh, that sounded bad. And judging by the grins on Logan's and Drew's faces, it would come back to haunt her. "Okay, you two need to get to school." She shooed them out of the room. "Do you have everything you need? Lunchboxes? Water bottles? Homework?"

"We're all sorted," Drew said as he headed for the door.

"You know," Darcy told her. "Those are stepmum questions. Are you sure you don't want to reconsider your position on this matter?"

Agnes gaped at her as the men in the family laughed. "Get out and get to school."

"Okay, but I want you to know that this whole thing is giving me very mixed messages about relationships," Darcy said as she followed her brother. "And I'm at such an impressionable age."

With that, they disappeared through the door.

Agnes let out a groan, picked up a cushion, and pummeled Logan with it. "There. Was. A. Rollout?" she said between blows.

He snatched the cushion from her and stuffed it under his head. "This was a better option."

"For who? Now your kids have the wrong idea."

"No, Agnes, love, they have the right idea."

"But I'm leaving Invertary!" Didn't he understand that this was all going to blow up in their faces? "They'll get hurt."

"And I'll help them cope with it."

"You are being incredibly stubborn and very annoying. Why won't you believe me when I say this thing between us has a definite 'best before date'?"

"Oh, I do believe you. And I won't do anything to stop you when you go. That's your choice, and you have the right to make it. But, you can't stop me from showing you just how good this could be while you're still here."

"You are driving me mad!" She lobbed another cushion at him before stomping from the room, only to find his mother in the kitchen frying bacon. "Don't you live next door? Shouldn't you be there making breakfast?"

"I would be, but you're here and I'm nosy." Shona smiled at her before reaching for the coffee pot, filling a mug and handing it to her. "Milk and sugar are on the table."

Agnes took the mug and plopped down in a chair. "Your son is driving me nuts."

"He gets that from his father," Shona said as she dished up food.

She put two plates on the table and took a seat facing Agnes. "Dig in and, while you're at it, maybe you can explain why my son's bum is all over the internet."

Agnes groaned. Shona was wrong—Logan definitely got his tendency to annoy her from his mother. "It was an accident," she said weakly.

Shona arched an eyebrow. "You *accidentally* slept with him and then kicked him out of your room so strangers could ogle him?"

"This whole family is evil," Agnes muttered as she cut up her bacon.

"No, dear." Shona reached over to pat her hand. "We just don't let crap slide. Don't worry—you fit right in."

A strangled little scream escaped Agnes. "Like I keep telling your son, I'm not staying in Invertary. As soon as the year with Dougal is up, I'm heading to warmer climes." *If* she lasted a year.

"Is that it? That's your reason for giving up on Logan? You want more sun?"

"I'm not giving up on him. There's nothing to give up on." Okay, so that was a lie and, judging by the look on Shona's face, she knew it. Damn McBride family, they were all annoying as hell. "I don't just want to leave Invertary for the sun. I want a career. I want stability. *And* I want more sun."

"You know, it's easier to achieve stability when you're part of a pair. I've been married forty-two years and I'm very stable."

"Yeah, I can tell."

Shona narrowed her eyes. "I gave you that bacon, and I can take it away again."

"Mine." Agnes pulled the plate closer. "Look, you don't know me, so I have no idea why you're so damn keen on getting me together with your son. But stability has nothing to do with being in a relationship. I just don't want to rely on anyone else. I did that when I was a kid, and I'm never doing it again. People let you down, they hurt you, and they leave you to care for yourself." As soon as the words were out of her mouth, Agnes wished she could take them back.

Shona's face softened. "Logan said your parents weren't there for you when you were a bairn."

"Logan's been snooping," Agnes said stiffly.

"He's an investigator. It's what he does. Always was far too curious for his own good, poking his nose in where it didn't belong." She squeezed Agnes' hand again. "And as for why I think you and Logan should try being together, well, it's because I've not seen him this interested in a woman since his divorce."

"Shona—" she started to protest that the woman's reasoning wasn't up to much, but Shona cut her off.

"You know, I had a bad childhood too." She reached for her tea. "I won't go into the details, but there was abuse. Took me a long time to trust anyone after that, but it's possible. Don't let your parents stop you from living a full life. Everybody needs someone to lean on, a partner to get through life with. Whether that's a friend or a lover, doesn't matter. We all need someone. Don't let them take that away from you."

"I don't want to talk about my parents. They have nothing to do with my life, and that's how I like it."

"I understand. But I'd hate to think you'd never trust anyone. You're a good girl. You're strong and capable, and more than a match for any man. Even if you were in a relationship, you'd never let someone neglect you or hurt you. You wouldn't put up with that from anyone. You aren't a helpless child anymore. You can do this. I believe in you. And even if the person you settle with isn't Logan, I still hope you eventually trust someone enough to let them in."

Agnes found herself turning her hand to hold on to Shona's. "Why? You hardly know me."

Shona's eyes twinkled, just like her son's did. "The big ball of wool in Margaret's basement told me."

Laughter eased the pressure in her chest some.

"What's funny?" Logan said as he came into the room, scratching his head.

Agnes slid her hand out from under Shona's and picked up her cutlery.

"Nothing," Shona said, angling her cheek for a kiss, which Logan promptly gave.

A pang of longing shot through Agnes at the sight. She wanted her morning kiss too. And she didn't want a nice staid peck on the cheek like he'd given his mother. Warm, dancing eyes met hers, and she couldn't help the heat that filled her cheeks. Damn man knew what she was thinking.

"You want to have a shower before we head to the hotel?" Logan said as he poured himself a coffee.

He was dressed in a long-sleeved T-shirt and jeans. Both looked rumpled because he'd slept in them. Beside her. A shiver ran up her spine, and she focused on her food again.

"I'll grab one there," she said. "I didn't bring a change of clothes with me."

"I can lend you some if you like," Shona offered.

Agnes smiled at the bright orange jumper Shona wore over lime-colored leggings. "I'd better wear one of my suits, just in case Dougal wants to nitpick."

"Okay," Logan said. "I'll jump in the shower, and then we'll head out."

"I have a car, so I don't need a lift," Agnes pointed out.

"You don't have a car," Logan said. "You have an accident on wheels. We're taking mine. The roads are icy and the last thing I want is to hear you wrapped that heap around a lamppost." He looked back at his mother as he sauntered from the room. "Tackle her and confiscate her keys if she tries to leave." And then he was gone.

When Agnes looked at Shona, the older woman smiled smugly. "What were you saying about people who leave you to care for yourself?"

"You're exactly like your son," Agnes complained.

"Thank you." Shona beamed.

CHAPTER 19

"Thanks for sorting out the sweatshirts for me," Agnes said once she was in the car with Logan. He was right—his vehicle was so much better than the heap she'd hired.

He shrugged. "That's what friends are for, and anyway, we had fun helping."

A strange thought occurred to her and came out of her mouth before she could censor it. "I've never really had any friends."

He shot her a sidelong glance. "Never?"

It was too late to take it back, so she shook her head at the same time as she wedged her hands between her knees to keep from touching him. "I had my sisters. We did everything together." More out of necessity than anything else. "There wasn't time to make other friends."

"Once you're settled in one place, you can make the time."

For some reason, the reminder she planned to leave sat heavily on her chest, making it hard to breathe. She searched for something to talk about, anything that would take her mind off the feeling crushing her chest.

"It's going to snow." She pointed to the heavy gray clouds hanging low over the town.

"If it does, you have to build a snowman with me," Logan said. "And have a snowball fight. Is it a deal?"

"I don't like being cold."

As they turned into the hotel carpark, his dark gaze caught hers. "I could warm you up afterward," the wicked man said.

Oh, she was sure he could. Just being in the car with him made her feel pretty warm. His proximity was driving her nuts, making her want to touch and taste when she'd resolved to keep her distance. Of course, spending the night curled up in his arms hadn't helped her plan any.

"It's playing in the snow, Agnes," he said when she didn't answer. "You'll enjoy it, I promise. And if you don't, I'll make you some hot chocolate to apologize for dragging you out into the cold."

Damn, he was irresistible. "Okay," she found herself agreeing.

As soon as they parked, Agnes opened the door to jump out, but Logan put a hand on her arm to stop her. "We *are* friends. You just don't realize it because you've never had any, but I can teach you how to have friends." He reached out and stroked her hair. "No matter what happens with us, learning how to be friends with someone will stand you in good stead for the future. Let me give you that."

The future she'd have without him. Her stomach twisted.

"Friends don't have sex." The words erupted right out of her, something they seemed inclined to do these days.

"Some do."

"Maybe we shouldn't." But her body screamed in protest at her words.

His fingers stilled on her hair. "Because it was too good?"

She nodded, her cheek brushing against his fingertips, the effect of his touch rippling through her whole body.

His gaze captured hers. "Some would say that we should do it again *because* it was so good."

Her resolve wavered as her hands inched toward him.

"Why shouldn't we have sex again, Agnes, love?" His voice, a low, sweet seduction, made her mouth water to taste him.

He was so close she could smell his unique scent, and she drew it into her lungs, holding it tight against her. Slowly, Logan reached past her and pulled her door shut. The heat of his body warmed her skin, making her long to curl into him and absorb it right into the heart of her so she'd never feel cold again. She was light-headed, every nerve in her body alert and aware of the man beside her.

"Tell me, Agnes, why can't we sleep together?" His hand clasped the side of her throat, his thumb stroking in a way that mesmerized her.

"You are so beautiful," she whispered. And it was true.

His lips quirked. "So are you."

"Your lips are amazing." Her gaze rested on them, remembering the feel of them against hers, against her body, and she shivered.

"They're better when they're on yours," he whispered, a hair's breadth away from her.

All she could do was whimper as her hands came up to curl into his jumper. "Maybe, we could kiss. I think kissing would be okay."

"Aye, kissing sounds good," he said, and then his lips were on hers.

The world around them swirled and disappeared as Logan deepened the kiss. It was a million times better than she remembered. Her body melted against him, and his arm wrapped around her, lending her his strength, keeping her upright.

"Tell me why we can't have sex," he whispered against her mouth, teasing her lips with his tongue between words.

She had no defenses against him. "Because I'm scared I'll fall in love with you."

The arm around her tightened as the slow, deliberate kisses worked their seduction on her senses.

"Would that be so bad?" he breathed against her mouth.

At that moment, she couldn't think of anything better, but she gave him the truth. "I'd have to give up everything to be with you."

"And you're worried I won't be worth it." There was no ego in his voice, only understanding.

How could it be that *this* man would be the one who understood her so well? It was the universe's joke against her. If only she could take him with her when she left. But that wasn't realistic. His life was in Invertary, with his kids.

"Don't overthink it," he said as he continued his sweet seduction. "The future will take care of itself. Live in the now, Agnes, love. With me."

"Yes," she whispered as she wrapped her arms around his neck and pulled him closer. He tasted of promises whispered in the dark, just out of reach. So close, she could almost touch them.

At last, breathless and with the windows fogged, they reluctantly broke apart. Logan pressed kisses to her forehead. "So, we're agreed," he said. "We're definitely having sex again."

"Oh, yeah," she said on a sigh.

With one last, gentle kiss, he moved away from her. "Better get out of the car—your meeting is in five minutes. I'll help you take the sweatshirts inside."

She blinked at him several times before her brain cleared

enough for his words to register. And then she scowled. "Five minutes? I had things to do before the meeting. Stop. Being. Irresistible. It's screwing with my brain." And her life.

He chuckled, and Agnes grunted with annoyance as she climbed out of the car.

Bloody man was driving her insane.

* * *

"I'M SORRY ABOUT YESTERDAY," Agnes said to Dougal as she rushed into the restaurant section of the pub. It was closed for a couple of hours while the chef prepared for evening service, leaving it available for a staff meeting. "About rushing off early like that."

Dougal waved a dismissive hand. "No need for apologies. Bernadette explained everything."

Agnes' eyes shot to her receptionist. "She did?"

Bernadette's expression was carefully blank. "Everyone gets headaches, and migraines are the worst."

"Yes. Yes, they are." As Dougal said something to Logan, Agnes mouthed, "*Thank you*," to Bernadette, who blushed and smiled shyly back.

It was the first time she'd had a friendly interaction with the young woman, making Agnes realize she hadn't had many friendly interactions with any of her staff. Logan was right, she honestly didn't know how to make friends.

She cleared her throat as she looked around at everyone. "I just wanted to say to all of you that you're doing a great job, and I appreciate how much extra work you've put into this market weekend. I'm sure Dougal appreciates it too."

"Very much," Dougal boomed, giving her a strange look as the rest of the staff smiled at her.

Agnes pulled out a chair at the huge table they'd made by

shoving lots of smaller tables together. She looked around in surprise when Logan sat beside her.

"What are you doing?" she whispered.

"Dougal asked me to stay. He wants us to update everyone on the thefts."

Great, something else she'd completely forgotten. One night away from the hotel and things were already slipping.

"You forgot, didn't you?" he whispered.

"This is all your fault."

"Aye, because I'm too sexy and irresistible, and it makes it hard for you to concentrate on anything else." He grinned smugly.

"I'll deal with you later," she threatened.

"Promises, promises," he teased, making her cheeks heat.

She glanced back around the table to see several staff members watching their interaction with smiles on their faces.

"I see you brought the jumpers," Dougal said. "Everybody grab one on your way out. We want to look the part this weekend and give everyone an amazing experience. It's in all of our best interests to go the extra mile because, if this year's market goes well, the council plans to extend it to two weekends again next year."

There were nods of enthusiasm from around the table.

"Attendance fell off for a few years," Logan whispered, his breath hot on her ear. "It ended up costing more to put on than it brought in, so they shortened its run time."

Agnes could well understand why people had stopped coming to the event. As far as she could see, the problem wasn't so much the market, but the fact it was a Christmas market, and those were a dime a dozen. Invertary needed something to make it stand out. Once upon a time, that had been the lingerie fashion show, but now, even that was old hat. The town needed a new approach to attracting people. The one they had just wasn't working.

As Dougal ran through the list in front of him and Agnes added input as needed, she was very aware of Logan lounging beside her, his thigh brushing against hers. She found it hard to concentrate when all she wanted to do was run her hand down his leg, feel the strength of his thigh beneath her palm.

"And Agnes and Logan have an update on that," Dougal said, turning to them expectantly.

Bloody Logan had derailed her again. She narrowed her eyes at him. "Why don't you start?"

"Happy to," he said with a knowing smile. "So far, the thefts have been a series of misunderstandings." Logan had morphed into business mode, and she found it sexy as hell. "Guests accessing the kitchen after hours, friends buying sundries but forgetting to have it noted in the books, that sort of thing. However, we still have concerns regarding the missing jewelry and the bar stock."

He cocked an eyebrow at Agnes, who took up where he'd left off. "As far as we can tell, there's no rhyme or reason to the jewelry thefts. It seems the thief is simply taking whatever attracts his or her attention. We've had reports of missing diamond rings as well as cheap plastic hair combs. All I can say is that we need to keep an eye open for any suspicious behavior in and around the guestrooms."

"Do you think one of us is doing the stealing?" one of the maids asked.

Agnes shook her head. "I'd be really shocked if any of you risked your job over a plastic hair comb. Plus, Benson Security ran background searches on all of us. And I'm pleased to say that we all came up squeaky clean. Except for you, Dougal," she joked. "You're as shady as hell."

Everyone, including Dougal, looked surprised by her

teasing, and then they started to laugh. Had she really been that uptight around everyone? Had her fear of losing her job taken away her personality? Probably. But equally, it could be the fact she mainly lived on sugar and caffeine. She was as jittery as a hamster most days, and she couldn't remember the last time she'd had a full night's sleep.

"And then there's the bar," Dougal said, his voice reverberating around the room, bouncing off the dark wooden furnishings. "We did a stocktake, and it seems we've lost a couple of bottles of whisky every month for the past few of years."

Shock rippled around the table.

"Is it the same whisky every time?" Logan asked.

"Aye, Glenfiddich."

"I'll need a list of everyone, outside of the current staff, with access to the bar," Logan said.

"You'll get it." Dougal was mad, which made Agnes wonder if that was how Santa looked when he read the naughty list. "This petty pilfering has gone on long enough. I want it stopped."

"Okay," Agnes said. "On that note, this meeting is over. Don't forget your jumpers, hats and headbands. Remember, everyone wears them starting from now right through until Monday morning. No exceptions."

"No exceptions." Logan's eyes sparkled with mischief. "Makes me wonder which one of our fantastic slogans you chose to wear."

"There's more to those sweatshirts than the stuff you and Drew wrote all over them."

"Aye, but you have to admit, the jokes are the best bit. Which one did you pick?"

"You'll need to come by later if you want to know."

"I can't tonight. I'm taking Darcy to a dance recital in Fort William. Will you wear it for me tomorrow night?"

"Weren't you listening? We're living in these things until Monday."

"I don't mean in the pub—I meant for *me*."

"Oh." Now that sent tingles up her spine. "What's in it for me?"

"Well, if you wear the sweatshirt and nothing else, there could be a lot in it for you."

She would have said something about him being awfully sure of himself, but he'd already proven he could put his money where his mouth was. "Throw in some chocolate, and it's a deal."

His eyes darkened. "You've got it. See you tomorrow, Agnes, love." And then he turned and sauntered off.

"Agnes," Dougal called. "Can I have a word?"

She tore her gaze from Logan's backside and went over to the bar where Dougal was holding court. "What can I do for you?"

"We had a council meeting the other night, where Betty held us hostage with a list of demands she says we need to meet before she'll consider selling any of her properties to us. The upshot of it is that I need to go to Spain for a couple of days and talk the old reverend into coming back here for a visit."

Agnes blinked at him. This was obviously another example of the ways in which they did things differently here in Invertary. "Can't you just call him?"

"I tried, but he told me he'd come back to Invertary in a casket, and not before."

So that was a firm no. "Why do you need him here?"

"Betty says she won't consider any offers on her properties unless Reverend Morrison stands in front of everyone and admits to having an affair with her."

"I can see why he'd rather die first."

"Aye," Dougal said in disgust. "Anyway, the only flight

available at short notice was this Monday, so I'll need you to look after everything while I'm gone."

"Dougal, that's why you hired me—to look after things when you aren't here. I can take care of the hotel and restaurant, and your bar manager can take care of the pub. You could disappear for weeks, and we'd be fine."

"Disappear? Leave the pub?" His voice was so loud it made the glasses shake.

Yeah, she shouldn't have brought that topic up. "I will definitely take care of things while you're gone. Don't worry about it."

But there was no distracting him. "What would I do if I wasn't here?"

"Play golf? Fish? Take up knitting? Whatever other people do when they retire."

"Retire?" The whole building shook this time, and Dougal looked like he might be having a heart attack. His face had turned a deep shade of red, and the vein in his neck throbbed. If she didn't put a stop to this soon, Agnes could see herself doing mouth-to-mouth on Santa.

"I'm joking." She forced a grin. "I don't believe in retirement. You enjoy being here, so why would you want to change that? And the community would miss you if you were gone."

"Aye, aye, you're right." The color faded from his face, but he still seemed uncertain. "I can see you're trying to be less intimidating and a bit more informal, but you might want to check your jokes are actually funny before you try them on people."

"Thanks." Agnes nodded solemnly. "I'll take that advice on board. Was that all?"

"There's one more thing—I need you to look after Arnold while I'm gone."

Oh, hell no. "I'm not really a dog person," she told her

boss. "I've never had one, and I don't know how to look after them."

"Don't be daft." He waved his hand dismissively. "You'll be fine, and you can always ask Mrs. Edwards for help if you get stuck."

There was obviously no getting out of it. "Fine," she said with all the graciousness of a teenager.

Dougal gave her a royal nod as though she'd done nothing more than her duty. "Thanks, Agnes. Now, if only getting the Reverend Morrison here was as easy as dealing with you."

And Agnes tried very hard not to imagine her boss's head exploding all over his precious pub.

CHAPTER 20

Officially, Agnes finished work around five, like most people. Unofficially, she was never off the clock. Living in the hotel until she found other accommodation didn't help—it only made her feel like she always had to be working. The fact that Dougal had his eye on her every minute of the day only added to the stress.

And that was why, instead of taking her time off on Friday night, she found herself in the bar, helping supervise the evening's entertainment. Her feet hurt, her eyes felt like they'd been rolled in sand, and Dougal didn't find her sweatshirt funny. She looked down at it. The man had no sense of humor at all.

The place was packed with people, some of whom she recognized. The women of Knit or Die were there, giving Dougal the evil eye and trying to get her to sit with them. The town's evil overlord, Betty, was there, enjoying the trouble she'd stirred up at the last council meeting. Lake and Kirsty Benson, Josh and Caroline McInnes, and Mitch and Jodie Harris all shared a booth at the back of the room. When Agnes went over to say hello, she found out Jodie owned the spa that housed the restaurant she'd enjoyed so much. And Mitch was Josh's manager but also ran a talent agency with Caroline. It seemed everyone she spoke to was somehow connected to everyone else. It was the way of small-town life.

As she circled the room, making sure everything was being taken care of, Dougal waved her over. Reluctantly, she went to see what he wanted now.

"Can you check with the sound person again and make sure this is the right volume?" It was the third time he'd asked her. Dougal didn't like it when something was louder than him, and he was too busy with the bar to check the sound for himself.

"I checked. It's fine. I don't want to bother them by asking again."

"It's awful loud."

It was on the tip of her tongue to say, so are you. Instead, she waited. Dougal's particular brand of micromanagement meant his questions and instructions tended to come in clusters.

"The kitchen's taking too long to get the platters of finger food out to the tables," he said.

"I'll have a word with them."

"Mrs. Docherty in room eight came up to the bar to tell me that there's a strange noise coming from her closet and the thermostat in her room isn't working properly."

"I'll deal with it." Because in a hotel that size, there weren't any housekeeping staff around overnight. Normally, a guest complaint would have to wait until the morning, when the reception desk was staffed, but everyone knew to speak to Dougal at the bar if they had a problem. And he knew to call on her—because she was so conveniently located in the building.

She really needed to find a place to live outside of the hotel.

"Also"—he frowned—"I have to question some of the jokes on the sweatshirts you bought." He glanced down at hers and his face turned red.

Agnes pulled it out to look at it. "What's wrong with it? It says *'Santa's little elf ho, ho, ho'.* What's offensive about that?" She gave him an innocent look. But she knew exactly what he meant. The elf part wasn't written in words. Instead, it was a small appliqué image in the middle of lots of huge text. From a distance, it read *'Santa's little ho, ho, ho'.* She found it funny.

"Never mind," Dougal said. Obviously deciding it wasn't worth getting into. "Mr. Thompson called to say he's run out of toilet paper."

"Again?" What the hell did he do with it?

"Could you drop some off to his room? I'd have one of the waitresses run up there, but they're busy." And why use a waitress when he had a hotel manager to boss around?

Actually, now that she thought about it, her job wasn't managing anything. Really, she was Dougal's hotel slave. No —she looked down at her sweatshirt—tonight she was his hotel elf. She blinked. She was bloody Dobby. And suddenly, she desperately missed her sister Donna, because she was the only one who'd get that joke.

"Anything else?" she said to Dougal, who was still standing there as if waiting for something. She didn't know what.

"No. Nothing. Except, did you make sure the Benson Security people are monitoring the cameras? Tonight seems a ripe night for theft."

"Logan rigged up a signal booster, so that someone in their office can watch them." So was she, as they were still set up in her bedroom. With the current state of the BBC, there was nothing else to watch when she suffered from insomnia.

"Okay," Dougal said. "That's all then." And she was dismissed.

As she walked away, she imagined all the ways she could torture the man with the soda gun behind the bar.

"Ah wouldnae put up wi' that crap," someone said as she passed, and Agnes turned to see Betty sitting on a stool, kicking her feet, while she ate a Scotch pie. A Scotch pie that wasn't on their menu. As usual, the cuboid-shaped woman wore a tartan tent of a dress in, what could only be described as an attractive mud color. There were black boots on her feet and a huge tatty black handbag in her lap.

Agnes had heard the rumors about that bag. People who got too close to it tended to get stun gunned. So she took a step back. "I'm sorry?" she said.

"Aye, you should be. You're letting Dougal walk all over you. It nearly put me off my pie." Betty waved the pie, sending beef mince flying. "You might as well roll over and let him scratch your belly, same as he does for that mangy dog of his."

Well, it turned out there was a limit to the crap she'd take for her job. And the limit was called Betty. Agnes glanced at the crowd in front of the stage. "Have you ever crowd surfed? Because I can make that happen for you." Although, she wasn't sure anyone would catch the woman.

"If you ever want to learn how to stand up for yerself, gimme a call."

"Do they have cell coverage in hell?"

Betty just cackled and carried on eating her pie. Agnes, meanwhile, went off to deliver toilet paper to an old man who spent far too much time in the loo.

* * *

BY THE TIME the last bell rang telling the patrons they had

one remaining chance to order from the bar before they shut up shop, Agnes was dead on her feet. All she wanted to do was crawl into bed, but as this was the hotel and bar's biggest weekend of the year, she knew she had to help clean up.

As customers drifted out, she settled up with the band and helped the waitstaff clear the tables. By just after midnight, they'd tallied the cash, cleaned and shut down the kitchen for the night, and the waitstaff were finishing up the vacuuming.

"Can you lock up?" Dougal asked, cradling his dog in his arms. "Arnold's exhausted, and I want to get him home to bed."

Agnes stared at him for a moment, waiting to see if he'd notice his hotel manager was exhausted too. He didn't. "Absolutely, Dougal. Take the dog home. We wouldn't want him overtired."

The sarcasm was lost on him. "True," he said. And with that, he was gone.

A few minutes later, the rest of the staff followed him, and Agnes was left alone. She locked the pub doors, turned out the lights, and sat in one of the booths, staring out over the black waters of the loch.

This had to end. Betty had been right—she was letting Dougal walk all over her. Partly because she knew he didn't mean to. He was still struggling with giving up any responsibility for his business, and it took time to settle into a new working relationship. And partly because this job was her only chance at having the career she wanted.

Only, she wasn't sure she wanted it anymore.

A noise attracted her attention, and she glanced over to the bar. As though her thoughts had conjured the woman, Betty walked out of the back of the pub and rounded the bar. She pulled over the small stepladder they kept for the staff to reach the liquor on the higher shelf, climbed up, and helped herself to a bottle of Glenfiddich.

Well, that solved the mystery of the missing whisky.

"Just what do you think you're doing?" Agnes snapped.

The old woman didn't even startle. She shielded her eyes and peered into the shadows. "I'm getting some whisky."

"Please tell me you aren't secretly paying for it, and Dougal's just forgotten all about it."

"No." She cackled. "I'm stealing it. Do you want some?" She grabbed two glasses and tottered over to join Agnes.

Betty seemed so blasé about the whole thing that, for once, Agnes found herself at a loss for words. In the end, she settled on, "Stealing is wrong." It lacked conviction.

"Aye, but it's fun. And that old bastard deserves it. He gets on my last nerve." She plonked the glasses on the table, unscrewed the bottle cap, and poured them each a drink.

Agnes considered it for a second before shrugging. What the hell.

She reached for the glass. "First thing in the morning, I'm telling Dougal you're the thief, which means he'll make you pay for this. You sure you want to spend the money?"

"I'm older than dirt. What the hell am I going to do with it? Save it for my retirement? Drink up, pansy arse, and tell me why you're still in this crappy job."

Tossing back the whisky, Agnes savored the burn as it slid down. She put her glass in front of Betty, who'd climbed into the seat opposite her, and without another word, Betty refilled it.

"I'm not spilling my guts to you," she told the town's resident evil genius. "Where were you hiding?"

Betty tossed back her own drink and refilled her glass. "There's a wee cupboard under the stairs. The lock doesn't work. When the last bell rings, I go in there and have a nap until everybody leaves, then I help myself and go home."

"What about the alarm?" There was no way Betty had the code.

"I switch it off."

Well, hell. "And nobody notices it isn't on when they come in the next morning?"

"Dougal doesn't always remember to set it." Betty's grin was a terrifying thing.

"I don't get it. You obviously have money. The way I hear it, you own half the town, so why don't you buy your own whisky?"

"Now where's the fun in that?" Betty finished her second glass and refilled it. "Hurry up, I'm drinking you under the table here."

Agnes refused to be outdrunk by a feral-looking cube of a woman. Although, in the back of her mind, a little voice wondered if she was thinking straight. It questioned whether her lack of sleep and intake of alcohol were impairing her judgment. She ignored the voice and emptied her glass.

"We need crisps," she told Betty and headed behind the bar to help herself to several packets of salt and vinegar crisps. Unlike Betty, she left money beside the till to cover her pilfering.

Agnes tossed the packets onto the table, vaguely noting her glass was full again. "Do you know what annoys me?" she said as she reached for her drink. "This isn't a hotel management job. It's only called that. Really, I'm Dougal's personal assistant, which totally sucks." She emptied her glass before slamming it on the table, and then she fell on the crisps like a starving dog. One who liked salt and vinegar flavor. She grinned as she chomped. "Potatoes are awesome."

"Aye, so is cake. How about we raid the kitchen and get some?"

Agnes cocked her head at Betty, suddenly wondering why

everyone hated the old woman so much. "I could eat cake. But we have to be very quiet, like tiny mice."

They climbed out of the booth and tiptoed through the empty pub to the kitchen out the back. Agnes fought the urge to giggle, as she tiptoed like a cartoon character, lifting each knee ridiculously high with every step she took. She reached for the keypad beside the kitchen door, covering it with her hand. "Don't look. You can't know the code is my birthday."

"I won't look. When's your birthday?"

"August fifth. I'm going to be thirty-three next year. Do you think that's old? Why am I asking you when you're so old you're practically mummified?" Agnes giggled as she pressed in the code. "Shh!" she hissed at Betty as she held the door open for the old woman.

Agnes retrieved the carrot cake from the fridge, while Betty raided the freezer, coming out with a massive ham.

"Put that back," Agnes said. "We can't eat it. It's frozen."

"It will defrost," Betty said, as she tucked it under her arm.

"Tell me the truth," Agnes demanded. "Are you stealing the ham?"

"Aye."

They stared at each other.

"Stealing is wrong," Agnes said at last.

"Come on." Betty headed for the door, carrying her ham. "Let's get some cake in us."

Taking the whole carrot cake, which was damn heavy, Agnes followed. Once they were back in their booth, she put the cake on the table between them. "I forgot forks."

"Just use your fingers," Betty said and grabbed a chunk of cake.

"That's unsanitary," Agnes said as she watched her eat. "We need napkins." She got up and retrieved some from the bar. They had Santa on them. She held them up for Betty to see. "We can wipe our faces on Dougal." She beamed.

Betty grabbed a handful and stuffed them in her bag. "I can think of other places I'd like to wipe with those."

"Here's to crappy jobs." Agnes lifted her glass.

"That's the only kind," Betty said.

And they both tossed back their whiskies.

"Do you know what?" Agnes grabbed a handful of cake. "I hate people."

"Welcome to the club," Betty said around a mouthful of food.

"I mean, I hate working in a hotel with them. I hate hotels. I hate this job. And there are days when I hate Dougal. Damn, this cake is good."

"Dougal is a pain in the arse—you should quit."

"I can't. Otherwise, I won't get a job in another hotel." Agnes frowned. "I don't know why I want a job in another hotel. Do you know why?"

"Stupidity?"

Agnes nodded. "Why won't you sell your land to Dougal so he can build his conference center?" She paused, gazed into the distance, and said, "So they will come…" Then she burst out laughing.

"Because it's a bloody stupid idea." There was cake smeared around Betty's mouth.

"Here, have Dougal's face." Agnes passed her a napkin.

"The only reason Dougal wants a conference center is to make himself feel important, and so he can hobnob with the big shots."

"That's a funny sentence." Agnes grinned.

"We'd be better off building something fun, like a shooting range. I need to practice with my guns."

"You have guns?"

"Only stun guns. Lake won't let me have anything else, but maybe if we had a shooting range, I could talk him into letting me loose in it. Bloody Englishman is holding me back."

"Men suck." She thought about it. "Except Logan. I think he might be a good one."

"Have another drink. You're still not thinking clearly." Betty filled her glass and Agnes drank. Damn, that whisky was smooth.

"I miss my sisters," Agnes said. "There's nobody to boss around here."

"It depends who you are. I don't have any trouble finding people to order around." Betty's smile was devilish. "Neither does Dougal. He can boss his manager whenever the need hits him."

"I hate this job. I want a job in…somewhere hot. I don't know where. Just a hot place. Not a cold place. I'm fed up being cold."

"Maybe you just need better central heating?"

They fell into giggles. Well, giggles for Agnes, cackles for Betty.

"I've just figured out who you remind me of," Agnes said, suddenly serious. "An evil Yoda! Same height, same hair, same green pallor. You could be twins!"

"I think you've had enough whisky." Betty confiscated the bottle.

"Did you know there's a karaoke machine in here?" Agnes said.

"Aye. I'm brilliant on it. Although nobody appreciates my talent."

"I will. Promise. Come on, let's go sing."

They zigzagged their way to the stage, which, for some reason, seemed really far away. Agnes tried to connect the machine to the sound system, but couldn't figure out how to do it, so they were stuck with only one speaker. It would have to be enough.

"I'm going first," she told Betty, as she brought up her song. "Wait. I need my phone for this."

She zigzagged back across the pub to get it and, when she returned, Betty was lying flat on her back on the floor. Agnes nudged her with her toe. "Are you dead?"

"No, I'm resting."

"Okay, I'm singing first." She climbed onto the stage, started her song, and dialed Logan.

"Agnes?" He sounded sexy when he'd just woken up. "What's wrong?"

"Nothing," she shouted at the phone. "This one's for you."

And then she launched into her own unique version of Stevie Wonder's 'I Just Called to Say I Love You.'

Someone had filled the sunlight with shards of glass that speared through Agnes' eyeballs and into her brain.

"Make it stop," she wailed. But it came out as a hoarse, whispered croak.

"Good morning," a cheery male voice said, before Logan's smiling face appeared in front of her eyes. "Did you have a rough night then?"

"Why are you torturing me?" Agnes asked. "What have I ever done to you? Just make the pain stop and leave me alone."

"Here." He held out a glass of water. "I've got some pills for you to take. Sit up."

Someone had covered her tongue in AstroTurf. "Turn off the sun first."

Mercifully, the light dimmed. Agnes cracked open her eyes enough to see her surroundings and was relieved to find she was in her hotel room.

Logan returned to her side. "Come on, let's get you sitting."

With his help, she managed to get somewhat upright, but

each tiny movement triggered a cacophony of percussion instruments playing in her head.

"Pills," Logan ordered.

"Not so loud." She took the pills and forced them past the grass growing in her mouth. The water was glorious, and she drank it down like she'd just come out of the desert. "More." She held out the glass to him, and he gamely walked to the bathroom to refill it. "What time is it?"

"Eight."

"In the morning?"

"Aye."

"What day is it?"

"Saturday."

"Market Saturday?" For all she knew, she could have lost weeks. It sure as hell felt like it.

"Aye." He sat on the chair beside her bed, studying her as she drank.

"Okay," she said at last. "Explain it to me. Why are you here? Why do I feel like a truck ran over me? Twice. What's going on?"

"Basically, you fell into a bottle of stolen whisky, ate a carrot cake with your hands, serenaded me over the phone with bad karaoke, and then passed out cold on the pub floor next to your partner in crime."

Oh no, it was all coming back to her. And it was horrific. "Betty," she groaned.

"Aye, Betty."

"Is she dead?" She remembered Betty lying on the floor. Had she let a woman die while she was singing?

"No, she isn't dead. Although, she might be once Dougal finds out she's behind the whisky thefts. Not to mention the cake and the frozen ham."

This just kept getting worse. "I need more pills."

"You need more water." He topped up her glass.

"How did you get involved?" She hated asking, but she had to know.

"Well, when you suddenly went silent mid-song, and it was followed by a thud, I figured there was something wrong, so I came to investigate, which was pretty easy because nobody had locked the hotel up for the night."

She ignored the implied reprimand over her lapse in security. "Where's Betty now?"

"Lake took her home."

"Lake was here, too?"

"Aye."

"Dougal's going to fire me, isn't he?" Weirdly, that didn't bother her one bit. "At least I won't have to look after his dog when he goes to Spain."

"Dougal doesn't know yet. Lake and I figured we'd let you tell him."

"Thanks." She closed her eyes and tried to come up with a plan to deal with this. Nothing came to mind.

"Do you want to know what you sang to me?"

"No." He didn't need to tell her—it was all coming back to her. And it was mortifying.

"Are you sure? Because it just so happens I have a recording. I can play it for you."

Oh, that was inexcusably cruel. "Leave me alone. I need to shower and then figure out what to tell Dougal."

"A shower would probably be a good idea. There's cake in your hair, stains on your shirt, and your breath smells like grass."

So, she wasn't imagining the grass thing. How the hell had that happened?

"I want to die," she groaned.

"Drinking a bottle of whisky will do that to you," he said cheerily.

She moaned and opened her eyes to try to glare at him.

That's when she saw movement on one of the monitors on the dresser facing the bed. Slowly, so as not to start the percussion instruments playing in her head again, she sat forward and stared.

"You have got to be kidding me!" she whispered.

"What?" Logan turned to see what she was talking about and started laughing.

"This isn't funny. I'm going to kill Dougal—and that bloody dog." She tried to scramble out of bed but got tangled in the sheets. "Don't just sit there. Help me," she demanded.

With a chuckle, Logan freed her and set her on her feet beside the bed. "I don't think you're up to this," he said.

"Thanks for the encouragement." She rummaged around in her dresser drawer until she found a pair of sunglasses and put them on. That was better. Then she grabbed her boots and shoved her feet into them. It would have to do.

Still wearing the Christmas sweatshirt and jeans she'd slept in, she staggered out of her room. It took holding on to the handrail with both hands to get her down the stairs, and every step drove a spike through her left eyeball.

Logan appeared beside her, looking fresh and awake. "Maybe you should do this when you're feeling better?"

"No. I'm doing this now." She made her way along the first-floor corridor to the console that sat in the middle of the longest wall. It held a vase of flowers and some magazines.

She'd always focused on the flowers, making sure they were fresh, and she'd never noticed what was under the table. Well, she was paying attention now. After getting to her knees, which took four million years and made her head throb like a bad disco beat, she crawled to the wall—where a tiny cupboard door stood ajar.

Agnes eased it open and peeked inside. Amongst the

cables and dust lay a treasure trove of stolen goods—and a bloody dog.

"That's it. I'm done." Agnes dragged the dog out of the cupboard and inched backward with it clutched under one arm.

Logan had to help her to her feet again and then hold her until she'd stopped swaying. "The lights in this hotel are too damn bright. Doesn't Dougal care about his electricity bill?" Even with the sunglasses, her eyes still hurt. "I'm okay now, so you can let go. I'm going to the bar."

"People say the hair of the dog is the best cure for a hangover," he said as he followed her. "Trust me—they're wrong. You'd be better off in bed with a glass of water and some ibuprofen."

"I'm glad you're having fun with my pain. I'm going to the bar to return Dougal's thieving dog to its owner and give my boss a piece of my mind. Believe me, it's long overdue. Now, are you coming or not?" She narrowed her eyes at him behind her sunglasses.

"Oh, I wouldn't miss this for anything."

Getting to the bar took longer than she would have liked. Each step was like negotiating a descent from Everest, all while holding a squirming canine thief and being monitored by Logan.

As she'd expected, her boss stood behind the bar, polishing glasses and checking the bottles for the day ahead.

"Would you believe it?" he said when he saw them. "Another bottle of whisky's gone missing."

"Oh, I'd believe it," Logan drawled.

"Look at you with Arnold." Dougal smiled at the dog. "And you said you weren't a dog person. You'll have no trouble at all looking after him while I'm in Spain."

"Dougal," Agnes snapped, then winced at the sound of her own voice. "I'm resigning. Effective immediately."

He gaped at her. "You can't resign—this is market weekend."

"Stop shouting!" She held up a hand as if to ward off the noise. "Whisper or die."

"What she means," Logan said, "is that she's got a stinking headache."

"Oh, aye, I understand," Dougal said softly, for him. "I need you this weekend. You can't resign. And what about while I'm in Spain? Who'll look after the place? Or Arnold?"

That reminded her. She handed Dougal his scabby dog. "You're not going to Spain, because, no matter what you do, Betty won't sell you the land you need. She thinks the conference center is a dumb idea." She paused and took a breath. *To hell with it.* She might as well get it all out of her system. "I do, too. It isn't going to bring business to town, not in a way that will revive it. But that's another issue. Your dog is the thief. He has a stash under the table in the first-floor hallway. And Betty's the one who's been stealing your whisky."

Dougal sucked in a breath. "I'm going to wring her scrawny old neck."

"On top of that, I ate the carrot cake with Betty last night while we were getting drunk on stolen whisky after hours. And she may, or may not, have left with a ham. Feel free to tell the planet I'm a useless, thieving hotel manager. I don't care, because I hate hotels and I'm never going to work in one again. Consider this my resignation. Not only from this job but also from this career." Although, why she was giving it to Dougal, she didn't know. She guessed it was the symbolism that counted. Turning to Logan, she said, "Can I come home with you?"

"Aye." He wrapped an arm around her shoulders and turned toward the door to the carpark. "We'll sort out her room later," he told Dougal.

"But she can't resign." Dougal looked a little shell-shocked.

"She just did," Logan said, opening the door for them.

Agnes was done with the hotel. "I want to sleep for a month. Can I sleep in your bed for a month?"

"Sure, but you should know it's Saturday and the kids are there. They'll think I've brought my girlfriend home."

"I'm past caring." If he wasn't bothered about parading her around in front of them, why should she be? "But I'm not having sex while they're in the house. That's just wrong."

"We'll see," Logan said ominously.

Snow fell over Invertary, and Agnes stopped to stare. It must have started sometime during the night because already a light covering lay on the hills beyond the loch. The whole scene looked like something straight off a Christmas card. The sky was painting everything new.

"You must be cold." Logan shrugged off his jacket and wrapped it around her shoulders.

Strangely, for the first time in a very long time, she wasn't cold. Settling into the passenger seat, she snuggled down in Logan's jacket, feeling his warmth and breathing his scent.

She was asleep by the time they'd turned into the road.

* * *

WITH AGNES SHOWERED and tucked into his bed, Logan went downstairs to deal with his kids. As meltdowns went, getting drunk with Betty McLeod was pretty unique, and entertaining to boot. But not as spectacular as watching her handle Dougal while dressed in yesterday's crumpled clothes, with half a cake in her hair, and wearing sunglasses. He grinned. He should have filmed it.

"Is Agnes staying here forever now?" Darcy asked as soon as he walked into the room.

"I don't know what she's doing." He doubted *she* even knew what she was doing.

Drew took off his headphones, obviously worried he'd miss something important. "You want her to stay, don't you, Dad?" he asked quietly.

Logan thought about fobbing him off with a non-answer, but that wasn't how he did things, even if it meant letting his kids see his vulnerabilities. "Aye, son, I do."

"Have you told her?" Drew toyed with the wires from his headphones as Darcy soaked up every word.

"No, and I won't."

"But, if you ask her to stay, she might change her mind and do it," Darcy said.

"That's true, but if I ask her, I'll never know if it was her choice, or if I influenced her to do it. I want her here, but only if that's what she wants too." He reached for the coffee pot and a mug. "Sometimes, people don't stay, no matter how much you want them to. And, in that case, it's better to let them go."

"Like Mum," Drew said.

"Aye, like your mum."

"So, what do we do?" Darcy asked.

"We play it by ear. One day at a time and see where it leads." But Logan had to be honest with himself too. Agnes had made it plain from day one that she planned to leave. Whether that was to go to another hotel or something new for her, it didn't change her desire to get out of Scotland.

"I want to know what's going to happen now," Darcy said.

"Me too, kid, me too. Now, who wants pancakes before we go to the market?"

"We can't leave without Agnes, Dad," his soft-hearted girl said. "She's never been to the Christmas market, and we should be the ones to take her."

"I suppose we could go later," he said. "After she's had some time to rest." And get over her blinder of a hangover.

"It's better in the dark anyway," Darcy said. "I like the lights. And we can play in the snow while it's still light."

"Playing in the snow is for little kids," Drew said.

"You're just mad because your day out with Zoe was canceled."

"Not Zoe. Zander and Harris."

"How about we try to get through breakfast without an argument?" Logan reached for the pancake mix.

The back door opened and his mother came in, shaking the snow off her hair. "What's this I hear about Agnes quitting?"

The Invertary grapevine mystified Logan. People heard rumors about things that happened when no one was around to witness them. His mother hung up her coat and took the pancake mix from his hands. Logan promptly took it back.

"I make better pancakes," she said with a frown.

"Then go make them in your kitchen." There were some drawbacks to having your parents living next door. A lack of personal space was one of them.

"Well," his mum said as she helped herself to coffee. "Is it true?"

"Aye."

"How did Dougal take it?"

"Silently. For him. Agnes didn't really give him a chance to say anything."

"What's she going to do for work now? We need to find her a good job in Invertary, so she won't be tempted to leave. We need her here. Margaret has her positioned to become the leader of Knit or Die when she pops her clogs."

"How exactly would that work? She doesn't knit, and she didn't want to join the group in the first place. And don't give me that rubbish about knitting choosing you."

"Basically, we plan to wear her down until she agrees she belongs here."

That sounded more like it. "Before you start job hunting for Agnes, bear in mind that she might like a say in what work she does. Then there's the matter of whether she even wants to stay in town. She really dislikes Scotland."

"I don't think it's Scotland she doesn't like so much as the memories it holds. She belongs here. That lassie fits into Invertary more than anyone who's turned up in the past twenty years. We all feel it, and I don't understand why she can't see it herself."

Logan didn't like the look on his mum's face. "Don't interfere," he told her. "Agnes has to make up her own mind about what she wants."

"And how will she know what her options are if we don't show her?"

Logan shook his head. There was no talking to his mother when she was in this mood. All he could do was remind himself that Agnes could stand up for herself. "After breakfast, I'm going to make a run to the hotel and clear out Agnes' room. I offered to do it so she wouldn't have to answer any questions from the staff until she's feeling up to it. Plus, Dougal could probably use the room this weekend."

"While you're there, give that idiot a kick from me," his mother said.

And his kids grinned at him.

* * *

AGNES STOOD up from the step she'd been sitting on. Her legs shook and her head throbbed, which is why she'd been on her way downstairs to ask Logan if he had some aspirin. As soon as she'd heard her name, she sat down to listen. She didn't even try to pretend she wasn't eavesdropping, or that she was doing it by accident. Nope, she'd wanted to hear what Logan and his family had to say about her.

The last thing she'd expected was that they wanted her to stay.

A tight sensation wrapped around her heart as she climbed the stairs to Logan's bedroom. Outside of her sisters, had anyone ever wanted to keep her around? And why would Shona think she belonged in Invertary? It was almost insulting—the town seemed filled with people who danced to their own special beats. Oh. *That* was why.

She crossed the room to look out the window. Snow fell thick and fast now, covering the town in a veil of white lace. Watching it from Logan's warm bedroom, she could appreciate the beauty without aching from the cold. There was something magical about having the world whitewashed around her. Everything looked clean and new—for a little while anyway.

Taking a seat on the bed, Agnes pulled out her phone and dialed Isobel. Her sister's smiling face made Agnes want to cry.

"Are you sick?" Isobel said as soon as she saw her.

"Hungover. And you'll never guess who I got drunk with. Betty!"

There was stunned silence. "No…You're right. I would never have guessed. Are you sure you should have been doing that? Betty tends to get people in trouble."

"Don't you worry. I can find my own trouble without any help." She took a deep breath. "I quit my job, Isobel. Tell Callum I'm sorry, will you? I know he pulled strings to get it for me."

"Callum won't care that you quit." Isobel waved a dismissive hand. "What are you going to do now?"

"I don't know, but I don't want to work in a hotel."

"Do you want to come to London? You're bound to find something you like here."

"No." Agnes started to shake her head, but pain made her stop. "I don't want to come to London—instead, I want you guys to come here. Can you come for Christmas, Isobel? I miss you all so much."

Her sister didn't hesitate. "Of course we'll come. Do you want me to call Donna and Mairi?"

"Yeah, I need to lie down for a bit."

"Okay." Isobel hesitated. "There's just one thing. Will you still be there at Christmas?"

Agnes started to say that Christmas was only three weeks away and she might as well stay put until it was over, but she stopped herself because that wasn't exactly the truth. Not anymore. And that meant, really, there was only one answer she could give. "Aye, I'll be here."

CHAPTER 22

The Christmas market was in full swing by the time Agnes felt well enough to go. Although barely teatime, the sky was already black—apart from the thick, white snowflakes that continued to fall silently and gather beneath their feet.

Shona had loaned Agnes a pair of padded snow boots, which kept her toes nice and toasty. And under her padded coat, she had on more layers than an onion. She could hardly move, but she was warm. To top off her look, Darcy had insisted on her wearing her fluffy pink earmuffs under her woolly hat. Nothing would have made Agnes disappoint the girl, so she wore the earmuffs, and every time Logan looked at her, he grinned.

"Nice muffs," he said, for the tenth time.

"That joke never grows old," she drawled.

"Hey, Logan," an older woman called out as she passed, "nice bum."

Agnes burst out laughing. It served him right.

"I'm getting the Benson Security tech people to scour the internet and take down those photos," Logan said.

"You love it." She bumped him with her shoulder. "Admit it."

"Aye, I love having my arse hanging out for the world to perv at."

"Knew it," Agnes said.

"Want some hot chocolate?" Logan asked, and she nodded.

As he headed over to a stall selling drinks, Agnes watched the market play out around her. Two rows of stalls, one on each side of the road, sold everything from handmade candles to elaborate cat scratching posts. There were paintings and secondhand books, beautifully turned wooden bowls and odd papier-mâché sculptures, knitted jumpers and quilted blankets. It was a celebration of the Highlands craft makers, and it was wonderful.

"Do you want to try some tablet?" a young woman asked Agnes as she held out a tray of Scotland's favorite candy.

"Absolutely." It melted in her mouth, making her groan.

With a knowing smile, the woman moved on, and Agnes wandered over to a stall selling handmade covers for e-books and laptops.

"These are lovely." Agnes ran her fingers over a beautifully detailed embroidered design.

"Thanks," the woman said. "I mostly sell them online. You can take a card if you like. I make them to order."

"You do?" As Agnes picked up the card and stuffed it in her pocket, a kernel of an idea she'd had for a while took root in the back of her mind.

"Here you go," Logan said as he came up to her. "I got you a sausage roll as well because we don't want hangry Agnes coming out and decimating the market."

"Funny." But she ate the sausage roll and, as they strolled down the high street, she filled her pockets with yet more business cards.

"Look what I got." Darcy bounced up to them. "I got a spinning top and a cool bag."

"Very cool," Logan and Agnes agreed.

"Where's your brother?" Logan said.

"He's flirting with Zoe." She pointed up the street and, sure enough, there was Drew hanging out with a cute young girl. "I'm going to talk to them." And Darcy ran off.

"Don't embarrass your brother," Logan called after her.

"You're wasting your time," Agnes told him. "Siblings live for these opportunities."

With caution and nerves dancing in her stomach, Agnes reached out to take Logan's hand. Thankfully, he didn't make a big deal out of it. He just gave her a smile and kept on walking.

"Nice bum," someone called to Logan as they passed, making Agnes laugh.

* * *

Logan felt ten feet tall walking hand in hand with Agnes. He wanted to wrap an arm around her and pull her into his side, but he was aware that his Agnes was cautious—unless she was drunk. Then, she was all about letting her emotions loose.

He wondered if she remembered what song she'd sung to him, and what she'd said after it. How she'd told him she was already falling in love with him, and how it scared the pants off her—her exact words. Glancing down at her as he held her hand tight, it seemed impossible to imagine what he'd do if she kept to her decision to leave. He suspected that getting over Agnes would take a whole lot longer than it'd taken to get over Danielle. Mainly because Danielle had been the love of his youth, and they'd outgrown each other, but Agnes was the choice of the man. And he knew he'd never grow so much that he'd leave her behind.

"You know that weird building behind the main street?" Agnes asked.

"You'll have to be more specific. This is Invertary—weird is a common descriptor here."

"The one that looks like lots of hexagons shoved together."

"Oh, the experimental school. Aye, that didn't last long. As far as I remember, it was the government doing what it usually does and trying out new ideas in the Highlands before inflicting them on the rest of the country. They called it pod schooling. Lots of little rooms with different subjects going on in them and the kids were free to float between them. Kind of like pick 'n' mix education. All it meant was that no one monitored the kids because the teachers weren't sure where they were supposed to be. So the kids spent most of their time hanging out and playing on their phones. Like I said, it didn't last long."

"What's the building used for now?"

"Nothing. There was talk a few years ago about turning it into an old folks' home, but the old folk didn't want to be dumped in there either. Why are you asking about it?"

Agnes shrugged. "It's just a weird building, even by Invertary standards." She grinned at him. "Not as weird as the folly, but close."

"Agnes," a distinctive voice shouted as they neared the hotel. "Agnes, can I talk to you for a minute?"

Agnes tensed and took a step closer to him as Dougal approached, looking more flustered than usual.

"Agnes, you have to come back. I need you."

"No, you don't," Agnes said. "That's the busy weekend talking. Let's face it, Dougal, you didn't want me there any more than I wanted to be there."

"That's not true—" Dougal started.

But Agnes held up a hand. "At least be honest with yourself. It might have seemed like a good idea to have a manager to free you up to do other things, but you hated every minute of it."

His shoulders slumped. "Okay, that's true. But I'm drowning right now. Would you at least consider coming back to work until I return from Spain?"

Agnes tugged on Logan's hand. "What do you think?"

"It's up to you."

She chewed on her bottom lip for a minute before looking up at him. "I know we haven't talked about this, but I don't want to move back into the hotel. Can I stay with you for a while?"

His stupid heart lurched in his chest. "Course you can," was all he said.

She turned to Dougal. "In that case, I'll help out until you return from Spain, but I'm not looking after your dog."

"But—" Dougal said.

"No." Agnes was firm. "Get Mrs. Edwards to watch him. She'll love it."

"But that means I'll have to talk to her," Dougal grumbled.

"I don't care what you do with the dog," Agnes said. "Just so long as you don't think you're foisting it off on me."

"Fine. Can you start now?"

She let out a huff. "I'm on a date, Dougal."

"You are?" Logan asked.

"Am I or am I not holding your damn hand?" Agnes held up their hands to make her point.

"And that means date?"

"Yes." She tapped her toe in the snow, which was a sure sign he should let things go.

But he didn't. "Well, if it's a date, there should be kissing."

And with that, he spun her into his arms and proceeded to match action to words.

"I'll be in the pub," Dougal said as they kept kissing. "Come on in when you're ready. Aye, I'll just go then. Bye for now." And at last, he stopped talking.

Logan didn't check to see if he'd gone, he just kept on kissing Agnes. Astonished that she was allowing it to happen in full view of all of Invertary. Slowly, reluctantly, they broke apart—to a round of applause.

That's when he spotted Darcy, standing wide-eyed beside them. "Does *this* mean you're his girlfriend?" she asked Agnes.

* * *

AGNES DIDN'T WANT to be back in the hotel and pub. She wanted to be in Logan's house with him and his kids. Drew had mentioned a movie that sounded good—they'd planned on watching it together. And Logan had promised they could make a snowman. It would have been the perfect evening.

But instead, she was in the pub, supervising the karaoke night and experiencing a weird sense of déjà vu. Her memories of the night before were foggy at best. She knew she'd sung, but that was about as far as it went. At some point, she'd have to ask Logan exactly how much of a fool she'd made of herself.

In the meantime, she had work to do and people to talk to. People she wanted to talk to for a change, and they were all sitting in their usual booth.

Weaving through the crowded room, she headed straight for the table with Kirsty, Lake, Josh, Caroline, Mitch, and Jodie.

"Hey," she said.

"Hey, yourself," Kirsty, Lake's wife, said. "I heard you quit."

"I did. I'm only filling in until Dougal gets back from Spain."

"Ah, the Reverend Morrison quest," Josh said. "And like most quests, it will be fruitless and pointless."

"Stop it," Caroline demanded, but she smiled at her husband while she did it. "He's only trying to help the town."

And there was her opening. "That's why I came over here. I have a few ideas on how we can regenerate the town, and I need backing. I hear you lot—and Flynn Boyle, who I haven't met yet—are where the money is at."

"I like you," Jodie said. "You just come right out and say what you mean."

"Usually," Agnes said. "Not recently, but I'm getting back to the old me."

"Do you have a business plan?" Mitch said.

"Nope, I have ideas and absolutely no money to turn them into reality."

They shared a look that didn't bode well for her, while in the background someone murdered 'Last Christmas' to a booing crowd.

"I don't think we—" Caroline started, but Agnes interrupted.

"I get it. I've only been here three weeks, and suddenly I'm an expert on what Invertary needs to survive. You see a stranger standing in front of you, asking for money for some cockamamie scheme she's cooked up. For all you know, I'm one of those weirdos who think rich people owe them money just for being alive."

They shared another round of looks and shifted uncomfortably in their seats. All except Lake.

Agnes spoke to him. "You know me and my family—you probably even know things about my family that I don't. Just give me five minutes to pitch my idea, and then I'll go. No obligation or bad feelings on either side." She glanced over at the crowd, happy and singing along to the music now that the last singer was gone. "I'm trying to stay here." She looked back at them. "I'm trying to stay when my instinct is to run, but I think I could maybe fit in here and, to do that, I need a place. A spot where I can work. And it isn't this hotel. Not unless you want Dougal drowned in the loch at some point."

"These ideas are really to help the town?" Caroline asked, reminding Agnes that she was a member of the town's council.

"Yeah," Agnes said. "But I can't guarantee it."

Lake wrapped an arm around his redheaded wife and pulled her into his side. "You can have my five minutes, but I can't speak for the rest of the group."

A little spark of hope ignited within her.

And was snuffed out by a voice that boomed across the room. "Agnes, I need you for a minute."

Swallowing her groan of frustration, she smiled at them. "Thanks for your time, guys, but duty calls. Lake, I'll take you up on that five minutes another day." After she'd tracked down the mysterious Flynn Boyle to see if he was willing to open his pockets or not.

Mitch leaned forward. "When you're done with whatever Dougal needs, come back. You've got your five minutes to pitch to all of us."

She looked at their faces, but they were all smiling at her, so it seemed Mitch spoke for everyone.

"I'll try," she said. "Thank you."

Rushing through the crowded bar, she spotted a familiar figure climbing up onto the stage to a round of groans— Betty. Agnes tripped over her feet as she reached Dougal. "I thought you would have banned her," she said to him.

"And then where would she go? This is Invertary, not

Glasgow. It's not as though she has a selection of places to socialize in. As much as she's able." He frowned in Betty's direction as she started to belt out Shirley Bassey's 'Hey Big Spender.' She sounded like she was in pain. Oh, dear heavens, it came with dance moves. "I will make her pay for the whisky, though," Dougal said. "Now, can you run up to Mr. Thompson's room with some toilet paper?"

"You have got to be kidding me!" She glared at Dougal.

His face softened. "I'm not messing with you. The man really does need toilet paper, and we're all run off our feet. You looked like the only one with a minute to spare."

"Fine." She hurried through the hotel and into the store-room, where she grabbed an industrial-sized pack of sixty toilet rolls before heading to Mr. Thompson's room.

When he opened the door, she thrust the pack at him. "This should last you a couple of days," she said with a smile.

"Where am I supposed to put that?" he asked as he took the toilet rolls.

"The same place you've been putting the rest of them." She turned back toward the stairs.

"That's not the right attitude for this job," he called after her.

"I know," Agnes answered with a smile.

The smile was still on her face when she made it back to the bar.

"What did you do?" Dougal demanded after taking one look at her.

"Let's just say, Mr. Thompson shouldn't be calling for more toilet paper any time soon. Now, I'm going to take a five-minute break, okay?" It was the first break she'd asked for since coming to work for him.

"Okay, Agnes," Dougal said gently.

She nodded, then made her way back to the table. "Is this a good time?" she asked.

"As good as any," Mitch said. "Pull up a chair."

But there were no chairs to pull up—the room was packed. "It's okay. I can stand. This won't take long. So, this is what I have. Right now, we can't attract businesses to town because there aren't enough people here to act as a market-place for them. Also, we're too far from the main centers to make transporting goods a cost-effective option for any manufacturers that might like to take advantage of our low property prices. And ideas like the conference center will bring money into the town for short periods, but won't increase local industry in the long term."

Plus, she wasn't even sure people would want to come to Invertary for a conference, especially when the town didn't have the infrastructure to support them.

"That's a good summary of the current state of things," Caroline said, eyeing Agnes with serious interest. "So what's your solution?"

Oh, Agnes liked Caroline. "We need to attract businesses that work local and sell international. Producers who'll spend locally and invest in the community but won't rely on it for their income. Which means we need small businesses, most likely crafters, who sell on the internet."

They were nodding, and she took that as encouragement, while also being aware the clock was ticking on her time and she really didn't want to go over it.

"What I want to do is open a communal business center. The idea would be to rent out space to these small businesses while providing resources that would be too costly for them to justify on their own. Things like a welding room, or a kiln room—things they could rent, instead of forking out money to set up everything themselves. We'd provide the facilities, the business support, and the equipment. And they'd run their businesses online, bringing money and an injection of new talent into town, as well as spreading the word about

Invertary internationally. Plus, the hope would be that each business would bring new families into town, growing the schools and providing more customers for local shops." She smiled. "That's it in a nutshell."

Six pairs of eyes stared at her, and she found it hard to breathe.

"I think," Caroline said at last, "that we need you on the town council."

"I'll help with your business plan," Mitch said. "Come see me Monday, and we'll bash it out."

Josh shrugged. "I'd give you my money."

"It's a good idea," Jodie said, studying her. "What else have you got?"

"Quite a bit, actually." Agnes said. "I grew up poor in a tiny town. I was always looking for ways to make money and noticing gaps where the town could have helped me do it. You could say I've been thinking about this my whole life." She glanced over her shoulder at Dougal, who for once wasn't frowning at her but smiling. "But right now, I need to work. Thanks for listening. I'll definitely be in touch about the help with a business plan," she told Mitch.

"Monday evening," Caroline said. "There's a private council meeting at the castle. Are you free to attend? I think it would be good for everyone to hear your ideas."

"Yes," Agnes said. "Yes, I'll be there."

And, with a skip in her step, she headed off to see what else she could do to help Dougal.

CHAPTER 23

Logan opened his front door as soon as he heard Dougal's car pull up, just past midnight, and leaned on the doorjamb to wait for Agnes. He liked that she hadn't wanted to leave Dougal in the lurch after he'd said he needed her help, but if the man had upset her again, he was going to kick his arse. Although considering their age gap, that would hardly be a fair fight. He'd get his mother to do it instead.

To his surprise, she gave Dougal a cheery, if somewhat tired, wave goodbye as she walked away from the car. He cocked his head and studied her. She looked...happy. No, more than that, she looked like a huge weight had been lifted from her and she was floating now. Her smile glowed as she came up the path toward him.

"Good night?" he asked, stepping aside to let her in out of the cold.

"The best." She surprised him again by going on tiptoe and pressing the sweetest kiss to his lips.

"Have you been drinking?" he teased.

She shuddered. "Never again."

He helped her out of her coat and boots. "I have a surprise for you," he said against her ear.

"I've got a surprise for you too," she said as she leaned into him.

"Mine first." Logan put his hands on her hips and guided her toward the stairs. "Up you go."

"I hope your surprise isn't of the naked variety, because I'm not doing that with kids in the house. It would be icky."

"Icky is not a word I remember you using when it came to sex. I believe it was two words—'too good'. And, for your information, the kids are sleeping next door tonight."

"Are they now?" She stopped on the step above him and turned to drape her arms over his shoulders. "That's a bit presumptuous."

"Not presumptuous. Optimistic." His hands rested on the full curve of her hips.

"I do like optimism in a man."

"I hope that isn't all you like."

"What else do you have to offer?" Agnes closed the distance between them and teased his lips with hers.

"Go upstairs, and you'll find out," he murmured against her mouth, before turning her and gently prodding her to keep climbing.

"You ruin all my fun," she complained as she put some extra sway into her hips.

He followed her into his bedroom and through to the en suite he'd added when he bought the house. His parents thought it an extravagance, but then, they weren't sharing a bathroom with two teens.

"Oh," she gasped as she halted in the doorway.

He wrapped an arm around her waist and pulled her back into him as he waited for her reaction. He'd be the first to admit his surprise wasn't the most original, but if an idea worked well enough to become a romance standard, Logan wasn't about to dismiss it.

The bathroom was full of the candles he'd stocked up on at the Christmas market, much to the delight of the woman who ran the stall. He'd chosen a variety of shapes and sizes and a myriad of fragrances, hoping it wouldn't all blend together and fill his bathroom with a toxic cloud. To his relief, the smell was heady but pleasant.

Candles burned on every surface, their light reflecting off the large mirror over the sink. In the corner of the room, his old clawfoot tub was filled with girly bubbles, and on a stool beside it sat a thermos of hot chocolate and a plate of shortbread.

Her smile was teasing when she looked up at him. "No champagne and strawberries?"

"This is winter in Scotland."

"You are such a wise man." Her attention drifted back to the room. "I can't believe you did this for me."

It was on the tip of his tongue to say it was only a bath, but it wasn't. It was him showing her that he thought of her even when she was out of his sight.

"You'd better get in before it gets cold," he said roughly.

Agnes turned and reached up to cup his cheek. "Thank you."

The warmth in her eyes burned a hole straight through to his heart.

"Anytime, Agnes, love." He kissed her forehead. "Now strip."

Without hesitation, she pulled off her jumper and tossed it at him before reaching for the snap of her jeans. For a second, he could only stand there, drinking in the sight of Agnes in a black lace bra.

"You're coming in too, aren't you?" she said as she shimmied out of her jeans.

"I'm not sure there's room in that tub for two."

"We'll make space." She licked her lips suggestively, a sparkle of pure mischief in her eyes.

He didn't need a second invitation.

"You get in first," Agnes ordered, "and I'll sit between your legs."

That was his woman, always in charge. She scooped a handful of bubbles into her palm and blew them at him, looking triumphant when they splattered on his chest. She stepped close, her fingers trailing through the smattering of hair that covered his pecs.

"Why is chest hair so fascinating?" she mused as she played.

Logan's hands came up to cup her heavy breasts, feeling their softness through the sexy black lace. "Why are women's breasts so fascinating?"

Her eyelids drifted down, and she gazed up at him through thick lashes. "Do you like having your nipples touched? Some men do, some don't."

She toyed with one as he rasped a thumb over hers. With a groan, she swayed in his hold.

"You like having yours touched," he said.

She rubbed a fingertip over his nipple. "Does that feel nice?"

"Honestly, I don't feel anything at all."

"Nothing?" Her eyes went wide.

"Nope. Sorry."

"That can't be right." She leaned in and laved at it, before adding a nibble for good measure. "Anything?"

"You might as well be doing that to my elbow."

Her frown was so cute it made him want to laugh. "These things really are pointless then, aren't they?"

"Okay, we're done here. Time to get in the bath."

With an irritated shake of her head, she moved aside to let him climb in.

He lowered himself into the lavender-scented suds and wondered how much mud he'd have to roll in afterward to stop from smelling like a girl.

"Hurry up and get in here," he grumbled. "Otherwise, I'm a guy having a bubble bath alone, and I don't think my testosterone levels can cope with it."

"Idiot." Agnes threw off her underwear and climbed in, her breasts swaying in front of him, tantalizing him. "There's nothing wrong with a man having a bubble bath."

"Maybe if it smelled like Old Spice. This is lavender and vanilla. I'm going to smell like potpourri."

"If you knew you were going to get in the bath, too, why didn't you pick a different scent?"

"Because you like this one." He'd thought that was obvious.

With a sigh of delight, she lowered herself to sit between his legs, making his dick stand to attention. The only thing his dick wanted more than to rub all over her was to be inside her. *That will come,* he promised it.

The sensation of her soft, feminine body against his settled something deep inside him. Something he hadn't even realized was tense until that moment. As her hands rested on his legs, his hands slid around her to cup her breasts. Now, he felt…content.

Candlelight danced over her skin as Agnes played with the bubbles. They existed in a cocoon of sensuality where nothing else mattered except feeling. Gently, he massaged her breasts, using languorous touches that made her melt against him.

"I could do this all day," he rumbled.

"The water would get cold." She rubbed the heel of her hands up his thighs.

"Are you sure you're comfortable sitting there? You might feel better if you put your legs over mine."

"You think that would be more relaxing?"

"Oh, aye."

She sucked in a breath but shifted to do exactly that. One leg hooked over each of Logan's, leaving her wide open in his lap. "Like this?"

"Exactly like that. Feel better?"

"Not quite. Something's missing."

"A pillow," he teased as he slid his right hand over her stomach and down toward paradise.

Her fingers dug into his legs as he toyed with the hair at the junction of her thighs.

"Are you going to tease me all night?" Agnes complained. "Should I do this myself?"

"Tempting, but trust me when I say that I have this in hand." He slid his hand between her legs to cover her, holding her to him.

"That better not be all you're doing." That snarky little bite that crept into her voice when she'd lost control of a situation was back, and he loved it.

"We really need to work on your patience." He slid a finger around her little clit, making her gasp and clutch his legs tight. "Happy now?"

"Not yet, but I'm hoping I will be."

Chuckling, he continued the slow circular dance with his finger as his other hand caressed her breast.

"Faster," she ordered on a moan.

"Not yet, there are some things I want to talk about first."

"You have got to be kidding me." She angled her head to glare at him, ready to argue her case, but he pressed that little bundle of nerves and got a groan instead.

"We need to clear up our living arrangement," he said as he continued his teasing strokes.

"What's to clear up?" She writhed against his hand, trying to get him to speed up his slow seduction. "All of my things are here."

"Aye, but have you moved in with me, or are you just staying for a few days? Are you going back to the hotel? Are you leaving Invertary? As you can hear, I have a few wee questions that need answering."

"How am I supposed to concentrate on answering them when you're doing this?" she demanded, but it sounded rather breathless.

"This is the only way I can pin you down long enough to get answers." Logan sped up his movements until she moaned, and then he slowed back down again.

"That is just cruel," she wailed.

"That's not an answer to my questions."

"Fine, okay. I've moved in."

His chest tightened. "For how long?"

"I don't know." She gasped, her nails digging into his thighs. "I'm trying to find a way to stay in Invertary."

And just like that, it became impossible to breathe. "Do you want to stay?"

"Yes!" The word exploded out of her when he changed the pressure of his stroke. "Yes. I do. I've thought about it a lot. I think I could fit in here, but I need a job."

There was no point in telling her that he'd happily support her for as long as it took to find work, as he knew Agnes wouldn't accept his offer. She needed the security of knowing she could provide for herself no matter what happened. And he understood that. Trust took time to build. It often took longer than falling in love and, sometimes, it was far more fragile. Instead, he rewarded her by speeding up and taking her right to the edge of release all over again—before he slowed.

This time, she wailed louder. "I'm going to kill you," she threatened.

"No, you aren't because later, in bed, I plan to do this with my mouth."

"I bloody hate that you're good at sex." She sounded so angry about it that he had to grin.

"I know. Now tell me this, do you remember what you sang on the phone the other night?"

"No." It came out too fast and too clipped to be anything but a lie.

He removed his touch from between her thighs. "Are you sure about that?"

"Logan, I swear, I am going to suffocate you in your sleep if you don't finish what you've started, right now. Oh, to hell with it. I'll do it myself."

"Oh no, you won't." He angled her forward, grabbed her arms, and tucked them behind her, then lay her back down so they were trapped between them. His arm snaked around her waist and held her tight, immobilizing her.

"What the hell? How did you do that so fast? And why is it so freaking sexy? That is just wrong." She sounded enraged, frustrated, admiring, and turned on all at once.

Logan couldn't help it—she made him laugh. Kissing her shoulder, he pressed his hand over her feminine heat, feeling all that wet lushness just for him. She lifted her hips and tried to rub against him, but with her legs over his, she didn't have the leverage she needed.

"I must be seriously sick in the head to be turned on by this," she grumbled.

"As sick as I am for getting horny when you kicked my arse?"

"Okay," she conceded, "not that sick."

He pressed his palm against her clit, delighting in the

little gasp that escaped her. "Are you going to tell me what you sang? I know you remember."

"Fine," she snapped. "I sang 'I Just Called to Say I Love You.' Happy now?"

She was priceless. "Aye, I'm happy now." He resumed his intimate stroking, making sure to add a little more speed and pressure than he'd done so far.

"Oh," she moaned, "that's much better."

"Let's talk about the song." Logan kissed her shoulder again, delighting in the wet, smooth skin beneath his lips.

"Let's not," she gasped.

"Interesting choice, don't you think?"

"What I think is that you're a teasing bastard of a man."

And she loved it. He nipped her neck, then kissed it better. All the while continuing his steady touch. Her breathing became more rapid, and her muscles tensed. She was getting close, making him itch to send her over and watch her come apart in his arms.

But not yet.

"Why did you choose that song, Agnes?"

"Because I know the tune," she said between gasps.

He lifted his hand and rested it on the side of the tub. Agnes wailed before cursing him out and threatening him with all sorts of bodily harm.

"Why did you choose that particular song?" he asked again, although he already knew the answer. She'd whispered the words after she'd finished singing—before she passed out. But he wasn't sure she remembered that part.

"Because I love you," she shouted. "Even though you're an evil, sadistic demon of a man. I also hate you right now too."

A surge of pure love swept up to meet her *romantic* declaration, and he kissed her neck. "Now, was that so difficult?"

Before she could say anything else, he used two fingers to stroke her hard. Her back arched, her muscles tensed, and she let out a glorious wail. And then she shattered. Panting and moaning as he gently slowed his caresses on her poor abused clit.

Listening to her labored breathing, he cradled her boneless body in his arms. Damn, she was perfect for him. And she planned to stay!

A smug smile broke out across his face, making him glad her eyes were closed and she couldn't see it.

"I'm not giving you your surprise now," she said huskily. "You don't deserve it."

"That's okay." He nuzzled her hair. "I don't think you could hold your breath under water that long anyway."

She barked a laugh and snuggled into him.

"I love you too," he told her.

"I know," she whispered before she promptly fell asleep.

CHAPTER 24

Agnes took a deep breath. Then another. She pressed her hand flat to her stomach and willed it to settle. This was ridiculous. She never felt nervous. Never.

"Are you sick?" Darcy asked as she came into the kitchen, where Agnes was going over her notes for the meeting with the town council. She checked the clock. In just over an hour.

"No. Just a bit nervous, and I don't know why. I don't usually get like this."

"I get nervous all the time," Darcy said as she jumped up to sit on the counter. "I was so nervous before a dance recital once that I puked all over my dance teacher. It stank because I'd had ice cream, and Gran says that curdles in your stomach. My teacher cried, and Dad had to sort it. You should get Dad to go with you to your meeting. He'd help you too. He always makes me feel less nervous when he goes with me to things."

"I don't think it'd be very professional if I brought him along."

"Well, do you want to talk about it? Gran says a problem

shared is a problem…yeah, I can't remember, but it's supposed to help."

Agnes couldn't help but smile. "It's that simple, huh?" She frowned as she noticed a mark on Darcy's face. "How did you get that bruise on your cheek?"

Darcy looked around the room before answering. "You won't tell Dad?" she asked cautiously.

All of Agnes' nerves disappeared as she focused on the girl. "I think your dad is going to notice that bruise anyway. Now spill, how'd you get it?"

"It's Samantha. She picks on me and, when no one's looking, she hits me."

Oh. That was *not* happening. Agnes got up out of her chair, crossed to the sink, and dampened a tea towel with cold water. "Hold that to it. Is it sore?"

Darcy shook her head. "Not now."

Agnes folded her arms over her gray work suit. The one she didn't bother wearing to the pub now that she was only there in a casual capacity. "Who's Samantha?"

"A girl in my class. She lives in Fort William, and she's pretty mean. She picks on all the kids that come from other places, but she really hates me, and I don't know why."

"Probably because she's a nasty little…girl." She'd been going to say bitch but caught herself at the last minute. "Hasn't Drew stepped in to stop it?" Agnes and her sisters had always stood up for each other when one of them was picked on.

"I haven't told him, because she's a girl and he can't hit girls. Dad says that's wrong."

She had a point. "How big is this kid?"

Darcy held up a hand, a couple of inches above her head. "To about here."

"Right." She took off her suit jacket and hung it over a

kitchen chair. "Come here. I'm going to show you how to hit back, but only on one condition."

Darcy eagerly jumped off the counter and rushed to stand facing Agnes. "Okay."

Agnes nodded. "I'll show you how to fight, but if this Samantha hits you again, you have to promise to hit her back and hit way harder than she hit you."

Darcy started giggling and covered her mouth with her hands. "I thought you were going to say I had to tell a teacher."

"Hell, no! I mean heck…heck, no. The only way to deal with bullies is to hit back and hit harder. They thrive on fear. Never show them you're scared. Plus, they count on you following the rules they don't follow, like the one that says you shouldn't hit people in school, and it gives them an advantage. She's using your good nature against you. That's why you need to hit back hard. One good punch, and she'll never bother you again."

It was tempting to tell her to punch that kid right in the throat, but that could kill Samantha, which was probably a step too far in dealing with a bully. Although…this was a bully who dared to mess with Darcy, and that made Agnes furious. She hadn't felt this angry since her sisters had been picked on. She'd always felt a ferocious fury when anyone messed with the people who belonged to her. Guess that meant Darcy was hers too.

She waited for the feeling of responsibility to squash her, but all she felt was a sense of rightness.

"Agnes, are you still going to teach me to fight?" Darcy said, making her smile.

"Was I thinking too much? That sometimes happens. I was wondering if I should go to the school and deal with this Samantha in person."

Darcy cocked her head. "You look kind of murderous. Maybe it would be best if I tried hitting her first."

"Fine," Agnes conceded, "but if this doesn't work, I'll deal with it."

Darcy got a scheming little look on her face. "Normally, only family are allowed to talk to the teachers about a kid. Does *this* mean you're Dad's girlfriend now?"

"I didn't plan to talk to anyone, and I don't see why we have to put a label on this thing with your dad. But fine. I'm his…" Yeah, she couldn't say it. "Whatever. Come here so I can show you how to knock this girl into next week. Nobody messes with *my* people and gets away with it."

And then she proceeded to show Darcy how to hit so damn hard, Samantha would end up in France.

* * *

"Dad?" Drew came up behind Logan as he stood in the hall, listening to Agnes instruct Darcy on the best way to pummel a girl in her class.

"Shh," he whispered. "I'm eavesdropping."

"I thought you said eavesdropping was wrong."

"I meant when you two do it."

Drew angled in beside him to peer through the crack in the door into the kitchen, where Agnes was explaining that if a good punch to the nose didn't sort things, Darcy was to aim for the eyes.

"Dad, your girlfriend is kind of scary." Drew grinned up at him. "It's cool."

Ah, like father, like son. Logan put a hand on his shoulder and squeezed. "It's definitely cool," he agreed.

"You'd better stay on her good side because if you get into a fight, she'll kick your backside."

Logan didn't bother telling his son she already had.

"What's going on anyway?" Drew said.

"Some kid in school has been hitting Darcy. Agnes is showing her how to hit back."

Although, he was in two minds about Agnes' plan. It was against school rules to hit another kid, but should it be if it was in self-defense? Did he really want to raise kids who were so frightened of stepping a foot out of line that they let everyone walk all over them? On the other hand, what if Darcy went wild and started bullying other kids? Naw, that would never happen.

"Somebody's been hitting my sister?" Drew's face was pure thunder. "Who? And why didn't she tell me? I would have sorted them right out."

"Because it's a girl."

He understood instantly. "I might not hit a girl, but I could still scare the crap out of her."

Logan wanted to say that wasn't the right thing to do either, that boys shouldn't go around threatening girls, but hell, the kid wanted to stand up for his sister.

"I wish parenting was clear-cut," he said on a sigh. "Let's see how Agnes' method works before we step in."

"You're going to let Darcy hit this girl? Do you think she'll be able to do it?"

They both peeked through the door again.

"Look," Agnes was saying. "This isn't about fighting fair. It's about fighting dirty. You want to take her down in as few strikes as possible, then walk away with your head held high. This is a message to all the other little shi…farts who think you're an easy target. We. Are. Not. Easy. Targets. Got me?"

Darcy nodded solemnly. "Is this what you did when you were in school?"

Agnes got a *very* scary look on her face. "I annihilated anyone who picked on me or my sisters."

Darcy's eyes went wide. "And did they stop?"

"Oh, aye, they stopped."

Drew shuddered. "No offense, but next time I'm in trouble, I'm calling her, not you."

Logan didn't blame him.

"Do you think she'll still be here if there's a next time?" It was clear that Drew was trying to look like he didn't care, but it was there all the same. In the solid set of his shoulders, and the blank look on his face.

"She's trying, son. I think she definitely wants to stay."

"How will we know for sure that she's decided to stay and that she means it?"

"I really don't know."

They watched Agnes and Darcy spar for a couple more minutes before Drew whispered, "I like her, Dad. I hope she stays."

"Me too," Logan said. "Me too."

* * *

AGNES GOT out of Logan's car, which she'd borrowed to get to the council meeting, and strode up the steps to the front door of the castle.

Yes. Castle.

Although not huge by castle standards, it was still impressive. Four stories tall and flanked by matching turrets, the gray stone structure sat in a park-like setting full of manicured hedges and huge old trees. Even if the castle and grounds hadn't been covered in snow, it would still have been gorgeous. It was a shame it was a private residence. If it hadn't been, she'd have added it to her list of ways to attract people to Invertary. Tours of this castle would have been a massive hit.

The large oak door with its brass knocker and stained glass might have increased her nerves if she hadn't spent the past hour teaching Darcy how to defend herself. Now, she felt nothing but confidence. She wouldn't let a kid at school intimidate Darcy, and she sure as hell wouldn't let anyone inside this castle intimidate her. Nobody messed with her or her family. Nobody.

Agnes stopped short of ringing the bell.

Her.

Family.

The one she'd chosen, not the one that'd been forced on her through crappy circumstances.

A clarity, the likes of which she'd never experienced before, settled over her. She loved her sisters, but the weight of having to care for them when she'd been barely able to care for herself had been a heavy load to bear. The kind of load no kid should ever have to deal with.

But she wasn't a child any longer. Her shoulders were broad, and she had more strength now than she ever did then. She could care for Logan, Darcy, and Drew without drowning under the weight of it. *And* she could choose her career now, instead of taking the first offer that came her way. Or working in a job she hated just because she'd spent time training for it.

Her dreams had changed. And instead of feeling guilty about letting her old dreams go, she would embrace the new ones. Which meant compromise. If she wanted *her* family and a life in a town that was every bit as crazy as she was, then she'd have to stay in Scotland. But she'd do it on her terms. And that meant making enough money to get her and her new family out of the country every damn winter! Because, seriously, there was a limit to how much rain and cold she could deal with, and she figured she'd reached hers about five years earlier.

With a renewed sense of purpose and a lightness she hadn't felt in years, she rang the bell to the castle.

A few moments later, the heavy door swung open, and Caroline smiled out at her. Today, she wore lilac cigarette pants with a matching cashmere sweater—total Grace Kelly. "Are you ready?" she asked.

"Absolutely," Agnes said.

She was ready for everything. It was right there before her, and all she had to do was reach for it. Which she intended to start doing straight away. With that thought, she followed Caroline into the castle, ready to pitch her ideas for town rejuvenation to the council.

CHAPTER 25

Agnes' sisters arrived in Invertary the day before Christmas Eve. Logan hadn't known they were coming until Agnes borrowed his car, went into town, and came back with them in tow. They'd then spent a raucous evening in his living room, catching up with each other and telling the kids stories. Ones that no doubt put ideas in their heads Logan would have to deal with for years to come.

Jack, Agnes' nephew, who was a few years older than Drew, had hit it off with his son straight away. They'd stood side by side, watching the women laugh together and talk a mile a minute, then looked at each other and said, "PlayStation." Since then, they'd been holed up in Drew's room, working their way through his stack of games.

Darcy, meanwhile, had taken one look at Isobel's daughter, Sophie, and pretty much adopted her. The four-year-old looked at Darcy as though she were her fairy godmother. And Darcy, for her part, had dressed Sophie like a doll before teaching her how to dance.

"You might need to extend the house if you're going to host any more Sinclair sisters' get-togethers," Keir, Mairi's

233

man, said to him once the men had retreated to the kitchen to drink beer and enjoy some silence. "You could knock out the living room wall and add a good few feet. Maybe a conservatory."

Unlike the husbands of Agnes' other two sisters, Keir was chatty. He also thought Duncan and Callum were hilarious. Probably because the two men had sat on the living room sofa staring at the women with a mixture of bewilderment and fear for the past few hours.

"I don't know how long Agnes is staying in Invertary, so this might be the first and last get-together that happens here," Logan said as he put a bowl of nuts on the table. He saw little point in hiding the fact that their relationship was still on shaky ground. Agnes had no doubt shared this information in one of her many phone calls with her sisters.

"She's got a job now," Callum pointed out, reaching for the nuts.

A taciturn Scot, the London boss of Benson Security rarely smiled, except with his wife and kids. He wasn't easy to get to know, but Logan had a lot of respect for the man. Not only had he survived a bomb in Afghanistan that had taken both his legs, but his introduction to the Sinclairs had involved a dead body and men with machine guns. And he'd still married one of them.

"Aye," Duncan said. "They settle some when they've got something to occupy them. A bored Sinclair woman is a dangerous thing." He would know. The artist had hired Donna as his housekeeper, even though she'd been ill-suited to the job. Now that she was studying to become an illustrator, she seemed much more content.

"What's the new job then?" Keir asked as he raided the fridge. A mechanic by trade, he'd sold his business and now traveled the world, helping Mairi sort out her business. "Last I heard, she was working in the hotel."

To be fair, he'd only arrived from Canada the day before, so he had an excuse for being out-of-date.

"No, that's done with," Logan said. "She lasted almost a month with Dougal, which is a damn sight longer than I would have."

"Never thought it was a good fit," Callum said.

Logan stared at the man. "You were the one who set it up."

He shrugged. "Agnes needed a job, and Isobel wanted her to stay in the UK. If I'd gotten her a job in London, there was a good chance she'd have been promoted to some far-off place. So, I talked to Dougal and shoved her here."

The three men stared at him.

"Does Isobel know that?" Logan asked. "Because Agnes sure as hell doesn't."

"She didn't need to know," Callum said. "She's pregnant. If she wants something, she gets it."

"Let's keep this between the four of us," Keir said.

They raised their beer bottles to toast their agreement, sharing an identical worried look as they did so. If this got out, they'd all be dead.

"So, she's not working at the hotel?" Keir said as he put a load of different cheeses and crackers, that Logan hadn't even realized they had, on the table. Either Agnes had been shopping for something she could cook, or his mother had been stocking up for him again.

When Agnes had moved in, Logan had told his mother he wanted her key back, but Agnes had stopped him. She'd grabbed his arm and whispered, "She brings food, don't be an idiot." So his mother still had her key.

"Originally, she wanted to start up a hub for small businesses and tried to get funding to get it off the ground. But when the council heard her other ideas, they decided to create a position for her and to run the hub under the council banner. So, now she's in charge of Invertary's industry schemes. She's supposed to find new ways to attract business to town and, as part of that, she'll oversee the business center."

"Did they rip her off?" Callum asked. "Would she have made more money if she'd kept ownership of the business center?"

That's what he'd wondered too. "She says no. The salary for the job is good, and she gets to stick her nose into lots of different areas. She won't be bored."

"Told you," Duncan said before taking a sip of his drink. "You need to keep a Sinclair woman from getting bored, or it all goes to hell."

"Aye, it's good for her." In all honesty, Logan wished she'd kept the business and run it herself. It was a whole lot harder to walk away from your own business than to quit your job and head out of town.

"You're worried she's still going to run," Callum said astutely.

"She never wanted to stay in Scotland." He took a sip of his beer as he leaned against the counter, trying to give the impression he was much more relaxed than he felt. Agnes was like water—every time he tried to grab her and hold on tight, she slipped through his fingers.

"People change," Duncan said. "I never thought I'd want to marry again." He waggled his ring finger to prove his point.

"I never thought I wanted to do anything other than be a soldier," Callum added. "But I enjoy being one of the Benson Security partners."

"I never thought I'd like beer," Keir said and held up his bottle. When they stared at him, he shrugged. "I'm at least ten years younger than the rest of you, and I have Mairi to cope with, so cut me some slack."

"How do I know she really wants to be here?" Logan asked. How did he know she meant it? Unlike his ex-wife, who'd said one thing but resented the hell out of him because she'd wanted another.

"You trust her," Duncan said. "It sucks, but that's the only option."

"I might have some trouble with that," Logan admitted. "Once bitten and all that."

"Welcome to the club," Duncan said.

"You get a T-shirt," Callum added.

"I'm way too young for this group," Keir said.

"Hey," Agnes said as she came into the room, grinning at all of them. She headed straight for Logan and wrapped her arms around him. "The pub okay for dinner tomorrow night?" she asked as she looked up at him.

"Aye." Damn, if she left him, he'd be broken. "The pub's fine."

"Good." She went on tiptoe to press a kiss to his jaw. "And since it will be Christmas Eve, we all thought it would be fun to dress up. You four have to wear suits."

There were unanimous shouts of outrage.

Agnes narrowed her eyes. "Wear suits. Or kilts. Or whatever. But we're going smart and fancy. It's one bloody night of the year. You can manage it for one night." With one last glare at all of them, she stalked from the room.

"She always was the scariest," Keir said as he watched her go.

"Aye," Callum said. "Good luck with that."

"Are you sure you want her to stay?" Duncan added with a grin.

Aye, he was sure. He just wasn't convinced it was possible.

* * *

"I CAN'T BELIEVE how big your belly is," Agnes said as she sat beside Isobel on the sofa. "Are you sure this isn't twins? Because you're way bigger than you were with Jack or Sophie."

"Definitely not twins," Isobel said. "It's because I got knocked up by a much bigger man this time. I'm going to give birth to a giant."

"I want kids," Donna announced from where she lay on her back in the middle of the floor. Agnes wasn't sure why she was there, but she seemed happy. "I think I should start popping them out soon. Duncan isn't getting any younger, and I want my kids to play with yours, Izzy."

"That will be hard when I live in London and you live in Glasgow," Isobel pointed out.

"One of us needs to move," Donna said. "There are art colleges in London. I bet one of them would hire Duncan in a second."

Seeing as her husband was a world-famous artist, Agnes was pretty sure she was right in her assumption.

"I could run my matchmaking business out of London," Mairi said. "But then Aggie would be alone, and that's not fair. But, I could also run my business from Invertary. Keir can open a garage anywhere, so he'd be fine. Does Invertary have a garage?"

"Not that I know of, but you can't move here just because you're worried that I'll be lonely."

"Do you want me here or not?" Mairi demanded, living up to her fiery red hair as usual.

"Yes," Agnes said.

"Then it's done." She grinned at all of them from where she sat curled up in one of the armchairs. "I'm moving to Invertary!"

"Yay?" Agnes said drolly.

"Keir?" Mairi shouted.

A minute later, he sauntered through from the kitchen. "What?"

"Want to move to Invertary?" The way she said it made it clear there was only one acceptable answer.

"Aye?" he said, looking bewildered.

"Good answer." She held out her arms to him and, with an indulgent smile, he leaned down to kiss her before sauntering back out of the room. "Guess I'd better go house hunting," Mairi said as she watched him leave.

"I wish we could all be in one place together again," Donna said wistfully.

"One day," Isobel said. "You never know. But in the meantime, we can visit lots."

"I think it's best if you two visit us, rather than the other way around," Agnes said. "Seeing as you both married money and can afford to fly up here whenever you fancy."

"True." Donna grinned.

"Hey," Mairi said. "I didn't need to marry money. My business is going to make me a fortune. I've already got TV stations clamoring to interview me and geeks queuing up for me to find them a wife. I can afford flights to London on my own. Don't worry," she told Agnes. "I'll pay for yours."

"Thanks," Agnes said drolly.

They lapsed into silence, each busy with their own thoughts. Looking around at her sisters, Agnes' heart swelled. They'd done good, and she was proud of all of them.

"We made it," she said. "We made it out of that house and away from those people who didn't deserve us. We have families of our own, careers we can be proud of, and most important of all, we have each other."

"Always," Donna said firmly.

"You bet," Mairi said.

"Don't make me cry," Isobel wailed.

A minute later, Callum rushed into the room. "Are you okay?" he demanded to know.

The four sisters had climbed onto the sofa and were hugging and crying in a huge puppy pile.

"I think they're fine," Logan said from behind Callum.

Agnes looked over at the man she loved and smiled through her tears. She was so far past fine that it made her ache. And he was the reason why.

CHAPTER 26

"Why am I wearing a kilt?" Drew complained from the back seat as they drove into town to have dinner at the pub with Agnes' family.

"Because," Agnes said from the passenger seat, "I asked you to."

"You didn't ask," Drew grumbled. "You handed it to me and gave me two choices, wear it or die."

"And you chose wisely." Agnes beamed. "I'm so proud of you."

Hearing Darcy giggle, Logan caught her eye in the mirror and grinned. There was no messing with Agnes—she'd win every time. And from the way his girl had dealt with that bully who'd been harassing her, she was another Agnes in the making. He wasn't really sure what he thought of that.

"This is so exciting," Agnes said. "I can't remember the last time I dressed up to go out."

Logan reached for her hand. "You look gorgeous."

"I should bloody well hope so." She waved a hand down her body. "This took hours."

Her pale green sheath dress shimmered in the light, showcasing her gorgeous figure with each step she took. Against Logan's advice, she hadn't put on her new snow boots, but wore delicate pink heels and carried a matching bag. She'd put pearls in her ears and draped several strands of them around her throat. Fake, she'd told him when he commented. One day, he'd replace them with the real thing, because Agnes glowed in pearls. Her messy, twisty, updo hairstyle looked sexy as hell, and her makeup made him want to see her face by candlelight. And, because the town was still covered in snow, she wore her big black padded coat over the whole thing.

"You look good too," she said with a heated smile.

She'd been hassling him all evening to find out what was under his kilt, and he'd promised to show her later.

"You'd better appreciate it," he said. "This isn't exactly the weather for a kilt."

Her gaze strayed to the snow-covered town spread out in front of them. The glittering lights strung across the high street looked magical against all that white. And at the bottom of the road was the ever-present blackness of the loch.

"I need to hire a decent photographer to take pictures of the town all year round. It would be good for marketing," Agnes said. "Americans love scenes like this. It's how they imagine the whole of Scotland to be. Either this or covered in heather, with grass swaying in a gentle breeze and men in kilts chopping wood under the sun."

"You've spent way too much time thinking about this," Logan said.

She ignored him as her eyes went wide, signaling she'd had another 'brilliant' idea. "We should do our own men-in-kilts calendar."

"No." He knew where this was going, and he wasn't posing for any damn calendar.

She narrowed her eyes at him. "We'll see," she said, and he felt the sudden urge to run.

The pub's carpark was full to bursting, but they were lucky and found a spot right near the door. Darcy leaped out first, excited to be dressed up and out on the town. Her pale green dress had been a Christmas present from his mother and it came with a full skirt that sparkled when it caught the light—something Darcy had told him at least half a dozen times.

"Hurry up," she called. "I want to see what everyone's wearing."

Logan shared a knowing smile with Agnes as they made their way into the pub. The place was packed and, as they made their way to the restaurant, everyone grinned and called out their hellos.

"Been a long time since I've seen it this busy," Logan commented.

"Where else is there to go around here?" Agnes grinned. "For now." She had big plans to totally disrupt the running of the town.

To his surprise, Agnes' sisters were waiting for them outside the restaurant doors. All of them dressed in various shades of green. He suspected it must be the family color, to match their eyes. When seeing them all together, it was hard not to feel a little stunned. With similar heights and builds, identical eyes, and startlingly different hair, the four women were breathtaking.

Agnes hugged her sisters, and they helped her out of her coat.

"You look beautiful," Isobel said.

"So do you. And you're out of Callum's sight! I'm surprised he allowed it."

"He's dealing with the kids," Isobel said. "And he made me

wear this." She tugged a necklace out of her dress. "It's a panic button. It sounds an alarm on his watch."

The sisters collapsed in hysterics over that, but Logan couldn't understand why. It seemed sensible to him. "Are we going in, or are we going to stand out here chatting all night?"

"You go ahead," Agnes said. "I've got a couple of things I need to tell my sisters first, without the men hearing." She caught Drew's eye. "I asked for a table near the kitchen, so better use the side door, it's closest. You know the one I mean."

"Sure." Drew grabbed Logan's arm and dragged him away.

"Don't be too long," Logan called. "I'm starving."

"Just a couple of minutes. Promise." She blew him a kiss.

They were halfway down the hall when Logan noticed Darcy wasn't with them. "Run back and get your sister."

"Don't worry. She'll come in with Agnes." He pulled open the door at the end of the hall and ushered Logan inside.

He took two steps into the room before he stopped dead. The room wasn't set up for dining, as it usually was. Instead, the tables were gone, and the chairs had been arranged in rows facing the front. There were pink flowers everywhere, and long lengths of green silken material draped across the ceiling in soft waves. Beside him, at the front of the room, was an arch covered in pink flowers and greenery.

And the new minister stood under it, a smile on his face.

"Drew? What's going on?"

The men in Agnes' family sat grinning at him from the first row, all wearing suits or kilts. The women of Knit or Die were there, as were the old men that made up the Domino Boys. Lake sat in the middle of the room, along with most of his work colleagues. In the front row were his parents, dressed in their finest. His father nodded at him, while his mother waved a handkerchief. He'd only ever seen her with a linen handkerchief once before…

He turned to his son but couldn't get the question out of his mouth.

Drew answered it anyway. "Welcome to your wedding," he said with a wide grin. "I'm the best man."

* * *

"If he runs, I'll puke all over your nice dresses," Agnes told her sisters.

"He won't run," Mairi said. "He loves you. Everything is going to be fine. The room looks beautiful, and everyone's in place, nothing is going to go wrong. Trust me."

"Trust you? You're the last person I should have asked to help organize this—chaos is your middle name."

"So is romance." Mairi looked pleased with herself. "I should put that on my business cards."

"I see him," Donna called from the door, where she was peeking into the room.

"Does he look mad?" Agnes wrung her hands. This was a dumb idea. The dumbest idea she'd ever had. Whatever had made her think she should stage a surprise Christmas wedding because her family would be in town? What if Logan didn't want to marry her? He'd been married before, and that hadn't turned out well. Maybe he didn't want to do it again? Maybe she should have had this conversation *before* she talked Dougal into holding the wedding.

"He looks shocked," Donna said. "The minister's going over to talk to him." She looked back at her sisters. "Can ministers date, or are they celibate like priests? Because that guy is seriously hot."

Isobel smacked her on the back of the head. "Don't let Duncan hear you say that, or he'll go mental." She waggled her eyebrows. "But Donna's right. That minister is totally a ten."

"What's going on?" Agnes snapped. She was going to pass out at this rate. Who the hell cared how attractive the minister was? What she wanted to know was whether Logan had sprinted off or not.

"Oh," Donna said, making Agnes' stomach lurch. "The minister just signaled me." She closed the door. "We're good to go."

Isobel burst into tears. "You're getting married," she wailed.

"Shh!" everyone, including Darcy, hissed at her. "We don't want Callum running out here."

"Sorry." Isobel dabbed her eyes. "Hormones."

"Okay." Agnes looked at her sisters. "Okay. I'm getting married. I mean, I must be, right? The minister wouldn't signal for me to walk down the aisle if Logan just wanted to talk."

Darcy put a hand on her arm. "Dad loves you. We all do."

"Damn it." Agnes pulled the girl into a hug. "Now, *I'm* going to cry."

"Don't you dare ruin that makeup," Mairi snapped. "Now, enough of this. Darcy, grab your flower basket, the music's started. Do it exactly like we practiced this morning."

"I've got this." She took the basket of rose petals and pushed open the door.

"You ready?" said a male voice, and Agnes turned to find her nephew, Jack, standing beside her, his elbow cocked waiting for her.

She took it gratefully, marveling at how much taller he was than the last time she'd seen him. "I'm ready."

"That's our cue," Donna said. "We go in by age. That means you're up first, Isobel."

Isobel kissed Agnes on the cheek, sniffed, and walked through the doors.

Donna smiled at Agnes. "I love you, sis," she said before she followed.

"Do not screw up my perfect wedding," Mairi warned before grinning. "Have fun!"

And then she was gone too. Leaving Agnes and Jack alone in the hall.

"I never thought I'd be this nervous," she said.

"Having second thoughts? I can get you out of here if you need me to."

She looked up into his beautiful, but very serious face. "The nerves are for Logan. I'm worried I've pushed him into this, and he doesn't really want me."

"At the risk of sounding like Callum, that's bullshit. Now, can we go?"

"Yeah." And with a smile, she pushed open the door. Her eyes went straight to Logan, who smiled at her as though she'd hung the moon and then shook his head. She hoped that meant he couldn't believe what she'd done, and not that he was going to tell her no when she got to the front of the room.

All she could do was walk toward him to get her answer.

* * *

A MILLION THOUGHTS raced through Logan's head before Agnes appeared and started down the aisle. Then, all he could think about was the woman he loved.

She positively glowed. Smiling at everyone as she passed, she overflowed with joy. The sight of her appeased his worry. His woman wasn't doing this because she felt she had to. She was doing it because she wanted to.

When she reached the front of the room, she kissed Jack's cheek then took Logan's hand.

"Good surprise?" she whispered. Her anxiety shone in her eyes.

"*Amazing* surprise."

He couldn't believe she'd pulled this off without him knowing, especially seeing as everyone in town seemed in on it. Staring at Agnes, drinking her in, he listened as the minister waxed lyrical about marriage. He listened, but he didn't hear a word, as his attention remained solely on the woman at his side.

When she cleared her throat and let go of his hand to rummage in her tiny bag, he realized she'd written her own vows.

Cocking an eyebrow at the minister, he asked, "What am I supposed to do?"

The minister didn't even try to pretend he wasn't amused. "Talk from the heart?"

"Helpful," Logan grumbled.

"Dearly beloved," Agnes said, then looked at the minister. "Oh, wait, that's your bit."

As the crowd laughed, she looked back at Logan. And everything within him stilled. The people in the room disappeared, and all that existed was Agnes.

"I never thought I'd be here," she said.

"Neither did I," he muttered, and Drew turned another laugh into a cough.

Agnes narrowed her eyes at Logan before continuing. "I never wanted to stay in Scotland."

He sucked in a breath.

"I never thought I could be happy here." Agnes blinked up at him. "I hate the cold. And the rain. And there are days when I'm not too fussy on the people either."

There was more chuckling at that.

"There is only one thing that could have made me change my mind about staying in Scotland, and that's you. Your love makes the winters warm and takes the damp edge off the grayest day. And knowing I have your love to go home to gives me the patience to deal with the most difficult of people. Scotland was a word that meant suffering to me, but now it means peace—because Scotland is where I found you, and where we make our home.

"In case you're wondering, all of this means that I love you, Logan McBride. And I have no regrets doing it. I don't regret staying in Invertary. I don't regret staying *for you*. *You* are my choice. You will *always* be my choice. And I can say right now, that I also *choose* to be a mother to Drew and Darcy—if they'll have me. They're my choice too, and I love them just as much as I love you."

Darcy burst into tears and ran from where she stood beside Agnes' sisters to wrap her arms around Agnes.

"Hush," Agnes said as she cuddled her close. "Nobody can hear my awesome vows over your wailing. And don't you dare wipe your snotty nose on my dress."

Darcy laughed and cried at the same time, which turned into a hiccup. Donna stepped forward and gently held Darcy as she led her back to the group. The women enclosed her at their center. Protecting her. Caring for her. Being everything that made them the Sinclair sisters.

"As I was saying," Agnes said. "I want *you*. I want your kids. I want this family. I thought I wanted something else, and I probably did at some point. But I'm smart enough to recognize a better opportunity when I see one. And that's what you are—you're the better opportunity. We can have a good life together, Logan. I promise that I'll treat your heart as precious, the way that you treat mine. I promise I'll compromise so that we can both do most of the things we want to do. I promise I'll care for you, the way you care for me. I also promise that I'll drag you out of Scotland every winter to escape the freezing rain."

Chuckles and sniffles rippled through the room.

"I promise I'll be crabby, difficult to live with, bad-tempered, and often irrational. But I promise to work on those things too. Mainly, I promise to give all that I am, to all that is you, for all the time we have left. If you'll have me."

Agnes folded the paper with shaky hands and returned it to her purse before handing it to Mairi. Emerald eyes stared up at him, and he felt like he could see all the way to Agnes' soul. She hid nothing, held nothing back. She was giving it all to him. Her love. Her life. All of it.

And there was only one thing he could say in reply.

Turning to the minister, Logan said, "I do."

AN EXCERPT FROM RAGE

Read on for a taste of Isobel Sinclair's story.

The village of Arness, Scotland

Isobel Sinclair should have contacted the authorities the first time she saw the boat sneaking into the cove. But she didn't. She should have called when there was a storm during the boat's third visit, and the crew lost some of their baggage on the rocky path up to Arness. But she didn't. Instead, she'd gathered their lost cargo, called it her own and sold it to help pay off her ex-husband's debts.

Which made her a thief, just like him.

And her thieving was the reason she still didn't call in the authorities the time the boat turned up in the dead of night, and there was shouting in the darkness. Or the time she'd seen evidence that someone had dragged something heavy over the beach.

No, she'd never called the authorities. Not once. Even though she knew the boat brought nothing but trouble each time it snuck into shore.

But she should have called, because the boat had come back.

And this time, they'd left a body behind.

"What are we going to do with him?" Isobel's youngest sister, Mairi, stared down at the man.

The dead man.

"I suppose we could bury him," Agnes, one of their middle sisters, said.

"We can't bury him here." Isobel gestured to the rock-strewn beach. "Even if we do manage to dig a hole, the tide will unearth him in a day or two."

Mairi looked up at the steep, rocky path behind them, the only route down from the bluff where the tiny town of Arness sat. "We'll never get him back up there. He looks like he weighs a ton."

"And he's wet." Agnes nodded. "That makes you heavier."

"Aye," Mairi said. "Water retention."

Isobel and Agnes stared at their sister.

"What?" Mairi said.

With shakes of their heads, Agnes and Isobel turned their attention back to the body.

"How do you think he died?" Agnes said.

"I suppose we should look him over and see if we can tell." Isobel didn't like the thought of touching the man, let alone examining him for clues as to his cause of death.

"Does it really matter how he died?" Mairi said. "I mean, it isn't going to change the fact that he's dead. Or that he was left here by the boat people."

"The boat people?" Agnes looked towards heaven and seemed to be counting to ten. Again.

Mairi shrugged, her long red hair shifting with the movement. "What else are we to call them? And he was left here by the boat crew. Isobel saw them while she was spying."

Isobel adopted her patented "haughty eldest sister" look—

it helped take her mind off her shaking hands and the fear gnawing at her stomach. "I wasn't spying. I was looking out of my window and saw them carry him off the boat and dump him here."

"You were looking out of your window with the aid of binoculars," Mairi reminded her.

She had a point. "What I don't get is if these boat people are so keen on going unnoticed, then why are they dumping bodies on the beach?" Isobel said. "I mean, they only come in the dead of night. And we know they're up to no good."

"Smuggling," Mairi said with a decisive nod.

Agnes walked around the prone man and looked back out at the choppy waters behind them, then up at the hill leading to town. "Do you think they meant for him to be swept out to sea? Or to be eaten by the crabs?"

"If they wanted him to be swept out to sea, why not dump him out there in the first place?" Isobel said. "And I don't think half a dozen crabs are enough to eat a full-grown body. At least not fast enough to get rid of the evidence."

"Even then," Mairi said, "there would still be the bones."

They nodded in agreement, and Isobel couldn't help but notice that her sisters were struggling to hide their shaking hands, just as she was doing.

"I think we should call the police." Seeing as Agnes wasn't the most law-abiding member of the family, it said a lot that she was the one to suggest calling them in.

"I can't." Isobel tugged at the sleeves of her oversized purple cardigan and wrapped her arms around herself. "They'll find out that I sold the stuff I found, rather than reporting it to them in the first place."

"I told you, you shouldn't have gone to the pawn shop in Campbeltown," Mairi said. "Too many people know us there."

"I wanted rid of it fast."

Plus, she'd needed the money to pay off the loan shark who was hounding her over her ex-husband's debt. Seeing as the man couldn't find Robert, he'd decided to make Isobel pay in his stead, with cash or her body, making it clear that her family would suffer if she didn't comply. That was the reason Isobel's moral judgment had been silenced when she'd found the stolen goods on the path—the thought of handing over her body to pay her ex-husband's debt made her ill. But she'd do it if she had to. She'd do just about anything to make sure her kids were safe.

"Enough of this." Agnes crouched down and turned the body over.

He flopped onto his back, and the cause of death was instantly clear. There was a wide, gaping slit where his throat used to be.

"I think I'm going to be sick." Mairi covered her mouth and turned her back on the body, making gagging sounds as she did so.

"Don't," Agnes ordered. "You know I'm a sympathetic puker. If you start vomiting, we'll both be doing it."

Isobel ignored her sisters as she stared at the body. It was the most horrifying thing she'd ever seen. She swallowed hard. "You can't accidentally slit your own throat, can you?"

"No," Agnes said firmly.

Aye, that would have been too much to hope for.

There was a scrambling noise from the bluff behind them. The women yelped and spun, to see their remaining sister coming down the rocky path.

Isobel put her hand to her chest. Her heart was racing hard. "You nearly gave me a heart attack," she told her sister.

Donna rushed up to them, her blonde hair flying out behind her. "Sorry. What's so urgent we had to meet in the dark on the beach? Did you find more bounty?"

It was then she saw the body. The colour drained from

her face, she turned and promptly vomited. Which, in turn, made Agnes vomit.

Mairi started making gagging noises. "I'm okay, I'm okay." She held one hand up, pressing the other to her stomach. "I can hold it."

"What a relief," Isobel told her.

Mairi shot her an irritated look. "I told you not to call Donna. She's vegetarian."

"I didn't expect her to eat him." Isobel glared back at her.

"That's just gross," Mairi said, and gagged again.

Isobel threw her hands up in disgust. "Why did I bother calling any of you? You're no use at all. We have a situation here and all you're doing is being sick."

"It's not like we can help it," Agnes said, looking decidedly green.

"Some warning would have been good." Donna swayed in place. Her eyes were on the water instead of the man.

"I did warn you when I called," Isobel said through gritted teeth. "I said, come quick, there's a dead body on the beach."

"I thought you were joking," Donna said.

"About a dead body?" Isobel practically shrieked.

"Right." Agnes held up her hands. "Everybody calm down. This isn't helping. It's getting light, and we need to deal with the body. It's not like people use this beach, but if someone did come down here, they'd call the police." She looked at Isobel. "And seeing as your house is the closest, you'd be first on their list to interview."

"That wouldn't go well," Mairi said. "Your whole face goes red when you lie, and you start stuttering."

"Then you just blab the truth and apologise for trying to lie," Donna added.

"Which means you'd get arrested for fencing stolen goods." Agnes nodded. "Something we're trying to avoid."

"Are you all about done?" Isobel put her hands on her hips

and glared at them. Was this really the time to bring up every single one of her flaws? "The kids will be awake soon. We need to deal with this now."

They all stared at the man.

"I've never seen a dead body before," Mairi said. "They look so lifeless."

"Idiot." Agnes smacked Mairi on the back of the head.

"What was that for?" Mairi rubbed her head.

"For being an idiot," Agnes said. "Now focus. Do we leave him here? Cover him and come back later to bury him? Bury him now? Or move him somewhere else while we think things over?"

"I think we need to move him. It would be too hard to bury him here, and we couldn't guarantee the tide wouldn't unearth him later." Isobel felt weary. She was sick of the stress in her life. Sick of dealing with other people's messes. Sick of struggling every single day just to survive. "Whatever we do, we need to do it fast, before the kids wake up. Either way, I want him off the beach. Jack sometimes comes down here with his friends after school, and I wouldn't want them to find the body."

"You could put him in the freezer in your garage," Donna said. "It still works, doesn't it?"

"Aye, but it's old, full of rust and smelly," Isobel said.

"I don't think he'll care," Donna said.

"What do we do with him once he's in the freezer? We can't leave him there forever." Isobel gnawed at her bottom lip and wondered how her life had come to this point.

She was a single mother of two, with two failed relationships behind her, a mountain of debt she hadn't personally accumulated, a minimum-wage job in the village shop and an ever-growing list of crimes under her belt. It was not how she'd imagined life would be at the grand old age of thirty-two.

"We need advice. We need someone who knows what to do with a dead body," Agnes said. "We need an expert."

"I'm not calling the police," Isobel said adamantly. She was the only stability her kids had. She couldn't even think of risking it.

"I wasn't thinking of the police," Agnes said. "I was thinking of an outlaw."

"Yes!" Mairi clapped her hands and grinned. "Great idea, Aggie."

"No." Isobel shook her head. "No. Just no."

Donna placed her hand on Isobel's arm. "Don't dismiss this idea just because you fancy the man. He used to be in the army. He's bound to have seen dead bodies during conflict. He must have an idea what to do with them."

"I-I don't f-fancy him," Isobel protested, but nobody was listening. No, she just dreamed about him every blooming night. What was it with her and bad boys? Hadn't she learned her lesson by now? Why couldn't she find a nice six-stone weakling of an accountant to fall in love with?

"It's well known he's dangerous," Agnes said. "Old man McKay used to tell everyone that his grandson was deadly. He was in the Special Forces. He knows about dead bodies."

"Plus," Mairi said, "there's a security company watching him—covertly." She whispered the last word as though it had special powers. "That must mean he's on the other side of the law now, which means he won't report us to the cops."

"I didn't know he was being watched." Donna's eyes went wide. "Maybe talking to him isn't such a good idea."

"I spoke to the woman who was setting up cameras," Isobel said. Of course she was going to grill a stranger who was setting up CCTV in the street, in the dark. "She showed me her ID and said he wasn't dangerous to the town. He isn't a criminal. She said he's only dangerous to bad guys." And then the blue-haired woman had laughed. It wasn't reassuring. Neither was the fact she was wearing a Wonder Woman T-shirt and a pair of pink, glittery Doc Marten boots. "She gave me her business card, in case I was ever worried about anything."

"Maybe we should call the security company instead?" Mairi said. "We can ask them what to do."

Agnes groaned. "I can just imagine that conversation— 'Hello, we have the body of a stranger in our freezer and we're looking for suggestions on what to do with it.' Aye, that would go well."

"It was only an idea." Mairi frowned at Agnes.

"Whatever," Agnes said. "I think our best bet is the outlaw. You said he's huge and there are weapons lying around in his house. He's obviously used to dangerous situations. I bet he'd know what to do with the body. You need to ask him for help."

"No."

Isobel had been delivering groceries to Callum McKay's house for almost four months, and she'd only seen the man three times. All three times, he'd scared the life out of her. Rage covered him like a shroud. But there was also something about him that made her heart ache. Maybe it was the utter desolation in his eyes, or the fact that the only people she'd seen near him had been from a security company that was hiding in the dark. She'd never met someone so completely alone. And so brutally raw. He was the embodiment of her own personal weakness—the tortured bad boy, with muscles like Thor. She didn't have to be massively self-aware to realise that he was the last person she should approach for help. No, for the sake of her sanity, it was best to keep far, far away from the man.

"Honey," Agnes said, "we don't have a lot of options here. Either you get help from someone who knows what to do with a body, or you keep the guy frozen in your old chest freezer for the foreseeable future."

"Aye," Donna said. "And what if this is just the beginning? What if the boat people dump more bodies? We need a plan. We need advice."

"Or we need to start our own crematorium business," Mairi said.

"Think of your kids," Agnes said. "This is getting worse every month. We're in way over our heads. We need help. If this guy can help, then great. If not, we'll try something else."

Isobel's heart sank. Agnes was right. They were out of options. Staying away from Callum McKay had become a luxury she couldn't afford. And it wasn't as if she wanted to start a relationship with him. No, she just wanted advice on what to do with the dead stranger who'd been dumped on her beach.

"You can do it," Donna said softly. "We have your back."

Isobel blinked back tears, as love for her sisters overwhelmed her. She didn't know how she'd survive without them. She needed to talk to Callum for their sakes. This situation with the mysterious boat was well past the point of being dangerous, and they were getting in deeper every month. No, they weren't —she was. And she was dragging her sisters down with her.

"Okay, I'll talk to him."

"You'll be okay, honey," Agnes said.

"Just keep your hands off him," Mairi said. "Maybe you could call him instead of talking to him face to face."

That caused Agnes to smack her again. "She isn't going to jump the man, idiot."

There was a pause as all three sisters gave her speculative looks. Isobel threw up her hands in disgust. "So I have a type. So what? It's not like I'm going to throw myself at him and offer to sleep with him in return for his help."

There was a shuffling of feet as her sisters cast sideward glances at each other.

"Thanks a lot," Isobel said. "Good to know you have so much faith in me."

"You tend to get physical without thinking it through," Donna said gently.

"I only did that once," Isobel protested. And ended up pregnant and alone at seventeen because of it.

Her sisters stared at her.

"Fine. Twice." And she had the ex-husband from hell to show for that little slip in self-control.

"If it's any consolation," Mairi said, "I've totally learned from your mistakes."

"No. It's no consolation. Now do you three think you could stop analysing my past mistakes long enough to help me get this body off the beach?" She looked at the sliver of light on the horizon. "Sun's coming. We need to get him to the garage and into the freezer before the kids wake up."

"This is going to be gross," Mairi said. "I'll need to burn my clothes after this."

"I might vomit again," Donna said.

"Get a grip," Agnes snapped, "and take an arm or a leg each."

With each of them clutching a limb, the four sisters carried the dead man up the hill to Isobel's house. Donna and Agnes were only sick twice.

Get Rage now to keep on reading!

ABOUT JANET ELIZABETH HENDERSON

I'm a Scot, living in New Zealand and married to a Dutch man. I write contemporary romance with a humorous bent – this is mainly due to the fact I have an odd sense of humour and can't keep it out of anything I do! If I wasn't a writer, I'd like to be Buffy the Vampire Slayer, or Indiana Jones. Unfortunately, both these roles have already been filled. Which may be a good thing as I have no fighting skills, wouldn't know a precious relic if it hit me in the face and have an aversion to blood. When I'm not living in my head, I'm a mother to two kids, several pet sheep, one dog, four cats, three alpacas, two miniature horses, eight guinea pigs and an escape artist chicken.

www.ingramcontent.com/pod-product-compliance
Lightning Source LLC
Chambersburg PA
CBHW021138110726
47900CB00002B/405